# REACH

A **FOR THE STARS** NOVEL

# REACH

## O McCARTHY

ISBN (paperback): 979-8-9908446-1-2
ISBN (ebook): 979-8-9908446-0-5

Editing & proofreading by Caitlin Miller
Cover design & typesetting by Benita Thompson

*All glory and honor to You who make all things new.*

*To Patrick, for believing in me with unwavering support.*

*To Gabriella, Maria, Pascale, Blaise and Paxton.*
*You are my sunshines on darkest days.*

*This book does not contain on page graphic violence,*
*but it does contain some content readers may be sensitive to.*

- Abuse of power by a government
- Psychological abuse
- Emotional abuse
- Capital punishment
- Limb loss

"It is not in the stars to hold our destiny
but in ourselves."

—WILLIAM SHAKESPEARE

# PART 1

# 1

THE PAWN IS the most powerful piece in chess. Its weakness masks the power beneath—the power to end everything. I study the chess board in our living room during my scheduled thinking period. A patch of late afternoon sunlight illuminates the table as I consider potential starting strategies. Mom and I play each evening after our daily science lab work is complete. She says it helps us connect, decompress, and that game theory is important. After years of playing, we're well-matched.

A low rumble diverts my attention and I gaze out the window, thoughts of pawn promotion momentarily forgotten. Dust swirls as a vehicle stops outside our quarters. The standard issue gray-and-white striped living room curtains conceal me as I peer out the large window. My fingers dig into the pocket of my navy blue student uniform, latching onto the paper that contains our weekly schedule. There is nothing out of the ordinary on it. The fact that a vehicle is here, on Compound, is remarkable; the fact that it is parked in front of my living quarters and *not* on my schedule is astonishing.

Compound is like a military base, but vehicles are a rarity. As the son of one of the most prestigious scientists in Nation, I live here, in an expanse of desert, helping Nation move forward into the future shaped by scientific knowledge.

A knot forms in my gut as I observe the car. It is boxy, navy blue, long, and raised about four feet off the ground. It is menacing, silent save for the crunch of gravel beneath its giant tires. The sound reminds me of bones breaking.

My hand grips the thin fabric of the curtain in my left fist. In my other hand, I clutch the pawn I was toying with. The knot in my gut is well and truly tangled now. Anxiety. Hello again, old friend.

My gaze catches on the chair across the room. It's the one my mother fills each evening when she returns from her laboratory job doing her "duty" for Nation. I'm not sure what she does exactly, but "duty for Nation" is how the secretive science work is explained. Mom served a space mission, making her part of the select group of men and women who work on the most advanced and secretive projects for the government. Compound is where these highly classified experiments take place.

I'm not the only scientist child on Compound, but I've always been set apart, different. My mother is the one of the only scientists here who served a space mission. She's a hero. And yet, despite having a famous mother, people stay away from me in general—except for the scientists working on the experiments I help with. I don't know what the experiments I work on are, but mine must have something to do with the human body, because my body has been studied in various ways for as long as I can remember.

All the children on Compound help with the experiments, but kids don't get clearance until they become full-fledged Citizens at age eighteen, the age of loyalty. I'm nearly fifteen now. The Citizenship process is highly secretive. Once I've passed Citizenship prep and shown my loyalty, I'll find out the details of my experiments, or maybe not. Maybe I'll have an entirely different purpose in Nation than science research.

In Nation, you do what you're told by the Citizens responsible for you, and after Citizenship, you do whatever the government says you should do based on your aptitude tests. My results have never been shared with me, so I have no idea what the government will require of me when I become a Citizen. I do know that these tests are nonnegotiable. Dreams don't have a place here. Everything is based on data-driven resource efficiency.

Security is scrupulously observed at all times on Compound, and the strict regimen of all the residents is entirely based on the schedules received weekly. The lack of cleaning, the normal light pink schedule this week, the way that this vehicular anomaly appeared during my thirty-minute afternoon 'thinking period'...a premonition, perhaps, but I shiver as I realize whoever is inside the mysterious vehicle is here for me.

At fourteen, I'm tall, thin, and shaggy. My dark brown hair falls over my hazel eyes. My hair is long, not cut to standard because, for some reason, the *scientists* don't want it cut. At my last *observation*, Dr. Jog announced, "The hair might have a different protein than keratin as its building block and should be allowed to grow in order to study longer strands." I still don't know why that matters. But I do get to skip the regular haircuts for now. I'm not sure if that's a good thing.

On Compound, uniformity is strictly enforced. The regulations are observed with the same strict enthusiasm as scientific protocol, and deviating from them can result in punishment. Having anything mark you as an individual draws attention and takes the focus off of learning. Whispers, scoffs, and dirty looks have always been tossed my way. It's worse when there's something that makes people notice you and you don't know what it is.

I ball my hands into fists, my fingernails biting sharp crescents into the soft flesh of my palms. When I was younger, the scientists wanted to study my fingernails. I had the unfortunate habit of biting my nails, so to prevent this, they put awful-tasting oil on them and then didn't cut them for eight weeks. After six weeks, I couldn't take it anymore. I endured weeks of taunts from my school comrades and stares from adults, so I picked them off. The scientists were livid, but I was relieved.

Scientists are usually curious, but when I looked at them, I saw only disgust. Bile fills my mouth as I remember the taste of the oil and the horrible sound of my own fingernails dragging against everything I touched while my classmates turned away, or worse, called me names.

I have approximately zero friends. Friendships in the kid world of Compound depend entirely on which science group you've been assigned. I'm in a group of one. Just me. I would let it bother me, but I don't mind being a loner. I do wonder sometimes if that's my experiment—being a social outcast.

I have Mom and I have myself. That's enough.

Movement at the vehicle jars me back to the present. A woman dressed in what looks like a black lab coat, wide-leg black pants, and black high heels sharp enough to be weapons climbs out as the vehicle door retracts. Her skin is olive, her hair jet black, and she wears jewelry. I have only ever seen one person wear jewelry: Leader. Jewelry is prohibited, not part of the standard clothing regulations and definitely frivolous when compared with the mission of Compound—classified science in the service of the government.

The sun glints off crystals dangling from her ears, and a small gold chain glimmers in her nose. The woman twists her head like she's cracking her neck. She squints at my door and steeples her fingers together as a smirk creeps across her face. Her heels sink in the sand and grit, making her take comically exaggerated steps. I would chuckle were I not subdued by a sudden and very heavy sense of dread.

The vehicle door rolls shut, revealing a watermarked seal. In a shade of blue just slightly lighter than the rest of the car is the seal of Nation: a falcon, wings spread wide, clutching a star in its talons, ringed by a wreath of DNA double helices.

The seal of the government?

"What the helix?" The words tumble out of my mouth in a whisper. I scan the room as tension fills every limb in my body; swearing is a punishable offense, and I do not want to clean the animal cages in the labs. No one is here, but I often get the feeling I'm being watched.

Shifting on my feet, I chew the inside of my cheek as I wait for the woman to arrive at the front door. A single knock sounds against the metal door. It's a shallow courtesy because before I have the chance to answer, the door swings open.

My mouth goes dry. *Where is Mom?* She was due home a few minutes ago. *Why am I alone in our quarters with a government official?* Fear roils up from my belly, settling in my throat as my heart beats faster.

The woman steps inside, her heels clicking on the cold white tile floor, and surveys the blank gray walls. Everything in our apartment follows the standard living regulations. The woman in black walks farther down the hall to the single wall niche, where personal items are allowed to be displayed. Ours contains one photograph of my mother and me. Black-and-white, in a round frame no larger than eight-by-ten inches, we stand together with the arid landscape in the background and desert blooms surrounding us. I'm a leggy eight-year-old in the picture, in awe of the flowers that only come out when it's rained in the desert. That was the last time we've had a rainy year. Despite the nearly seven years that have passed since that day, it is etched deeply into my memory as one of the few instances where something unexpected happened in my life.

The day of the photograph, the scheduler machines malfunctioned, and the pages delivered blank ones. It was chaos on Compound, and Mom said we would gather knowledge while they sorted out the problem. I sense now that she wanted to get away. She took a picnic with us, and we went deep into the desert before finding the blooms. Mom brought a camera and rigged a rock, fork, and shoelace to take our own picture in front of the flowers. Years later, there have been no more malfunctions, no more rainy years, and no more blooms. All that's left of that day is dry dust and a strange woman from the government studying the photograph.

I move forward from the shadow of the curtain, my fear flaming into irritation and then anger at the stranger standing in my home like it belongs to her, like she belongs here. The flicker of movement catches the woman's attention. Her eyes find me, scan me up and down, as a broad smile breaks out on her face. It does not make her look beautiful. It makes her look calculating.

"Hello," she says. Her voice is quiet, yet strong. It has the timbre of a lead pipe wrapped in velvet. I sense immediately that this woman is harsh, uncompromising, and uses her authority. She is not to be trusted, and certainly not trifled with.

"Hello," I repeat, and I'm ashamed it comes out an octave higher than I'd like. My voice has been changing over the past year (Mom calls it 'puberty'), but when I'm anxious, which is rather often, it squeaks higher. I try to save face by introducing myself. "I'm Reach." I hope she'll give me some answers as to who she is and why she's here without me having to ask directly.

"Yes, I know." Her reply gives away nothing. She proceeds into the living room and sits on the white couch facing the window. She crosses her legs at the ankle, making the blade-like high heels visible, and consults the watch on her wrist. "Your mother is late."

I gulp. This woman is bad news. My mother *is* late. I check the communication device I wear on my wrist. There are no messages reporting any accidents or quarantines in the labs. I don't know who this woman is, but I know enough that being late is *bad*. Every fiber of my being is screaming to get away from her, to protect the mother I love. But I can't move. A government official has arrived in my home, and I'm alone with her.

This is not good at all. There are no protocols for this. When Leader visits Compound, we practice different scenarios in school. Most importantly, the government is always right. If you disagree, you are wrong. I struggle to think of something I can say to admit that she is right, that my mother is late, but also provide Mom with an out. I don't trust this woman, government official or not. "Perhaps she had to clean up an experiment at the lab?"

"Perhaps, Reach, perhaps." Her velvety voice can't completely drown out the menace underneath. I can tell a lot about people from how they talk. When you're an outsider looking in on every group in a highly classified facility, how people talk often gives more information than what people say.

Silence stretches between us as she leans forward. "Sit, Reach." She points to the chair across from the couch. Only the coffee table will separate us and I'll have to look her in the eyes. She reminds me of a rattlesnake, waiting for its prey to slip up and become a meal. My thoughts whir as I contemplate what to do. I know that this woman is important, and not offending the government is imperative. I need to listen, and promptly.

Hoping to buy some time, I blurt out, "Something to drink?"

She looks at me, rattlesnake black eyes piercing my own hazel ones as if she had taken off her shoes and driven the heel through them. "No," she replies coolly. She snaps her fingers and points to the chair. "Now sit."

I am trapped. With a calm I do not feel, I lower my body into the fake leather upholstery. The back of my thighs squeak against the chair when the front door opens and my mother walks in.

"Hello," she calls, breathless as she rushes into the living room. She smiles at me, a strange, fake sort of smile. She turns to the woman in black. "I had to put the samples away properly at the lab. I'm sorry I'm late, but I couldn't ruin the experiment we've been working on for years by mismanaging the samples."

The woman in black looks at her with one eyebrow raised. "Human samples or others?"

My mother swallows. "Non-living."

"I see. You have the numbers for the log books I'll need to verify for your tardiness?'

"Yes, ma'am. Would you like them now?"

"No. I see you received my message and are here. Of course, your tardiness in official matters has been noted."

My mother, usually calm and collected, swallows again, unease rising to the surface. "Yes, ma'am."

"Sit," the woman in black says again with the snap of her fingers. My mother passes in front of me and sits in the chair next to mine. It groans and lets out a little puff as it accepts her frame. "You are, I'm certain, aware of the terms in which your most unique situation was permitted fourteen years ago."

Confused, I look at my mother. She nods and gazes down at the floor.

"You'll be fulfilling those terms now," the woman continues. "You have twenty-four hours until a crew arrives. At that time, the specimen known as Reach becomes the property of the government, and you will relinquish said specimen from your care." My mother's gasp seems to bring the woman in black a measure of happiness. She appears to grow larger, and her velvet voice is back. "I'm sure you recall these special circumstances necessitate the personal sacrifice of our *brave Citizen* and government control over the specimen." Her white teeth gleam as her smile stretches wide.

My heart pounds, the thumps sounding an irregular drumbeat in my ears that must be audible to everyone else. The words *Reach, property of, specimen,* and *relinquish* echo around the room. I follow the woman's flashing eyes, see the answering spark of anger in my mother's, and the moment when the mysterious government woman wins the power struggle.

My mother breaks eye contact with the woman, bites her lip, and nods. She's had her hands clenched so tightly on the edge of the chair I can see the bones in her hand. A perfect X-ray image of bones. She shakes them out and wipes them on the front of her scientist uniform, a standard-issue white lab coat. This agitation is shocking. My mother is unflappable.

She rises, her posture mimicking her voice, growing louder the taller she stands. "Yes, I remember. Surely you can understand that, despite the unusual circumstances, I have cared for this specimen like a child, like a future Citizen. I have an affinity for Reach. He is my son!"

"Of course. Those were your directives as outlined in the protocol given fourteen years ago." She lifts her voice into a mocking falsetto. "Treat this specimen like a child, raising it as a Citizen child of Nation would be raised." She drops back to her normal lead pipe tones. "Except for the directives stating otherwise." She smiles her predatory smile, flashing blindingly white teeth as she stands. "I will be returning with the crew tomorrow. Twenty-four hours."

She turns the doorknob, her words lingering in the air like smoke. Before she can leave, my mother speaks. "That's it?" My mother's shoulders are slumped, her voice wobbly, the strident tones she took before long gone.

"Dr. Impart, I am not completely heartless. My orders were originally to bring the specimen in immediately. I delayed the departure by twenty-four hours because I also am a mother…of sorts." She rolls her eyes and gives a small snort. "I understood this parting would be difficult for you. Science is coming closer to understanding love, but you've not yet determined the chemical components in your *lab*."

She stalks through the door and begins her bizarre high knees walk back to the blue vehicle.

# 2

My brain is hazy, my body stiff, and mentally processing the past twenty minutes is the most taxing thing I have ever done. The click of the front door closing triggers a nervous tic. I try to master it, but I can't sit still—my feet begin tapping, black shoes of my Compound uniform hitting the floor in a rhythm of their own volition.

Mom still stands, scowling at the door as she clenches and unclenches her fists. I try her name, but it comes out as a squeak. "Mom?"

Her head turns sharply and her gaze lands on my tapping feet. Regret flashes over her face. Her eyes meet mine.

"Reach," she says. "Oh Reach. I thought we'd have more time."

Looking at my mom is always a bit disconcerting; it's like looking in a mirror, only seeing a differently gendered version of you staring back. Commentary on my appearance is part of daily life on Compound. Even the non-scientists are constantly remarking that I look just like her. Today, I want to see everything. To commit everything I ever thought mundane to memory and hold on to it forever.

Her dark hair is long, her face oval, and her eyes dark hazel, nearly gray. As a scientist, she is required to wear her hair pulled away from her face, braided in one long strand down her back. My hair is not that long, but it is just as dark. My face is the same shape, with the same high cheekbones and round, dark hazel eyes. Even our clothing is similar. She wears a white lab coat and wide-legged pants. I wear a navy blue jumpsuit, complete with black sneakers. We each wear a communication device on our wrist.

Mom starts to speak, then stops, removes her communication device, gestures for me to do the same, and holds out her hand. I pull the strap away and remove the device. The sun glints off the black glass screen, blinding me momentarily as I pass it into her open palm. There is an important rule on Compound: Do not remove your communication device. No amount of preparation can prevent accidents from happening in a science-based community, and you never know when you might need to be quarantined or notified of a disaster. Personal messages are never sent through the communication devices, only immediate government messages. It also functions as a regular watch.

Mom is a rule-following scientist. She achieved a high rank in the community as a Citizen who served a space mission when she was younger. Serving a space mission cements you as a hero in Nation. Space—the final frontier, not just the physical location, but also knowledge and human understanding. Taking off her communication device signals an act of defiance on its own, but when she takes a blanket from the basket next to the couch and rolls both of our devices into it, my eyes nearly pop out of my skull. This is unprecedented. I'm aware enough of people and behavior to know that hiding communication devices is rebellious—and illegal.

"Reach. I'm sorry."

I stare at her, willing my voice to work. I open my mouth, but the words stick in my throat.

"You have questions."

I nod, because even saying 'yes' is impossible.

"You're feeling anxious."

That's a statement and not a question.

"We need to—" She heaves a large sigh as she brings her palm to her brow. She tries again. "We need to talk. Come with me?" She spins on her heel and walks down the hall to her bedroom.

Unsure, I follow. I pause in the doorway because my mother's bedroom has always been off-limits. As a child, I could knock on the door, but when I tried to enter, she told me, "Everyone needs a place that's just their own. This is mine." Being invited into her sanctuary now is a significant moment.

"Reach, come on," she whispers. Her room is dark, the window shades closed. In the dim shadows, I can make out her profile sitting on her bed. "Shut the door," she hisses. I do. She flips on the lamp beside her bed.

Immediately I am awash in color. I can see why Mom never let me in here before. For a woman who follows the standard regulations in every regard, from decorating our apartment to the length and style of her hair, this room is the opposite of my standard regulation bedroom in every possible way.

She has a wider bed than I do, and while my bedsheets are all crisp and white, hers are the color of the desert sky on a hot summer morning before the blistering sun has burned the blue to a haze. Her walls are colored with flowers that have been painted onto the white cinderblock.

I recall the phrase given to us about the standard regulations when we learned about them in school: "Efficiency found in regulation leads to discovery." This room is not regulated. Which means it's not efficient. So why does it still feel like a discovery?

I quirk my eyebrows at the wall. Who knew Mom had a rebellious streak.

"Reach, come sit here." She pats the bed. "We need to talk about things." It's an ominous statement at best. The bed offers a small creak as I lower my weight onto it. "What are your questions?"

My mother, the scientist, always starting with the scientific method, even for important conversations. I'm not sure I have the ability to form a coherent question, but when I try to use my vocal cords, my efforts are rewarded. "Who was that woman?"

Mom's face screws up like she just ate something sour. "Enforce." I stare blankly. "You know that Leader, Legislate, and Litigate are the Three Powers of Nation's government. Because you aren't at the age of loyalty when you're in school, you only learn partial information about the government structure. Certain, more volatile aspects of Nation's government are kept secret until you publicly pledge your loyalty and begin Citizenship training. Enforce and her role in government is one delightful surprise that awaits the future Citizens of Nation."

If her facial features hadn't already, the sarcasm in her voice would have exposed my mother's true feelings about Enforce.

"What does she do?" I whisper, half-awed that there is more to the government than I'd been taught and half-terrified by Mom's reactions to talking about it.

"Enforce is the head of the government's Punishment and Retribution System."

I blink. "There's a Punishment and Retribution System?"

"Of course. You don't learn about it at school because it might encourage rebellions. I believe you studied a few rebellions, but they were all from long ago, right?" I nod. "Did you really believe that there are no active rebellions happening now? That there has been a single government in the entire history of humankind that did not fear rebellion?"

I shrug. "I guess I never really thought about it. We're so much more civilized than people were back then."

"That is exactly what they want you to think! No one challenges the status quo because the current status quo is so much better than anything from history. Becoming a Citizen naturally feels very safe, stable, desirable, right?" I nod again. "There are active rebellions, little ones each day, and sometimes even larger ones. These rebellions are a threat to the government. In order to maintain power and control, Enforce and her department carry out the punishments for any acts of insurrection. The fact that you are surveilled and responsible for keeping Enforce from punishing you is hidden until after completing stage one of the Citizenship process. You don't know this. I've never told you. Everything I say to you from now on never happened."

"What sort of punishments?"

She closes her eyes and takes a steadying breath. "Removal of Citizenship, pain, prison time, in some cases…death."

"But—I thought. We. Wait. What?" My words are stilted, and my breath hitches as I try to make sense of Nation's dark secrets.

"The government surveils Citizens regularly. Since all you've ever known is safety and security provided by the government, the pre-Citizens have no problems signing away certain rights in the name of government safety and cooperation. It is patriotic to become a Citizen, and there's a fervor to the ceremonies that is intoxicating. In the ceremony, the pre-Citizens sign one final paper before they are presented with the secret inner workings of Nation's government. This paper is the Citizenship paper. It's signed with blood. Once you've signed, you're a Citizen, meaning you've agreed to surveillance and pledged your life to serving Nation. The fine print explains anyone deemed a threat or not useful to Nation will be eliminated.

"Here on Compound, we have even stricter surveillance rules than the general population. Your communication device is a way for government officials to keep tabs on you. There are always ways for them to listen, but the wrist device is one that they use most regularly for spying."

"But I thought you designed it?"

"I did."

"So, you made a device that spies on people? But you sound like you're against spying? Do you…not…like the government?" I want to ask if she is dissenting, but that word feels too volatile, too explosive.

She hesitates. "It's complicated. I designed a device that would allow the leaders to spy on us because if I didn't, who knows what would have been created. It was a way to preserve some dignity for everyone on base. I designed it to be the least intrusive as possible. I've been a scientist for decades, and I served a space mission. I have known many, many, overly ambitious scientists." She shudders.

I blink, confused. "But what about the Citizens? I don't understand. What does any of this have to do with *me*?"

She inhales, and I can tell she's filling her lungs with courage rather than air. "I rebelled. I am still rebelling. We've been in a game of power with the government your entire life." I feel my facial muscles twitch involuntarily. She continues. "When I was in space, I was sent to Station 15." I shake my head because I know this. Space missions are high priority and considered heroic. There are 51 stations, numbered from closest to Earth to farthest. 51 is extremely deep space. "Station 15 is near Mars," she says so quietly her voice is nearly inaudible. I lean closer. "While at 15, I made contact with a group of people that the government does not have jurisdiction over."

"Martians?" I breathe the word out contemptuously. Aliens and Martians are the stuff of children's stories.

"Yes. Martians. Except these people were not Martians in the sense you think of. They were—and are—completely human. I met your father when he was scouting for his people, and we fell in love. His people have a deep love for exploration and science. We were compatible and shared much scientific data. He challenged me to think critically, and proposed ideas about our government I had never thought of before—*treasonous* ideas, the kind that result in death from the Punishment and Retribution Department.

"His people are the descendants of those who fled Earth before the Scientific Revolution. They believed that the new regime would result in complete tyranny, and they were right. They are *defectors*."

"What do you mean?"

"This government is about complete power," she explains. "Anything that challenges that power is removed. There is no accountability. They direct the Citizens to the pursuits of science, which are glamorous and exciting. All the while, they are quietly establishing their dominance and power over the lives of the people of Nation. It's broken. Greg told me about his people and how they live. People are valued there not just for what they produce, but for *being*."

"Greg is my..."

"Greg is your father."

My eyes grow wide. I've wondered about my father—who he was, his name, his story. I've studied biology at school. The truth is that some kids never get to meet their fathers. It's rotten luck, but I'd accepted it as my lot in life. Mom never talked about him, and I never asked.

I finally manage to squeeze out a single word: "How?"

"We fell in love. He left for the colony before I knew about you. He had to maintain secrecy about the colony location, so I don't know exactly where they are in the universe, but I'm certain they are on Mars. I had to think of a lie so that the government would let me keep you."

"Why wouldn't they let me stay with you? They love babies."

Mom takes a moment to draw in a breath. She grimaces, the words coming out of her mouth adding to the pained expression on her face. "The government of Nation loves babies from approved 'matches.' They do not love rebels. All the children on Compound are the result of government-approved matches. You have been in the unique position of being a symbol of rebellion without even knowing it."

"Why would they...I'm...Mom, I don't get it."

She meets my eyes and then looks away. "I fell in love with a defector. To them, nothing is more dangerous than a rebellion. I had a highly publicized science career before I was selected for space missions." Mom's gaze tracks upward until she lands again on my eyes. Her voice lowers. "I followed the rules and was loyal beyond question. I was cheered and displayed as an example of what we could *become.* To have me, the poster child for Nation's government, do anything that could be conceived as turning against them…it would have resulted in my death. It still will, but you have a chance because of the lies I told." She slumps like the cinder blocks that make up our structures on Compound have been dropped onto her shoulders.

"Death? Lies?" My head spins as I try to understand everything. "Reach, you are completely human. But to the government, you are half-Martian. *That* was the lie I told that would allow me to keep you, to raise you, to give you a semblance of a regular childhood. The terms of the agreement were just as Enforce said. I could be your mother, raise you just as any other child on Compound, as if you were destined for Citizenship, unaware of your Martian heritage, until a time when they decided to take you for further study and use you to further Nation's scientific understanding of the universe. In return, you have been studied. You are *the specimen* of a highly classified project named Global 1."

I may be only fourteen, but I have had a rigorous education. I have also been around scientists my entire life. They know how to sniff out errors, and do so relentlessly. "I'm the experiment? How would they not have figured it out? I know I've been studied, and a lot, so how do they think I'm half-Martian?"

"Dr. Jog has been instrumental in assisting with data manipulation."

"The hair scientist?"

Mom smiles warmly. "Yes. Dr. Jog is the only person to ever return from Station 51. He's been an ally. He's going with you to Hub. Remember, allies are not necessarily friends. I like Jog, though. I've never told anyone but you the whole story. Jog has just suspected and picked up on the hints I've dropped." Her countenance falls and her eyebrows pinch toward her nose, pained. "I know he has a plan. You'll need to listen to him when they take you."

"Take me where?" I whisper.

"Hub, the city where the government Capital is located, as well as more active projects. They train for space missions there. I have no information—my contribution to the project is completed when you leave tomorrow—but my guess is that they want to send you on a space mission to try to make contact with the Martians that you are supposedly related to."

"They haven't talked to the Mar—my father's people?"

"No, there has been no contact, although they have tried. It's all been unsuccessful. I'm confident that it's because the colony simply does not want to have communication with Nation." Suddenly, she claps her hands onto her white pant legs and stands. "That's the back-story. We need to figure out a plan for your survival in the next phases now. We have twenty-three hours. Questions?"

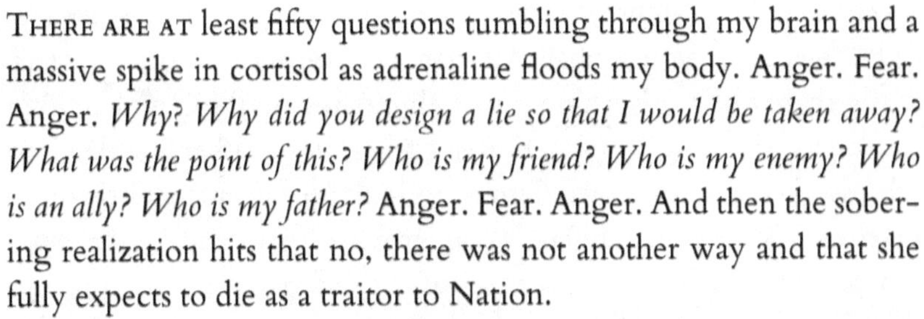

THERE ARE AT least fifty questions tumbling through my brain and a massive spike in cortisol as adrenaline floods my body. Anger. Fear. Anger. *Why? Why did you design a lie so that I would be taken away? What was the point of this? Who is my friend? Who is my enemy? Who is an ally? Who is my father?* Anger. Fear. Anger. And then the sobering realization hits that no, there was not another way and that she fully expects to die as a traitor to Nation.

"I'm going to make us some dinner now, Reach. Our rations got restocked today, so we'll have something tasty and nutritious." Mom has always been stoic, but when I meet her eyes, I can see that she is holding herself together by sheer will.

Despite the anger coursing through my veins, it hurts to see her pain. I direct my sentence to the floor. "I'm sorry, Mom."

"Sorry for what, Reach?" Her quiet voice penetrates the gloom that has flowed down my body like an icy shower since I remembered her pronouncement of death.

"For being born. And for causing you…" I chance a glance at her face, which is contorting through different emotions. Anger, fear, sorrow, regret—each emotion flashes across her countenance with raw passion.

"Don't you ever, *ever* even think that your life is something to be sorry for." Her statement is delivered calmly with conviction, and it hits me in the heart. It's as if someone whacked me with a concrete block. I am overwhelmed. I can't help feeling hopeless any more than I can help the tears now falling down my cheeks.

We are not affectionate people on Compound. So when Mom sits back down beside me on the bed and pulls me into a hug, I'm first surprised and then even more distraught.

"Reach." Her breath tickles my cheek as her arms tighten around me. "I didn't have many choices that would have protected you. I'm the one who's sorry." She hands me a handkerchief with a watery smile. "You need to eat. We can figure this out. You are highly intelligent, and all your aptitude tests show us that you have what it takes to be and do anything you want. The government is excited about how they can use you to further their influence into space because they think you are half-Martian. Do you want to be a *specimen* at the mercy of a government that eliminates anything and anyone it deems a threat to its power? Remember, your father is a defector who swayed a highly loyal Citizen to look further into government practices. Who you truly are is dangerous to them and tyrants anywhere." She draws in a shaky breath. "It's all game theory, playing their game until you find a weakness and exploit it. It's dangerous, but it's the only way. I'm so sorry that your life only has value as a science experiment to them. We have to keep up the game if you want to live. Do you want to live or let them win?"

It is such a simple question, it's almost rhetorical. Almost, but not quite.

"Yes, I want to live."

Mom's eyes meet mine, piercing my irises with hers. "Good. Your father would be very proud. And I am too."

"I don't know what to do," I whisper. "This feels impossible."

"Reach, why do you think we spent so much time learning

chess? You know game theory. You'll figure out what to do when you see their moves." Her thumb lands next to my eye, her cool skin wiping away an errant tear. "Reach, you know that scientists name their children things that relate to their interest of study, usually, or a verb, since science is about action. I named you Reach because it is a verb and also because Greg taught me an old saying that his people held on to from before the Scientific Revolution. Before space travel was common, people would say 'reach for the stars' whenever they were attempting to do the impossible. Reach, yes, what you'll have to do seems impossible to a fourteen-year-old, but your name's a reminder of what else lies among the stars. An entirely different people, an entirely different way of life, *that* is your heritage and right. You can do this. You were born to do this."

I still don't understand what I'm supposed to do and what the government wants to do with me, but my stomach chooses that moment to rumble loudly. Mom's affectionate eyes glance down at the source of the noise, and she gives me a small smile and removes her thumb from my face. I miss the contact.

"I'll go make dinner." She stands and leaves the room, but before she does, she turns over a picture frame from her nightstand and unlatches the back. She slides a photograph out, removing it from under a pressing of a desert flower. "This is Greg, your father." She pushes it into my hands. "Everyone always said you look just like me, but it's because they never saw him."

I study the photo. My father and mother, together. My father happens to be the reason I am a top-secret science specimen. I didn't even know I was a specimen. I thought he was dead. My father is apparently not only alive but in another universe, and a defector from a government my mother just told me is tyrannical. It's a lot to take in.

My eyes seek out the man in the photo. He is taller than Mom. It's hard to see his build under the spacesuit, but I would guess he is lean; being in space is taxing on muscle mass. Astronauts have to train for years to build up strength before they can go on a space mission simply because they lose so much muscle in space. I briefly wonder how the colony maintains muscle before I resume my perusal of Greg's—my father's—face. I spy my nose, my full lips, my right ear that holds a notch in the lobe, my prominent forehead. My mother is right, per usual. I look like her, but I look just as much like *him*.

The photograph is on a type of paper that feels soft, like linen, with muted colors. My mom's spacesuit is white, stiff, and large. There are knobs and dials behind her, cords and tubes folded into neat loops by her feet. In contrast, my father's spacesuit is silver, slouchy, and much slimmer than my mother's. It still looks bulky, but she looks like a marshmallow next to him. It's impossible to miss the adoration on her face as she grins up at him. His mouth is set in a half-smile, and while his eyes are on the camera, they are turned down in the corners as if they are looking at Mom from his periphery. I don't know this man, but he has a hint of mischief in his expression. I like him.

"Ready to eat, Reach?" Mom's voice penetrates my perusal of the photo. I tuck it into the front pocket of my navy jumpsuit and tread to the kitchen. She looks worn, but I offer her the photo and she smiles, unmistakable joy at the memory flitting across her face. "It's yours. Keep it. Actually, bury it. You'll have no privacy at Hub. But hold it in your mind, keep it in your heart."

I nod and slump into one of the simple wooden chairs as Mom sets a plate of unidentifiable meat in front of me. "What is it?"

Our rations are delivered weekly. We can determine what to make with the rations in our own apartment blocks, but what is delivered varies based on our nutritional profiles. Nutrition is the cornerstone to optimizing efficiency, and efficiency in research is what drives Nation into the future. *Progress, progress, progress.*

"Some kind of meat; it wasn't labeled in the ration delivery—potatoes—and I was saving something for another day, but this *is* the day." She holds out a sleeve of chocolate circles with a crunchy mint in the middle—celebration cookies. Cookies are delivered five times a year: on our birthdays and three important holidays, one of which is Leader's Day. Seeing the dessert unlocks questions.

"Mom." I set my fork down and push my plate away. I'm not hungry. She pauses, her fork midway to her mouth, and lowers it as she waits. "Mom, am I a pre-Citizen? They called me a specimen, but I get cookies too?"

Her fingers run through her scalp as she considers her answer. "No."

I gulp. In Nation, there are two classes of people: the Citizens, who have prestigious careers that further Nation's scientific advancement, and Noncitizens. Citizens live in the city centers of Nation. Nons live in the Wards. They are the people who do hard labor and are not protected under the law. My education at Compound's Educational Facility instilled a certain fear of being a *Non*.

Our government is comprised of three strands: Legislate, Leader, and Litigate. Legislate is responsible for creating laws, Leader for signing them into being, and Litigate for understanding them when harm befalls a Citizen. Leader has the ultimate power. As a Citizen, there are protections in the laws. Citizens are the future; Noncitizens exist in a support role. With no legal protections, Nons are expendable, while Citizens are supposedly cherished.

Citizenship can be revoked. Citizens are superior to Nons, and since everyone fears revocation, Citizens stay as far away as possible from them. Nons are criminals, or the children of criminals, or the people who didn't have enough aptitude to be useful to Nation in any scientific way. They are the people who do not advance the good of Nation under their own merits. So, Nation finds a way to use them for progress.

If I'm not a Citizen, I have no protection under any laws. A Citizen or a fellow Non can do whatever they want to me, and I have no recourse. I am defenseless.

The anxiety that often fills my body comes coursing through. "So I'm a Non?"

Mom's fingers still. "No. You're a half-Citizen. It doesn't mean anything, but I was able to secure you a status, based on your being a long-term scientific experiment specimen and my service to Nation. There was no reason to relegate you to a Non. I had to argue that you were half-human and should be given a half-status."

"That's something then, isn't it?" I hate how unsure my voice sounds.

"It's something..." Her voice trails off and she grimaces. "I tried to protect you as much as I could, Reach. But you're the *only* half-Citizen in Nation. It means *nothing*. When they take you tomorrow afternoon, they can do whatever they want to you. You are going as a specimen, which is a scientific prisoner." Tears pool in the corners of her eyes. She clenches her jaw. The words grate out. "I'm not trying to scare you, Reach. I'm trying to prepare you." She softens. "I-I love you, Reach, and I have high hopes for you and Nation."

"What hopes?" I form the words cautiously. They feel heavy and wrong on my tongue.

"I hope that you can make a real difference. Greg showed me how broken this society is. How tyrannical. How people in power do not exist to serve, but to be served, and how everyone else is just a cog in the machine of their ambition."

"That sounds like you want a reb..." I choke on the word, knowing that it is punishable to discuss. "Rebellion," I whisper.

"I do." She says it flatly, without emotion.

"But I thought rebellions were criminal and you would become a Non if you tried anything."

"They are. But I won't become a Non. I'll die for my rebellious lies. They will find out eventually that I used you to undermine them. But in the meantime, I have given my life to make sure that this system has a chance to be defeated." Her voice is gravelly, her tone heavier.

"How? How am I supposed to do anything? I'm being taken away from everything I've known tomorrow. Do you know anything? Can you help me?" The words are gushing, a torrent of phonemes. I despise the fear in my voice.

"Reach. I don't want you to go. But this is literally what you were born for."

"I was born to be a science experiment that gets you killed?" I snap.

"You were born to be the change."

I blink as the implication of her words hits me. "That's why you had me, so I could be a pawn in a power game with the government." My hands ball into fists beneath the dinner table. "Do you even love me?"

"You were born *because* I love you. But when I discovered I was pregnant, I needed a way to make your life valuable to the government. I played a long game, gambled on something I knew they would want, and exploited a weakness. They will know, eventually. But they couldn't know before I had a chance to raise you. I owed that to Greg. His way of life is so much more than ours. We all deserve better than this system. And Reach, yes, I love you. How could I not when I have been reminded of *him* every day I've had you?"

The panic rising in me is calmed by my mother's demeanor as she delivers her words.

"Here's what we are going to do, Reach." She leans over and grasps my hand in hers. "We are going to follow along and do what we are told. You are going to Hub, and I think you'll be training for a space mission. Since all Martian contact efforts have failed, you are their only hope for finding the colony and bringing the Martians under Nation's rule, or at least infiltrating their scientific advances. You are going to cooperate. You are going to bide your time. When it is time, you'll have to start making choices. I can't make them for you. But you can choose to thwart their plans in little ways and, eventually, big ones."

"But what will happen if they are training me for a space mission?"

"Jog has implied they will be, but you're too young to go right into space anyway. Becoming an astronaut takes years of preparation. There's the educational phase—you have an excellent start because of Compound's high-achieving Educational Facility—then the physical phase, and finally, a lengthy simulation-based phase. You will need to excel. You can't think beyond being excellent at every task they set before you."

"Will I see you again? Or talk to you? Can you help me?"

Her face falls. "Probably not. Your leaving marks the end of your childhood. You'll see that family ties don't matter when you're serving the government. That's expected to be the highest honor, to fulfill you to such a degree that there is no reason to look back. Also, Reach, remember that to them, you are a scientific specimen. You're half-human, which is to say, not as human as they are."

I shake my head slowly to signal my understanding, but my reality is blurred in the way that dusk and sunset don't have clear parameters but slowly bleed into one another until darkness falls.

"There's not much more I can tell you. Jog has been Global 1's head scientist since he returned from 51. With Global 1 being such a top-secret project, we have been surveilled closely. We know that our work on Global 1 is of the highest interest to the government, and we have had one conversation privately in all these years. The rest of my understanding of him- it's just a hypothesis based on observation." She sighs.

"So how can you trust him?"

"I don't have another choice. I know he caught some of the data manipulations I made and let them slide. He also advocated for the most humane treatment possible. Some of the experiments they wanted to run were"—she grimaces—"invasive. He's loyal to the government even more than I was, but I get a sense there's more to his mission than meets the eye. He's an ally, not a friend." She picks up the foil-wrapped sleeve of cookies, the packaging making a zing as she rips it open. "This is all I can do for you now, Reach. You'll have to make choices every day. Whose side are you on?"

I point to hers and she smiles. It's weak, but there is a resoluteness behind it. "Well then, let's enjoy our last night together. Chess?"

# 4

THE NEXT DAY dawns like a calico quilt. Streaks of red, wisps of white, and robin's-egg blue create a breathtaking patchwork across the sky. I have never seen the desert as a beautiful place. When we studied biomes at the Educational Facility, I was drawn to the mountains and oceans. *Desert* was just a synonym for a place with tumbleweeds, sand, and scratchy cacti. My mother liked the desert blooms, but those only happened when conditions were just right, which was rare. The only reason I found them interesting was because they broke up the monotony of the tumbleweeds and sand. Familiarity breeds contempt—with landscapes, anyway.

I stand before my window, leaning against the frame and looking out at the shadows cast by the rising sun. I am conscious of a sense of awe welling within me, an appreciation for a place that has been my home. A home that I am leaving today, and no one asked me if I wanted to go. Truthfully, I do want to leave. I've never been anywhere but *here*. A sense of adventure and excitement about all the new things I will experience simmers below my skin. I feel a little bit guilty about that feeling. Is it wrong to feel excited about a new life?

The word *life* brings the word *death* to mind, and suddenly I am terrified. I can't let them hurt my mom. She protected me. She wants me to go to my father. To make a difference here. I have to. She can't die. I have to protect her.

The thoughts circle the drain in my mind. *Protect her. I owe her what she wants. She protected me.* I know I'm only fourteen. I'm young, but I've been educated by the best scientific minds on Earth. Scientists expect the best education for their children, so the Education Facility on Compound is staffed by the most cutting-edge teachers. Only the best for the children of the best minds. I can figure out this game. I can beat them at it. I have to.

Last night, Mom and I played chess. We discovered chess while reading historical books about the culture before the Scientific Revolution for a school project. The school, a gleaming structure of glass and stone, has an extensive library. The library serves all of Compound, so it was never an unusual thing to see scientists in the building checking out books. We had gone to the library to work on my project, a comparison of life before the Scientific Revolution to life now. It was obvious that life now was an improvement, but the game of chess was briefly mentioned as a form of popular entertainment pre-revolution. I showed the page explaining the rules to Mom, and she was fascinated. This led to a year-long deep dive on all things chess and creating a board and pieces. Since chess is a two-player game, I had to learn it too. Not that I minded. Now I can see that Mom saw more to the game. She saw the theory, the way the principals of the game could be used in what I never knew was a deadly situation.

Mom is one of the leading scientific minds of Nation for a reason. As her name—Dr. Impart—aptly implies, she *imparted* knowledge without nagging or harping. She taught chess calmly, and with conviction. She never said what to do, but allowed me to make mistakes and figure out what I needed to do. When I made a mistake, she would dissect my moves with me. I learned strategy, and how to think like my opponent. All that time, she was using chess as a way to prepare me. In her own way, she has calmly gone about doing her duties to Nation while giving me an education in how to manipulate powerful people. She has done her best not to die.

Despite never knowing a single person who held to any religious belief, I utter a plea to something. Someone? The universe? The ether? Stars? Clouds? I have no idea. There is no religion on Compound. Our schooling made brief mention of religion as a substitute used to distract people from the real goal of science and exploration.

I whisper it aloud, because saying it makes it real. "Please, please, don't let them hurt her." The words hang there like music notes in the early breeze and then gently waft away on the ever-shifting grains of sand.

Up to this point, I have been a child. Today, I lose the protection of my mother, and the last vestiges of my childhood slip away. I become responsible for myself and Mom. Maybe if I play this right, I can win. Maybe I can give her what she wants. It's the least I can do for her, to try—really try—to undermine the three strands of leadership. I vow to promise her whatever she wants. I feel a sense of restitution, a rightness, as I consider a promise that binds us together not only now, but in the future.

I softly step down the cool tile hall to the kitchen. Mom is there, dressed as usual in her scientist clothing. I'm in my navy jumpsuit and socks. Peeking out of her lab coat pocket is a flash of orange paper, the official schedule color for government visits and notifications.

"Hey, Mom."

She looks over at me, a small smile forming on her lips. "Hi. Good game last night. I was impressed."

The air is tense, but I grin. Mom is not easily impressed.

"What's on the schedule for today?" I gesture at the orange paper in her pocket.

"It's a 'Day of Reflection' for both of us until four p.m. Then it's your departure."

"Day of Reflection?" I test out the words; they sound foreign to my ears. "Is that even a thing?"

"It is now." Her shoulders lift and fall in a resigned shrug. "It's our time together, so what would you like to do?"

"Mom." I check to see if she's wearing her communication device. I'm not. I will have to return it when I leave Compound, so I left it in my bedroom on the charging module. She is, so I gesture for her to remove it. She does and passes it to me. I want to smash it with a hammer, but settle on placing it on the charging module next to mine. When I return, I find her smiling broadly.

"Yes, Reach?" She's quiet, but I can sense the adrenaline thrumming through her. The words we say to each other have more meaning today than ever and we both know it.

"Mom, I—I'm going to do it."

"Do what, Reach?"

"I'm going to do what you said. I'm going to make Nation better. And I'm going to use game theory to do it." The promise is out, words I can't retract floating like dust motes in a patch of sun between us.

Her grin turns so wide that the corners of her lips are parallel with the corners of her eyes. It's strange and rather scary, but I know I've pleased her. "That's *my* boy. Now, what would you like for breakfast?"

# 5

THE HOURS PASS in fits and starts. A 'Day of Reflection' before being taken away is not something I'd recommend. There is nothing to keep me or Mom busy. I find myself second-guessing everything. My mind pulses with thoughts: *You're fourteen. You don't know enough. You'll never be able to make it to a space mission. How can you make changes? You're nothing, no one. Why didn't Mom just tell them you were human?*

I know the answer to the last question. She was trying to protect me. I don't know what they would have done to me if she had told them the truth, but she made that much clear.

I'm slumped in one of the chairs in our living room. Mom is reading an original scientific research paper for peer review. If it wasn't for the intrusive thoughts, it would feel almost cozy. Even on holidays and our *break day*, the one day a week we are not required to work or attend school, we receive schedules that group our time into specific tasks. Staying efficient is key to a healthy, productive society, and the schedulers ensure that efficiency.

I catch Mom's eyes lingering on my face. "What?" I'm like a rubber band pulled taut, dealing with all these feelings and thoughts, so I snap the word at her more sharply than I intended. She flinches at my tone.

"I just want to remember you."

*Great.* Now I feel all watery from her love. This is not what I need before entering into the longest game of chess I've ever played. I can't be crying when they come for me.

Mom leaves her chair and crouches down in front of me. "Reach. You are *not* weak. You can do this. You *have* to do it. Don't give them the satisfaction of knowing you're bothered. You have to be half-Martian, so you need to *not* have human emotions. You have to keep up the facade. It's the only way to make all this worth it!" She gestures around the room. She hisses, "You promised!"

Surprise at her vehemence stops my tears. She places a warm palm on my arm. "You have a part to play. I have a part to play. They're coming. Are you packed?"

Of course I'm packed. It took me four minutes to place everything into the travel bag. I have one small orange duffel bag sitting on my standard regulation bed. In it are my three navy blue jumpsuits and backup pair of boots, my comb and toothbrush, and a tube of deodorant from the rations. The picture of Greg and Mom has been carefully rolled into a tight tube and placed inside the deodorant container, hidden under the wax. I know she told me to bury it, but I couldn't let it go.

"Your emotions, Reach. You'll have to control them to succeed at this," she whispers, her voice soft but firm. She glances out the window at the sun. "Time for me to put the communication device back on. They can track that I'm in the apartment with it, but I need to have it on when they come."

I nod, understanding that what she really means is that it's time to stop talking about anything dangerous.

It's four p.m. exactly when two sharp knocks sound on our front door. Mom strides to the door and opens it. I hear murmurs, followed by voices. Enforce is back. "Is he ready?"

I stand and make my way behind my mother.

"Yes, madam Enforce." The deferential tone in my mother's voice makes me cringe.

"Good. We don't have much time." A new woman is speaking. I can tell she is important, because she wears the uniform of a high-ranking government official. She has wide-legged black pants, a black button-up shirt, and a black coat that is structurally the same as a lab coat but has much fancier buttons. The buttons look like pearls. Her uniform is similar to Enforce's, but Enforce has no fancy buttons. She has a larger communication device on her wrist and rings on each of her fingers. She is small and slight, and the rings are heavy, clearly weighing down her hands. Her blonde hair is swept up off her neck in some sort of twist, and I catch a black pen tucked behind her ear. I remember Enforce's shoes and glance at the mystery woman's. Her shoes are plain and black. They look comfortable, practical.

While I'm observing shoes, I glance at Enforce's. Today, they are not high heels; she wears flat black strips of leather wrapped to make a cocoon around her feet. I can tell they are designed to be stealth shoes. She shifts slightly and I see the flashes of small silver spikes attached to the insteps.

Dread, grief, remorse, fear—it all washes over me as the reality of going anywhere with this woman becomes apparent. I freeze.

"Are we ready, then?" a deeper voice booms into the hall. I know this voice. Relief instantly flows into my veins. Dr. Jog. I forgot he was coming too. I've seen Dr. Jog every day while working on my experiments, but other than an occasional word or two, I've never spoken with him. My mother sort of trusts him. I won't be totally alone with a woman who looks like she wants to destroy me and use my bones for musical instruments. Actually, Enforce does not look like someone who would play music. She would turn my bones into weapons, though, that I can believe.

"We have a schedule to keep if we're going to make it on time." The mystery woman speaks in an oddly clipped voice. Her consonants are too harsh, vowels too liquidy.

I step forward to give my mother a farewell. She just told me not to have emotions in front of these people, but I have to say goodbye. I *have* to. If only I could figure out an appropriate way to touch her, to be affectionate. I'm saved from my doubts when Mom reaches out and wraps her arms around me.

Between yesterday and today, this is more physical touch than I've had since I broke my arm learning how to balance on a bike when I was four. The touch unlocks a memory and my emotions rise up, swelling like the rogue ocean waves we spent an entire year studying. I'm four years old, in the Preparatory Division of the Educational Facility, balancing on a two-wheeled bicycle. Other children are riding their bikes around the floor. I haven't mastered the skill yet, but I'm close, I can tell. I get going, slowly, slowly, slowly. And then I am doing it! I am riding. I pick up speed until I arrive at the corner. I slow down to turn, but as I do, three children crash into my back tire. I fly off the bike headfirst, but my arm lodges under the handlebar and bends backward. I hear the gravelly crunch of the broken bone, but am too dazed to cry as I lie in a heap. They transported me to the hospital wing and Mom arrived, running in and giving me a hug in front of everyone. It was the hug that unlocked my tears then. It's a hug that unlocks my tears now.

"Thank you," I whisper, the words muffled in her arms. "I—"

She pulls back and meets my eyes with her own, something inexplicable within her gaze. "Be brave, Reach. Make me proud."

"Touching." Enforce's softly cultured tones meet my ears, her voice laced with sarcasm.

"It's time to go." The mystery woman's voice tone isn't sarcastic, it's annoyed. "Get your bag, Reach."

There's nothing for it. I retrieve my orange bag and sling the strap over my shoulder. Enforce talks to Mom as I pass them by on my way out the door. I hear two words before the vehicle's engine starts with a loud popping gurgle: "You better…" Enforce threatens.

The blonde woman and Dr. Jog are already climbing into the vehicle. I take a breath and bravely march across the sand. By the time I'm seated, Enforce slips into her seat. The door retracts from its open position and I watch everything I've ever known disappear.

# 6

No one drives on Compound, so I've never been in a vehicle. Everything is within walking distance, self-contained. I've seen pictures and diagrams, so I do have a frame of reference. This vehicle is arranged differently than the diagrams I saw at school. There are two benches with three seats each. The benches face each other, unlike what I had seen when we studied vehicles. In that unit, every car we saw had the benches all facing forward.

I peer around the vehicle, looking for features. When I'm anxious, I try to hone in on small things. My anxiety is roiling, and I know I'm not supposed to show it. I can't be weak in front of these people. Anxiety is weak. I instinctively know I'm not supposed to ask questions. I'm also not supposed to talk to Enforce or the mystery lady. Dr. Jog is an enigma. My mother's warning flickers in my mind: *ally, not friend.* How am I supposed to interact with him? Am I supposed to interact with him?

Questions form rapid fire as I drag my eyes over the vehicle interior. *Black fabric. Black leather seats. Wood trim. Glass windows on the sides. Air conditioning.*

Dr. Jog's voice startles me from my inventory of the vehicle features. "So, Reach," he says as his gray head moves slightly in a bobbing motion. "I imagine you haven't seen much of Nation."

I find my voice, and I'm pleasantly surprised that it's not squeaky. "No, sir. Only Compound and a bit of the desert near it."

"Yes, of course. That's all in your files. When we arrive at the checkpoint, you'll have lots of interesting things to observe. Riparian habitats are quite shocking when all you've known is desert flora and fauna."

I can't find any words, so I sit there wondering what *riparian* is as I stare out the window.

"Second?" Enforce gently taps on the mystery woman's hand with one finger. She speaks with a previously unheard deference in her menacing voice. The mystery woman I assume is called Second removes an earpiece. I focus on the unending sandy landscape outside of my window but listen harder.

"I assume you took care of the loose end, Enforce?"

It's quiet for a beat.

"Yes. She knows what she must do, or she will suffer the consequences."

"Excellent. Leader is expecting us tomorrow at five fifteen. Reach will need to be made presentable for the occasion. I've arranged for him to be groomed to standard when we arrive. Dr. Jog will supervise the taking of samples. You have several calls to make tomorrow. I'm sure your schedule will enlighten you."

At the sound of my name, I lose my focus and find myself watching Second. There are notes of dismissal and scorn in Second's voice. She jams her earpieces back in before disappearing behind a handheld screen and removing the stylus from behind her ear. She begins furiously circling, writing, and sliding things on the screen.

My voice and body language reading skills tell me that Second is more powerful than Enforce. This is interesting. Enforce is intimidating and oozes menace. Second is not exactly intimidating, but she has more authority. Enforce pulls a tablet out of her black leather bag and begins mimicking Second's behavior. The taps on glass screens and the low whir of electronic fans are oddly soothing when set against the backdrop of a rolling vehicle.

I must fall asleep because the vehicle jerks to a stop and my forehead bumps against the window. I open bleary eyes to see Dr. Jog looking at me, bemused. He gestures with one finger out the window. "Checkpoint."

Up ahead is a stile gate with a metal boom arm. I estimate the fencing on either side of the stile to be twenty-five feet high with barbed wire not only looped and rolling at the top but intertwined throughout the wire mesh of the fence. There is no scaling *that* for even the most serious of climbers.

Enforce and I sit on the vehicle bench, facing forward. Second and Dr. Jog sit opposite us, facing back. From my viewpoint, I can see the driver rolling down his window and presenting a card. It has the official insignia of Nation on it. The guard snatches it and carefully inspects it.

Nation does not have a military, it has Citizen Guards at strategic checkpoints along travel routes. These guards wear tall white hats with folds along the brim and one navy stripe vertically stamped on the fabric down the middle. The stripe highlights the symmetry of the human face. They also wear long white lab coats with hems that fall just below the knee, white slacks that taper at the ankle, and white lace-up boots that cover the foot and shin.

"Passengers?" the guard speaking barks as the other guards mill around the back.

"Enforce. Second. Global 1 business," the driver answers, his voice gravelly.

A shrill whistle escapes the guard's mouth before he speaks. "They told us that's the most classified project there is." The guard peers into the vehicle, trying to see something. It dawns on me that the something the guard is trying to see is me. I shrink a little in my seat.

There's a tap on the window glass, the sound only metal colliding with glass can make. The window in between our passenger benches rolls down.

The guard's eyes round as he blinks in surprise and salutes crisply.

"Citizen Guard Bowlin, is it?" Enforce's voice is eerily calm.

"Yes. Yes, ma'am," the guard says.

"Do you know who I am?" Enforce studies her lengthy fingernails as she asks this seemingly innocuous question.

"Yes…ma'am." Bowlin's voice trembles. He definitely knows who Enforce is.

"Why are you delaying official business?"

He shuts his gaping mouth. "I'm sorry, ma'am. My apologies, ma'am. We don't get much excitement here, ma'am."

"So we're excitement?" Enforce presses. "We have titular value to you and your comrades? We're scintillating? Something to chat about later?" Enforce emphasizes the consonants in a way that's menacing.

I shrink lower, feeling the embarrassment pouring off of Bowlin.

"No, ma'am. Of course not, ma'am."

"Do you *like* being a Citizen Guard here, Bowlin?" The overly precise words grate against my eardrums.

"Yes, ma'am, it's an honor. My sincerest apologies, ma'am." Bowlin steps back from the vehicle, then nods to another guard, and the boom gate opens. Our driver pulls through the stile and onto a track of packed earth. Enforce taps on her screen furiously, and before the window is even rolled up, I hear a click–click–click sound, and then a scream.

A man's scream.

Bowlin's scream.

I jerk around, looking for him, trying to see what happened, but Dr. Jog pushes me down.

"Keep looking forward," he mumbles through gritted teeth. "You don't need to know."

Sweat forms on my brow, but I obey. Thoughts of Citizen

Guard Bowlin and whatever made him scream like that ricochet through my mind as we traverse sand, and sand, and more sand. I focus on my breathing—in and out—as long as I'm breathing, I'm not panicking.

An abrupt change in the scenery takes me by surprise. It's beautiful, and I've never seen anything like it. Lush green ground, bushes, and trees suddenly appear. The packed earth track becomes harder, until eventually the tires roll over smooth pavement. The road gently winds along trees moving their branches in a breeze, and I glimpse a river cutting curves in the ground.

"Riparian." Dr. Jog gestures out the window. I say nothing. "Reminds me of home."

I've never heard any scientist mention anything about where they came from. An assignment on Compound is a high honor; many scientists work their entire careers in the hopes of going to study and learn there. If you can't go to space, time at top-secret government science facilities is a decent consolation prize.

I have said less than ten words since entering this vehicle, but since Dr. Jog is obviously trying to have a conversation, I'll play. After whatever happened with Bowlin back at the checkpoint, I feel like curling into a ball and hiding. I don't really trust Dr. Jog, but he's the only familiar person in this vehicle. I remind myself of the game theory: *Gather information. Think about your opponents, your enemies. Learn how they think.* Even though Dr. Jog is more of an ally than an enemy, the theory is still applicable.

"Dr. Jog, where are you from?" I'm proud of the way my voice comes out, even and strong.

He smiles and responds with a number. "Eleven."

Confusion flashes over my face. I've been given a puzzle and asked to assemble it, but there's no image to follow and all the pieces are blank. "What is Eleven?"

"A place you'll never see and a place I was glad to leave. Although I miss it sometimes." He offers me a sad smile.

Enforce snorts. "You would *want* to go back to that—" She looks at Second, who has not glanced up from her screen even once this entire time, then says, "That hole?" The disdain dripping from her voice is poisonous.

Dr. Jog gives an imperious look over the rim of his glasses. "Of course not. But the scenery was significantly more interesting to study and observe than the desert. I thought Reach here might be interested, since he's never seen anything beyond Compound."

"I'm sorry, Dr. Jog, but what exactly is Eleven?" I ask. "A place? Where? For what? How can you be from a number?"

Enforce mutters, "She did her job well if he really doesn't know."

"Jog," Second's voice cuts in. It's an obvious warning meant to silence her. "It's all *classified*."

I startle. This whole time she has been tapping on her tablet with some device in her ear. I assumed she couldn't hear us with it in. She heard Bowlin's scream and didn't even react. Assumptions are dangerous, and apparently so are numbers.

Anger bubbles in my chest, along with fear. These two women in the vehicle are monsters. The logical part of my brain is in overdrive, trying to fight off the primitive part that wants to flee. I know that's not an option, and I know that I need to know everything I can if I'm going to survive. I am highly educated for fourteen. On Compound, education is a priority. I hate not knowing facts.

I run through everything I know about Nation. Geography is considered a very advanced subject; it's not taught until the age of loyalty. Geography is classified. Students don't study any maps of Nation or learn anything about the Cities beyond the basic facts. There's Hub, the Capital, Cities scattered across the landmass that are home to Citizens, and then the Wards for the Nons. You get assigned to a city once you're a Citizen, based on your aptitude tests. You go where you can most efficiently further Nation's progress. I don't know if *Eleven* is a region, a city, a science compound, or anything. Feeling left out always shakes me. In a science community, there are things that are classified—I have always understood that fact—but a morsel of something that may be important to my survival was just dangled in front of me and then snapped away. My ignorance taunts me.

"Eleven is the past, Reach," Dr. Jog says. "It's best to focus on the future, not the past. Forget I mentioned it and forgive an old man for his reminiscence."

I keep my expression icy as I level my gaze at him. I will *not* be forgiving. *Whose side is he on anyway?* Dr. Jog brought this number Eleven business up. He had to *know* the conversation was going to get shut down, or that it was classified. Or that it was…my brain reminds me that Dr. Jog is an *ally*.

An ally calmly reminiscing about his classified past in front of two government officials who enjoyed a man's scream of pain and remained unfeeling to human suffering.

My mind is clear on one point: I don't know what Eleven is, but Dr. Jog is an ally I don't trust.

# 7

THE MOOD IN the vehicle has soured. Dr. Jog seems to be watching me, but I ignore him and look out the window. Several hours pass. I feel naked without my communication device, which also functions as a watch, but I can make out the face on Second's wristwatch periodically when she shifts her tablet.

The vehicle continues along the river, following its meandering course until a sudden change in direction takes us away from the *riparian* habitat. Instead of lush green trees and grass, we now pass squares of brown, gold, and light green. These colors spread across the horizon, fading into a murky gray at what I imagine is the edge of the world. As we crest a hill, a flock of birds rises up from the brown square at the bottom. I imagine what our vehicle would look like to a bird. Just a speck—a tiny, insignificant speck. Before yesterday, I thought I was insignificant, just a kid raised by his scientist mother on Compound. One of countless kids there. That's how it was, and that's how it would always be. But now, for reasons beyond my comprehension, I've been thrust into the reality that I *am* important. I'm in a role I'm not ready for. I should have been better prepared for this.

My thoughts fly unbidden back to my mother. Mom. She assured me of her love, but I feel a hollow aching inside when I remember that she was trying to prepare me. She tried to shelter me. She tried to give me a childhood. She tried to instill in me a strategy and understanding of how to make moves. What sort of a childhood was that, really? Being raised just to be taken away? How can you feel love and bitterness for someone at the same time? It's an itchy, burning sensation, these thoughts about Mom.

I don't have nearly enough facts to be successful. I'm not sure what I'm supposed to do. *Game theory. Game theory. Game. Theory.* The words become a mantra. I think them over and over again as the weight of helplessness and hopelessness descend on me and press suffocatingly on my chest.

Our driver stops the vehicle in the middle of a field populated with golden stalks.

"Everyone out," Second says smoothly. The golden stalks sway in the breeze. Second leads us down a path. Dr. Jog follows along behind me. I really despise enclosed spaces, and not seeing where we are going is tortuous. No one else seems bothered.

The path swerves and turns unpredictably. I am disoriented and claustrophobic and the emotions I've suppressed all day threaten to make an ugly appearance. After another sudden, sharp turn, a giant silver structure comes into view. It reminds me of an airplane hangar.

Space travel is a keystone of Nation's progress, so we spent a lot of time learning about the history of flight at the Educational Facility. The large structure is made of a type of galvanized metal. It looks wavy. It is exceedingly tall, casting the nearby path in shadows.

We curve around the back of the building and enter through a door that has been rolled up and secured. My eyes take in the dim fluorescent lighting, the concrete floor, and several men and women wearing a light yellow uniform. It looks just like mine, except for the color. A tall man approaches us. He places his pinky above his right eye and brings it down across his body in a diagonal zip where it ends at his hip, saluting Second. I can see the way his breath makes his mustache flutter slightly.

"Captain Loyal," Second acknowledges, and he relaxes slightly. "We have a schedule to keep."

The man nods once, then, in a languid voice, says, "Follow me." He leads us through the building, past a small prop airplane, through a maze of cans and tools organized on rolling carts, then stops in front of a machine that sends my mind racing for identification features. I'm not sure what it is. I've never seen anything like it before. It's here with an old-fashioned airplane, so my best guess is that it's for air travel.

Dr. Jog sucks in a breath from behind me. I turn. He stares at the gleaming thing in front of us. It's jet black, shaped like the letter *u*, and two stories tall. The bottom half is completely black, but the upper legs are covered in a clear glass dome. The curve of the *u*-shape is covered in colored glass. It's too high up, and from my angle I can't see inside it, but I want to know what's in there.

"I didn't know they built it," Dr. Jog whispers. I raise an eyebrow. "I designed it. It's a futuristic aircraft for ease of travel over lengthy distances while under the Earth's gravitational pull and atmospheric pressure."

"Does it work?" The words, heavy with sarcasm, fly out of my mouth before I can reel them back in.

Dr. Jog's features are still awestruck, but he looks at me with such sympathy it makes me uncomfortable. "Of course it works, Reach! What you must think of us all."

I don't know what to do with that statement, so I follow Enforce up the ladder rungs that lead to a door along the second story of the *u*-shaped aircraft.

Captain Loyal stands just off to the side, nodding at us as we enter the aircraft. The inside is surprisingly spacious. There are comfortable chairs clustered in small groups around tables.

Enforce sets her black leather bag on one table and slinks into a seat near the entrance. Second is a few clusters away, already tapping on her screen with the stylus. I want to be as far as possible from everyone, and no one has said I can't explore. I have a hunch that there will be more clusters and tables on the other side of the curve, so I pass through the curved portion of the aircraft. The space changes. A passageway leads up to two sliding metal doors. On the outside, there's a box with a button, and a small light next to it reads 'locked for flight.' This must be where the pilot's cockpit is.

I keep going, following the passage until the curviness becomes the symmetrical straight arm on the other side. Sure enough, there are more clusters of chairs. I drop my orange bag next to my feet and slink into an armchair. It rocks back and forth in a surprisingly comforting motion. Alone at last, I feel free to indulge my curiosity. I look out the glass but can only see more tools and equipment hanging on the walls in the hangar.

There is a horrific screeching noise as the ceiling of the hangar slides open. I'm still trying to figure out how we are going to get out of the hangar when the craft gives a momentous heave and lifts straight into the air. A completely vertical takeoff. I know from my studies about flight that key scientists have intensely studied vertical ascent and descent. There was always debate about whether it was possible, many leading minds claiming it was not. Apparently, Dr. Jog proved them wrong.

Thinking of Dr. Jog makes me wonder where he is. I half-expected him to follow me and sit by me here. *Ally, not friend.* Something about the way he told me not to look at Bowlin felt protective. I don't know what to think of him. He's got the government's trust. Mom's too. It feels like playing chess with a third player. I can't figure him out, and I don't know how his pieces move.

I clear my head with a small shake. He's not here. I'm alone. I don't need to figure this out right now. I just need to learn more about what they want me to do. My stomach gurgles loudly. *Great. I'm hungry.* I am not going to go anywhere with Enforce or Second if I don't have to. I don't know when I'll eat again or where we are. I need to distract myself, so I think of everything I can remember about airports and aircraft.

My memory summons the time when the children in EF11— that's Educational Facility for eleven-year-olds—were given the assignment of creating a miniature version of an historical airport. I worked for weeks on a to-scale model replica of the Denver International Airport.

I didn't know anything about where Denver was located since maps were highly classified, but we studied old photographs of the structures and the surrounding landforms. History books mentioned various conspiracy theories that intrigued me, but most impressive to me was the high mountains surrounding the airport. With primitive flight technology, the pilots had to know exactly what they were doing to get enough altitude over the mountains in such a short time from take off. Not to mention, pilots landing those behemoth jets had to descend over the mountains.

Scientists on Compound anonymously judged the model airports. It was a Compound-wide big deal; the contest was in preparation for Leader's last visit. The pride I felt when I walked into the building and saw that my airport had been awarded the blue ribbon for first place was immense. I couldn't wait to go home and tell Mom that I had won. For the first time ever, I didn't feel like a total outsider amongst the kids on Compound. I felt happy. The next day I begged her to come with me to the Educational Facility on her way to work. We walked through those glass doors and marched right up to the display cases to find my airport gone. Disappeared. Instead of my airport, the second-place model had slid into my spot, a blue ribbon adorning it. A replica of some place called Atlanta. I hate that place, wherever it is.

Standing there, crestfallen, Mom did something I couldn't understand at the time. She placed a hand on my shoulder, looked at me, and said, "This is prejudice."

The memory has always had blurry edges, like I knew something important was missing but I didn't know how to make sense of anything. Now I know what she meant. She meant that once they knew *who* I was, someone decided that I didn't deserve the first-place prize. Because I'm not fully human.

You'd think scientists are open-minded. Sometimes they are, but when it comes to their children, scientists are extremely competitive. Anything they can do to give their child a leg up in the world of education, they will. It's hypocritical, but it happens all the time. It just took eleven years to have it directly impact me.

The memory of Mom's sorrowful face as she uttered the word 'prejudice' pushes the emotions I've been holding in check up out of my clenched muscles and into my eyes. Tears start to fall. I let them.

# 8

Hours pass, or maybe minutes. My tears are still falling while I rest my forehead against the cool glass window and ignore the world going by underneath the flying machine. The thrums and vibrations of the aircraft are more intense than the simulations we watched at school. I never thought I'd miss *school*, but here I am, missing everything about my old life.

A hand on my shoulder startles me. I look up into Dr. Jog's warm brown eyes, which brim with sympathy. He offers a small smile and holds a foil-wrapped rectangle in his hand.

"I thought you might be hungry."

I nod, embarrassed that I've been caught crying and that he came in search of me.

He adds in an undertone, "You know, you can live off these." He slides into the chair next to mine and begins unwrapping his own rectangle. "It's a perfectly portioned fiber, carbohydrate, and protein bar. They are truly a marvel." He takes a small nibble and grimaces.

I wonder why he's grimacing as I take a bite that befits a fourteen-year-old boy. Basically half the bar is in my mouth. It takes less than a moment later for me to understand why he nibbled. The worst, driest, most flavorless heap of chalk powder and dust and gravel is in my mouth. I want to spit it out but there's nowhere for me to except in my hands, so I chew. Methodically, slowly, feeling the grit turn into smaller, dust-like pieces.

Dr. Jog laughs at the expression on my face. "It *is* terrible, isn't it."

"I don't think I could live on that," I blurt out after choking my bite down. Instead of feeling satisfied, I feel like I ate dirt. Actually, concrete.

Dr. Jog grimaces as he nibbles yet again. "It is best to take it in smaller pieces. Otherwise, it just kind of—"

"Sits there in your stomach for hours?"

"Pretty much. So, Reach. You've had a lot happen in the past few days. How are you doing?"

I am surprised by the kindness in his voice, and I almost answer him truthfully. *Ally, not friend.* My mom's phrase about Dr. Jog flashes a warning before I reveal that I'm not fine, that I am confused and angry and don't like Second at all and think Enforce is terrifying. Instead I opt for questions. Having been raised on Compound, there is one thing that I know all scientists love: a teachable moment.

"I'm really not sure what..." I pause as I consider my words, chewing on the inside of my cheek. "I'm not really sure what to expect. Or what's happening."

Dr. Jog nods, his graying hair swaying just a little with the motion. "That's perfectly reasonable. There are many things you'll be learning about Nation in the next days, weeks, months, and probably years. I'll be your project supervising scientist. We'll have to work together. I can probably help clear up confusion if you have questions."

I don't know why, but his words feel wrong. He's insinuating something, but I can't tell what exactly.

"Reach." His voice has dropped to a whisper, and he glances around the craft before he speaks again. "I can *help* you."

My stomach swoops with the clandestine words he issues. I know I shouldn't ask, but I do anyway. "With what?"

"Whatever comes next."

"You don't know?"

"We never really know. But we can make hypotheses."

I shrug. "You're one of *them*."

He has the decency to look abashed. "Things are never just the surface all the way down, are they?"

I bite my lip, considering his words. "I don't follow. But I'm here, so I guess I'll just have to see what happens next before I know if I need help."

"You shouldn't trust anyone, and I understand that. But maybe you should consider what you'll need to *survive* this." My eyes snap to his face. "I know enough to know what comes next for you is not going to be easy. I'll do my best to help you. But you have to let me in. I can't help if you won't see me as a mentor, and if not a mentor, a friend, and if not a friend, an *ally*."

The emphasis on that word throws a metaphorical stick in the wheel of my thoughts. "Did *she* say that?" My whispered words are harsh, ground out in a mixture of fear and sorrow and remorse and every other emotion that I've tamped down.

"I'm not sure whom you're referring to by the word *she*, but I have reasons for wanting you to be successful that are similar to your mother's."

"You know my mother's reasons?"

He shrugs. "I have vague ideas about that and other things. But of course, you don't know anything—yet."

"Couldn't you tell me?"

"I will. Reach, I promise. I will tell you when you need to know. Right now, it's best if you know absolutely nothing. Your mind is a blank slate. Wipe whatever you think you know away and prepare to learn everything."

I want to answer him with a rebuttal, but the sound of footsteps in the corridor effectively silences me. Enforce and Second round the curve and step into the cluster of seats Dr. Jog and I occupy.

"We'll be touching down in thirty minutes," Second announces.

Enforce narrows her eyes as she looks at us. I'm not sure what that means, and I have reached my limit for travel for the day. Having never left Compound, now I've driven in a vehicle, flown in an aircraft, and had to muddle through whatever is going on with these powerful people who've taken me away from everything I've ever known.

"Where?" I snap at Second, the frustration of the day spilling into my voice. I know the moment the word leaves my mouth that my tone is not appropriate.

Shock dawns on Second's face before she recovers her typical flat persona. Enforce's narrowed eyes widen as she licks her lips. There's excitement on her face; from what I've observed, the woman is excited by conflict. That scares me even more than anything else.

Second's eyes now regard me coolly. "Hub. You'll be meeting a Sty to get you ready for the Inaugural Science Banquet. Enforce, we have work to do. There's a request for your department that I need to discuss with you."

Second turns to leave, but Enforce stares me down. Her eyes penetrate mine and I know she is waiting to strike, like a cobra waiting for prey to wander into the kill zone. I feel Dr. Jog's keen gaze as I shudder under Enforce's intensity.

"Enforce." Second doesn't raise her voice, but the sharpness in it is unmistakable. Enforce smiles a slow, menacing smile before twisting her mouth into a smirk and leaving what I'm now thinking of as *my side* of the craft. It's quiet for several beats.

"Don't push her." I'm almost certain I hear Dr. Jog say this, but he's looking out the window.

I angle my body to look at the now-pink and dusky sky we're floating through. Nothing about anything makes any sense.

# 9

Our ride on the aircraft ends when it descends vertically into a green square located between many tall buildings. As with everything related to the government that I've experienced in the past thirty hours, there is no warning beyond Second's announcement thirty minutes prior. It's alarming to be floating along horizontally, parallel to the ground one moment and then, without any advanced notice, to drop straight down. Dr. Jog's lack of concern is the only thing that keeps me from screaming. I swear I can see the faint hint of a smile on his face as we lower to the ground.

Our group of four exits the craft and I find myself standing in the bright light of a park. The colors are too bright; it feels artificial. Everything is perfect—the blades of grass are all the same height, width, and shade. My first instinct is to pinch my arm, but I opt to lean down and pull a blade of grass from the ground instead. It's not fake, but it's also not quite real.

"You've never seen grass before?" Dr. Jog stands beside me.

"Not in person. It seems…"

"It's going to take time to adjust. Hub is proud to be the center of the government. Everyone takes their roles here very seriously. Even the groundskeepers."

"But it's not like a real plant," I point out.

"It is, it's just a special hybrid. It requires less maintenance since it's been modified. Efficiency is key."

I nod, glancing around, trying to take everything in. Second is motioning to a woman who is moving quickly toward us. The new woman is not running, but she increases her pace as Second waves her over.

The woman approaches. I can see her dark, long hair. It's so dark it could almost be midnight blue. She gives a small, stiff bow to Second and then another bow to Enforce. Second gestures toward me with her stylus. The light glints off her rings and sunspots blind me momentarily. "Sty. This is your charge. The banquet is tomorrow. Your instructions are in your portal." And then Second walks off, disappearing into the evening sun.

Enforce grins at Sty; it's slow and menacing and full of authority. Sty looks at Enforce expectantly.

"You'll need to follow *every* instruction. I'll be checking. Leader has a special interest in this. I know your type."

The dark-haired woman, *Sty*, looks down at the ground as she bobs her head in assent. "Yes, madam Enforce." Her voice is dispassionate; she sounds flat. Enforce strides off, disappearing the same way Second did.

Sty's posture changes the moment Enforce is out of sight. "Hey." She sticks her hand out in my direction, and I notice her voice is no longer flat; she sounds more excited than anything. "I'm your Sty. Let's get going. Looks like I have some work cut out for me."

Dr. Jog jumps in to respond. "Great, thank you, Sty. I'm going to supervise collecting bio samples for study. So I'll be with you for a bit. Are we going to the studios?"

Sty shakes her head. "No, they want to keep things buttoned down tightly until the banquet. We're going to a private space. It's in the Sty school building."

Dr. Jog nods in approval and begins walking. I know nothing about where I'm going, and even if I wanted to run away, the threat of Enforce finding me and her punishment of Bowlin make it clear. I have no choice but to follow.

I get a good glimpse at Sty's clothing as she walks with Dr. Jog in front of me. She's wearing a washed-out red top with a pair of black pants that taper at the ankles. Her feet are clad in black boots that lace. I can't tell if it's a uniform or if she has the ability to dress according to her personal preferences. I want to ask her, but we leave the path from the park and turn onto a sidewalk next to a road, which distracts me.

There are hundreds of buildings in various hues of green, black, and blue as far as my eyes can see. The buildings are taller than anything I've ever seen, except for the astronomy and meteorological tower on Compound. As we walk, I notice the streets meet in perfect ninety-degree intersections. People walk in orderly lines on the sidewalks: all those heading south are on one side of the street, northbound pedestrians are on the other. The organization of the throng of people feels sinister. My body shudders with an involuntary wave of fear.

I've been so focused on the surroundings that I don't notice Sty falling back to walk beside me. "I already told you, I'm your Sty."

My head jerks toward the sound of her voice, which I thought would be in front of me but is now directly to my right. There's a slight accent to her voice which sounds simultaneously very proper and stiff. I've deduced that this woman is not a government official and that Enforce doesn't like her, but other than that, I have no context for who this woman is and what she has to do with me.

"Hi," I squeak out. I clear my throat and try again "Hi, Sty. I'm Reach."

"Reach. You have a name. That's a good thing, I guess." Her tone holds an undercurrent of longing, but since I don't know this woman, I can't think of anything to say. "We have to get you ready."

She turns off the sidewalk and leads the way toward a dark green building. As she approaches the door, she waves her wrist at a sensor. I don't see a communication device on her wrist, but the sensor makes a beep as the door slides open.

"Security," she mumbles as I step through. The door slides shut and beeps again. "For the banquet, Reach. It's not every day a major science operation begins here at Hub. You'll be in the place of honor with Leader, Second, Enforce, and visible to the head scientists from the sixty Compounds across Nation. It's all hush-hush to everyone except those with the highest levels of clearance, but those of us who are allowed to know are pleased. You bring a lot of opportunities with you here."

I scrunch up my nose as I try to digest her words. Dr. Jog joins our conversation. "She's right, Reach. You bring a lot of opportunities with you. It's something the heads of the science department want to celebrate, and Leader wants to accommodate them. You'll be highly visible for one evening before you disappear into the first phase."

*Oh no.* I have memories of Leader's last visit to Compound. The formalities required were exhausting to learn, and Leader never directly interacted with the children. We had to practice what we would do for weeks in all the circumstances our teachers could come up with. Never once did we role play sitting with her in a place of honor at a banquet. Weeks—it took weeks to learn the etiquette for her visit. Now I have less than a day to learn what I need to know for a banquet next to her and Enforce. This is worse than a nightmare.

But then I wonder: *What's worse than a nightmare?*

Sty continues to lead us down a cool tiled atrium. There are glass doors leading to 'suites' periodically. She keys in a code on a box and a door swings open. She flips a light switch on the wall and begins to descend down a curving set of stairs. This set of stairs isn't tiled, it's raw wood. The handrail is made of the same rough-hewn wood. I'm concerned about tripping in the semi-gloom, so I grab hold of it. I slide my hand along the wood as I move down the stairs and am rewarded with a splinter.

"Ouch!" I hiss.

Sty and Dr. Jog look back at me with quizzical expressions on their faces. "What's wrong?" they say in unison and I would laugh, except I'm trying to spot the sliver of wood in my palm.

"Uh. I got a splinter from the railing."

"Oh. We'll get that out when we get to the salon." I notice that Sty has not been holding onto the railing. I get the feeling that she knows better than to touch it from experience.

We reach the bottom of the stairs. It's darker here. The fluorescent lights overhead are turned off. A light beckons from under a door at the end of the corridor Sty leads us toward. She pushes the door open and ushers us into a white room. The white tile is on the floor, the walls, and the ceiling. The long tube lights are turned on in here, and there's a drain in the center of the floor. There's a chair and a metal table on wheels, a cabinet along one wall with various clear containers, cups, and a cup of markers.

"We're here. Have a seat, Reach." She gestures to the chair in the middle of the room next to the drain. She's produced a tablet like Second's from somewhere and scans the screen. She turns to Dr. Jog. "Do you know what samples you need?"

He nods and begins pulling cups from the cabinet, labeling them with a marker.

"So, Reach," Sty says. "We're just gonna get you ready. We'll work through the night until you're ready. I'm sure you're tired, so I'll try to finish in time for you to sleep before the banquet." Her voice is soft and caring, and I find myself wanting to trust her. I blink at her soothing tones, feeling the heaviness of my eyelids as I think about sleep.

Dr. Jog clears his throat. "I just need a few samples: nails, hair, a skin scrape, and some measurements."

Sty purses her lips in a thin line before she nods. She pulls out a pair of scissors and begins running her hands through my hair, which is still too long. She sprays something that smells like oranges onto my head, then begins cutting. Dr. Jog uses tweezers to extract several hairs Sty trims and places them into a container. Sty rubs the bottom of my feet with a rough piece of sandpaper, and my skin flakes off. Dr. Jog collects several flakes before he begins taking measurements. He has a rope-like ruler hung around his neck. He measures as Sty still works on my hair, typing numbers into the tablet each time.

"I'm done now, Sty. I'll see you at the banquet, Reach. And this Sty"—he indicates her with a nod—"is a good *friend*. Maybe even an *ally*." Dr. Jog leaves with the containers in his lab coat pockets.

Sty blows out a breath before she speaks. "He's the nicest of them."

*Them? Who is them?*

Sty uses a brush on my head. Each stroke leaves my scalp tingling, like tiny lightning bolts are striking my head and giving a gentle zap. It's not unpleasant, and I can tell that she's working hard not to hurt me.

"I guess." I'm not sure who is more surprised by my response, her or me.

"I only know what I've been told about you, but you're not what I expected."

"How do you mean?"

"Maybe you're not fifty-fifty."

"Do you know math?" I snort.

She stops and comes to the front of the chair, crouching down to meet my eye. "Do *you?*" Her tone has gone from caring to biting.

I feel ashamed. This woman is being gentle and kind and wants to ensure I get some sleep. I look away. "I'm sorry, Sty."

She places a hand on my knee. "I know you're nervous. But you cannot act like you're superior to anyone here. There's a very specific order of things. But you *know* that. Where I fit into the order is complicated, and there are plenty of people who harbor ill will toward me. But I'm in charge of you at the moment. If you can't treat me with deferential respect, you will certainly not be successful with Leader and Enforce and Second. You already *know* they are unequivocally in charge. You can't challenge them. If you try, you'll end up..." She lets her sentence drop for a moment. "Not—"She swallows. —"Not here."

She brings my face to her golden eyes. "Look. It isn't going to be easy, but you'll eat, drink, and say thank you to Leader. You'll be charming. Always take the lowest place, the one furthest from Leader. They will tell you exactly what they want in some way. You might have to decipher their head nods or other gestures, but they don't want to be embarrassed in front of the scientists. It's important that they keep the scientists aware of their power. You might see a show of force from Enforce. It's pretty common at these banquets. Prepare yourself. But don't let them see your fear.

"I'm not an idiot, despite being a Sty. So, I always assume the people I meet in this capacity aren't idiots either. I know only bits and pieces, but you are here in Hub for the long haul. And *I'm* the one they asked to get you ready for *them*, so I think that gives you an idea of the order of things."

She has a point. Actually, she has more than a point, she has the whole pencil. She's in a position of authority, and I had the audacity to think of her as less than me. Teenage snark is not easy to control, but I'm going to have to master it.

Sty stands me up and leads me out of the room. She pushes open a different door and I enter a bedroom. There's a narrow bed with a striped blanket, a white cotton shirt and a pair of black shorts. "You can sleep here, and in this. You won't be wearing that anymore. I'll burn it if you'd like me to."

I can't tell if she's joking about burning my Compound uniform, but maybe they just incinerate all the trash here.

"Thanks," I murmur.

She closes the door gently behind her and I sink onto the bed, feeling the exhaustion from the past few days wash over me. I'm asleep before I can even think to change or pull up the covers.

I wake to a rustling sound. I'm now under the blanket, but still wearing my Compound uniform. Rubbing my bleary eyes, I look around. There's a small light with a pull chain hanging next to the narrow bed it's on. It casts the rest of the room into a murky shadow. There are no windows.

"It's time to wake up, Reach." Sty places a hanger with a black button-up shirt on a hook on the back of the door. There's a clear bag around it, which explains the rustling.

I wipe the sleep from my eyes and say, "Hey, Sty. I need to wear that?"

She frowns. "Yeah. I'm sorry."

"Why?" It looks like a regular shirt. It has buttons, so it's more formal than my everyday Compound uniform, but I'm going to a government banquet tonight, so I would expect more formal attire.

She doesn't say anything, just holds up something long and smooth. I can't see perfectly, but I think it's a necktie.

"I've never worn one of those before. But it can't be that bad, right?"

She shakes her head and walks forward, holding it out and passing it to me. It's smooth, black, and feels nice against my skin. And then I see it, spelled out vertically along the length of the tie in green letters: SPECIMEN.

# 10

Sᴛʏ ʜᴀꜱ ᴍᴇ dressed in a black suit and tie before my car arrives. She washed my hair in the room and rubbed copious amounts of gel into it. It sticks up at odd angles, and when I looked in the mirror she offered, I laughed.

I can't figure out Sty. She was visibly upset by my *specimen* tie, but she's also here and working for the government. If that's not conflicting enough, Sty is also giving me advice about the banquet. I hold on to every word.

"Reach." She holds a comb in her mouth and rubs something on the back of my neck. "You're something to celebrate for Hub. The person to the left is always less important than the person to your right. There's usually a…"

"Show of power? By Enforce?" I cut in.

She nods in agreement. "It's designed to be alarming. You won't know when or where or who, but you will know when it happens. Keeps everyone on their toes." She glances at her wrist. "It's time for your car. Let's go up and get you settled. You can do this. You're the main attraction, so you *have* to do it."

I stand in the shadows. It's what I do. It's how I've always been since I could move and understand that people looked at me differently. I'm left wondering how I stay hidden when my tie screams that I'm a specimen.

Sty leads us out to the front of the building, where a vehicle will arrive to transport me to the banquet. I'm nervous, but Sty will help me. I know she will. As long as she's with me, I'll be all right.

We wait behind the glass wall in the atrium, which offers a view of the road. Precisely on time, a white car pulls up in front of the building.

"That's you, Reach." She presses some buttons and ushers me out.

As we walk into the afternoon sunlight, I notice the dirt. Or rather, the lack of dirt. The vehicle is pristine. "That would never work on Compound." I point to the car as I look over at her. She returns my look with her own quizzical one. "Dirt," I offer.

"They don't sweep at your Compound?" She sounds positively horrified.

"We sweep inside, but not outside."

"No street sweepers? No PSABT?"

"What's a…a PSABT?"

"Pedestrian Safety and Beauty Team. They keep everything clean."

"No." I gaze around and the word *sterile* flashes in the front of my mind. There is no dirt, no grime here in Nation Hub. This too-perfect environment cannot possibly be real. It's like a scientific control; there are no variables here. It unlocks a new fear. *Am I an experiment within an experiment within an experiment? How many layers deep am I?*

I rub my thumbs across my cheekbones to relieve the mounting pressure. Sty is staring. I try to play it off like I, too, abhor dirt. "Well the roads are packed with dirt and sand, so…no. A street sweeper would be…inefficient."

Her eyes scrunch and her mouth sets into a thin line as she undoubtedly imagines *that* gigantic mess. She gives her head a shake and turns back to me. "You can do this, Reach. Act like this is the biggest honor of your life, because it is. If they ask you, you can say something about honor and sacrifice for science."

When we arrive at the car, the door retracts into the open position and I begin to climb inside. Sty brushes nonexistent specks from my black coat. I slide all the way over and the door begins to lower. "Wait! Aren't you coming too?"

She shakes her head and gives me a look. "I'm nobody, Reach. Just a Sty."

The door clicks closed and I begin to move. I'm confused and alone without her. I don't know where we're going, but a glance to the front of the car shows there is no one here for me to ask. The vehicle is driving itself.

I have a thousand new questions I may never get to ask.

# 11

My DRIVERLESS CAR pulls into a paved loop at a tall building made of jet-black obsidian. The loop curves around a pavilion that holds a pool with many flagpoles, the flags waving in the breeze. I sit inside the car, wondering what to do and where to go when the door retracts. It seems obvious enough that I need to get out. The moment I stand in the dusky sunlight, the car speeds away.

The entirety of my life has been predictable. I have been given a weekly schedule and I'm used to a thirty-minute "reflection period" each afternoon. Somehow, finding myself in a situation without a schedule feels both freeing and stifling. I can't plan for what needs to happen next without a schedule. The worst of it is that I *know* there is a schedule, and that I need to follow it. This would be much easier if anyone had bothered to share such a document with me.

The flags snap and wriggle in the air behind me. I feel exposed, small, and very powerless. There is nowhere to go but forward. I approach the door. It slides open with a hiss, and I enter the towering building.

A man stands facing the door at a desk. He's dressed in a green suit. His lab-style coat is shorter than mine, hitting at the top of his hips. His pants and coat look furry and velvety, and his shirt is starchy white. The word *concierge* is embroidered on his left breast pocket. He doesn't even look up as he speaks monotonously. "Hello. They are expecting you in Banquet Room Three."

I desperately search for a sign that might tell me where Banquet Room Three is. I find nothing. "Err. Where is…Banquet Room Three—"

He sniffs in indignation and cuts me off. "Banquet Room Three is that way." He jerks his thumb over his right shoulder and looks up from his desk. His gaze travels from my tie to my face and he colors, cheeks and forehead turning a bright red. He snorts a string of obscenities.

"Thanks." I move to pass his desk, and he shuffles to the farthest corner while not making eye contact. *Prejudice.* I walk past and take a few steps, then turn so I'm facing his green back. He has resumed his post at the desk.

"I'm not contagious." The words come out, startling me, but certainly startling him. He snaps around so quickly I think he may have broken his neck. *Serves him right.*

I face forward and follow the hall until I arrive at massive wooden doors. They are at least twenty-five feet high, made of carved panels, and contain ornate metal handles that run the length of half my torso. A small plaque by the side of one door reads 'Banquet Room Three.' There's no one to ask what to do in this situation.

I take a deep breath, willing myself to feel courage, and pull the door open. I am immediately hit with a wave of hot air. It is stale-smelling and yeasty. There are scientists milling everywhere in their white lab coats and wide-legged pants. I stand there for a moment as I try to make sense of my new environment. The sea of white makes my black attire even more conspicuous. I am meant to stand out, to be visible. I hate it.

I sweep my gaze over the room and realize it's actually a series of rooms. There is this area, by the door, but then there is a small set of steps leading to another room. After the first set of steps, there are long tables in each room. This continues until it finally ends in a room with a semi-circular table on a raised dais. It's hard to tell since it's yards away, but there seem to be people sitting at the table.

The hot air rolling out of the banquet hall must have been met with a wave of cooler air from the hallway when I entered the room. The doors swing shut slowly behind me. The scientists nearest to me look over, and a murmur begins to overtake the crowd.

"It's here."

"Really? Where?"

"What does it look like?"

Directions would be extremely helpful right now. I have none, so I stand there staring at the many eyes examining me. Scientists crowd me, talking about me as if I can't hear.

"It looks more human than I'd thought."

"I can't believe it's *that* tall." This comment gives me pause. I can't figure out why. At first, I think it's about my height. I'm taller for my age than most of the boys on Compound, but I'm not unusually tall. I stand at a respectable five feet nine inches and will probably grow more. Then I realize that these people referred to me as an *it*.

"I wonder when I'll get to work on it."

"I'm going to try to get it for my experimental research on…"

My anxiety roars. No one here sees me as a human. I'm a specimen to all of them. It says so. It's emblazoned on my tie.

A woman, also dressed in black, makes her way through the crowd of white. I'm relieved at first until I see who it is. Enforce. Her nose chains glint in the light as she pushes people out of the way with her elbows. Her shoes click-clack on the floor. The sea of white parts, those closest to the channel rubbing the various places on their bodies where she made contact. She's grinning. It's a gigantic, cat-got-the-cream grin, and it's terrifying.

"Reach." Her voice is even scarier than I remembered, lead-pipe intense. She gestures to the scientists. "These are the top scientists in Nation Hub. You'll only work with some of them, but these ones were granted the opportunity to see the specimen in person."

Her lips curl in a half-smirk, half-snarl, and I feel panic rising. Her eyes bore into mine briefly before she stares down the scientists closest to us. "Get a good look. Specimen coming through." She turns and begins walking back through the path she created. Over her shoulder, she barks, "Come on."

I follow her like a stray puppy, and as I pass through the crowd, I am subjected to more whispers and even an occasional unwanted touch. One scientist has something like a nail file, and he reaches up and catches my right cheek with it. I pull back in shock as the gritty texture painfully scrapes my skin.

"Ow!" I look around for the culprit, but Enforce is already there. The scientist tucks the object back into his pocket. A few of the scientists are laughing. Enforce is not.

"Dr. Whatever-your-name-is, was that an approved contact? Are you part of the team?" The menace in her voice makes it clear she knows he isn't and that it wasn't. The doctor shakes slightly as she speaks to him. Enforce does not speak to people, she speaks *at* them.

"N-n-no." His voice is shaky and he sounds weak.

She pulls a red marker from her pocket, reaches into the scientist's pocket, and extracts the device he used to scrape my cheek. She places it in her pocket, and then, with slow, deliberate movements, she draws a large red *x* on his breast pocket. She smiles. It lights up her face; she's genuinely happy. She could be a very pretty woman if she wasn't so menacing.

The other scientists look on with wide eyes, backing away from the man. He hangs his head in shame, but a glint of hatred pulses from his eyes.

Two muscular men in black jumpsuits with the letter *E* stamped on the lapel and the back penetrate the crowd. They arrive at the humiliated scientist and each grabs one of his wrists. Enforce watches while she casually places her hand on her hip. I can see her itching to mete out punishment while the bruisers do it for her. She furls and unfurls her fingers, stretching them. She tries to maintain a bored expression, but she is not bored. She is watching too intently for boredom. She is riveted.

One of the bruisers catches the scientist on his instep with his heavy boot while the other twists his wrist up and backward ninety degrees with a sickening crunch. I haven't eaten anything since the aircraft, and thank goodness. I feel my stomach heave, but its lack of contents keeps me from vomiting. He screams and falls to the ground. The two men grab him by the armpits and shuffle out of the hall.

"Second," Enforce says quietly, but it's so silent in the rooms that everyone hears. "Revoke. In full." I don't know what that means, but I know it's bad. And I know that my cry caused his humiliation. My pain, which was sharp and fleeting, caused his, which is definitely calculated and lengthy.

I drag my eyes away from the man and back to Enforce. I can see a tiny earpiece in her ear. She's quietly communicating with Second across a room of hundreds of people. Something about that fact makes me feel even more afraid of her than I had been before.

She doesn't stay to watch the scientist leave through the doors. Instead she marches forward, climbing up the set of steps into the next room. That scientist had no right to touch me, but the response was unpredictable and harsh.

Enforce keeps going, passing through all the rooms and right up to the dais. Seated at the table on the dais is Leader. Flanked on her left is a small man with glasses and no hair. To her right is another man, this one tall and wide, with gleaming white teeth and beady colorless eyes. Directly to the left of the man with glasses is Second. The seat next to the tall man is empty—it's Enforce's.

Enforce gestures for me to step into an opening in the circular table. Leader looks me over and folds her fingers together in a be-mused sort of way. "Welcome, Reach." She says it in her raspy voice, the one I've heard before from visits to Compound. Her gold bangles catch the light. Her black clothes seem to shine. There are golden hoops all along her ears and a dainty gold chain with a small clear diamond around her neck.

"I see you made it in one piece." She gestures at my cheek. I place my hand on the throbbing skin, and when I draw my hand back, I see blood. "This is the first time you've ever met the Three Powers in person?"

I nod, blood pooling on my fingers and rolling in beads onto the ornate carpet.

"This is Litigate." She points to the man with the glasses. Her fingernails are unnaturally long and pointy. They are painted a dark red color and almost perfectly match the color of my blood as it drips to the floor. "And this"—she points to the man with the glasses and her voice curls into something akin to a purr—"is Legislate."

I know who Litigate and Legislate are. I live in Nation and attended a National school on Compound. They are the lesser cords in the "three-stranded cord" that makes up Nation's motto: "A three-stranded cord is not easily broken." Leader is the most important, but these two men are also not to be crossed.

Leader travels Nation, keeps abreast of latest scientific progress and organizes security and temporal needs. Leader signs off on food and clothing distribution, building projects, and anything to do with living. If you need something, Leader provides it. Leader can't do it all herself as an individual, but she oversees the large offices dedicated to helping her with the responsibilities of her post. Second is her second in command. She's more of an administrative assistant than anything, but she holds more keys than anyone else in Nation. She greases wheels and gets things done, all on Leader's behalf. Second stays out of the spotlight, but I've observed her the past few days.

I didn't know about Enforce until she showed up on Compound, but I know now that ignorance truly is bliss when it comes to some people.

Leader's dark eyes are looking at me, narrowed. Stark black eyelashes slowly open and close as she watches me turn toward Litigate and Legislate. Leader has high cheekbones and an almost hollow face. Her skin is porcelain white. She's tall and slender. She has remained seated, but her posture conveys authority. I stand a little taller. "Say hello, Reach."

My mouth is dry, so I will it to form saliva. I press my tongue to the roof of my mouth and croak out "Hello" as I nod deferentially to Litigate and Legislate. I remember to dip my head toward Leader as I half-bow. It's an odd movement, but I saw Director do it once on Compound when Leader came to visit. I hope that was the right thing to do. I really do not want to be dragged away from the banquet with a broken arm; a cut on my face that no one seems concerned about is bad enough.

"Very good, Reach," Leader says. "Are you hungry? It's a banquet. Eat."

I am hungry, but the sound of the man's body hitting the carpet and the crunch of bones breaking has made eating significantly less appealing than usual. I haven't responded, but Leader snaps her fingers and another man in a dark green suit appears with a place setting. More green suits come carrying trays brimming with food.

"That one," she says dismissively as she points to me, then leans over and whispers in Legislate's ear.

There is no chair. I look around for an extra seat I could pull over to sit in. It's awkward to be the only person standing at the table.

Leader stops, her long fingers resting on Legislate's shoulder.

"Is something wrong, Reach?" Enforce sits with a smirk on her olive skin, using her right thumb to crack her knuckles.

"No, madam Leader. I…chair?" The room is stuffy. I can feel the eyes on me from every direction.

"Eat." Her commanding voice allows no argument.

I'm sweating from discomfort and the hot material of my suit. It's too hot, too prickly, too close to my skin. The tie is too tight, the shoes too heavy. I need to sit, but no one will let me. I'm supposed to eat this food like an animal at the zoo—on display. I focus on cutting a bite of my chicken, but the edges are moving on the plate and I swear I see the fork tines bend and wave one by one.

"Reach, you need to drink some water." I hear a voice, but I can't find the person speaking because of the echo. I try to pick up the glass, but as I'm bringing it to my lips, my palms sweat so profusely that it falls, shattering into pieces and puddling over the tablecloth and my food.

Everything goes blank as I have one final thought: *I'm falling.*

# 12

Pinpricks of light dance across my eyes in the dark. I struggle to open them. *Did Enforce glue them shut?* Enforce. The banquet. Goodbye to Compound. Goodbye to Mom. The volume of events in my life the past three days has been denser than Osmium. Of course, Osmium occurs naturally, and everything that's happened to me has been exceedingly unnatural.

I manage to open my eyes a sliver, and what greets me is a blur of alabaster, black, and dark brown. Squinting, I try again. A person is right in front of my face. Actually, scratch that. A very pretty person is right in front of my face.

Her blue eyes are framed by thick, dark lashes. Her skin is extremely white, while her brown hair hangs past her shoulders in a braid. Her pale skin makes me wonder if she's ever been out in the sun.

"Look who's finally joining us." Her voice is odd, nasally, with emphasis on the vowels. "You've been out for two days."

My voice comes out as a croak. "Wh-who are you?"

"Llama. And you're the new one."

"New, what?" The creases on my skin from the pillow pull taut as I massage my forehead and try to guess how old this person is. She isn't old enough to be a scientist, and she's not dressed like one. My eyes snag on her outfit.She's wearing a white hospital-style gown. It buttons down the front with big white buttons and hits just below the knees. Her feet are bare, which seems odd. I guess she's sixteen. I'll be fifteen in a month, so she's not much older than me.

"You're one of us."

"Us?"

"Research Assistant. You're an RA. Welcome to the heartbeat of progress."

"Wait. Your name is…?"

"L-L-A-M-A."She spells the name of an animal. "You have a name?"

"Err. Reach."

"Weird name."

"What?"

"Your name. It's weird. I like it."

"Ok. But isn't your name…uh…Llama?"

She grins. "Yep." She gets closer to my face, her blue eyes arresting me with their intensity. Cotton balls have invaded my mouth. I can't swallow; I have no saliva.

I force words out of my throat. "Your name is weird."

She laughs loudly. "My mom named me. Reminded her of home. The double l's looked like eleven to her, I guess."

My brain searches for something, a fuzzy memory enshrouded in a haze. "Eleven," I state slowly. "E-lev-en. I know Eleven."

Llama's eyes rake over my face in derision. "Trust me, Reach. You do not know about Eleven."

"But I've heard of it."

"You haven't heard about it."

"I heard Enforce thinks it's a hellhole."

Llama's eyes squint while her mouth turns into a frown. A muscle in her cheek ticks.

I shrug, closing my eyes against her intensity. My head hurts. This woman is eccentric.

"Everyone's thirsty when they get here. Here." She hands me a cup and I down the liquid, feeling relief as it cools and soothes my burning throat. "So, Reach." She flicks her tongue out and catches the corner of her mouth. "You're an RA."

"I didn't know that. What does it mean?"

She rolls her eyes as she tips her head backward, thinking. "What does it mean to be a research assistant? Or is your question more existential?"

"Uh, the research assistant one?"

"Practical. Getting your bearings. I can appreciate that."

I bring my palm to my face to rub the disorientation from my eyes. This person, *Llama*, is not helping. As I scrape my palms up and down my face, I feel small neat hatches. Stitches.

"Did I get stitches?"

"That is not what we were talking about. But, yes, you have stitches on both sides of your face. I overheard the medic teams talking. Do you want to know what happened?"

I really do want to know how I ended up here, in this sterile-looking place, on a thin bed with scratchy white sheets and a pretty girl standing next to me. I nod.

"Yes," I say, then remember my manners. "Please. I'd like to know everything."

Llama cocks her head to the side and fixes her eyes on mine. I don't flinch, even though I'm confused about my role here. Am I a specimen or a research assistant?

"Well no one can know *everything* here, but I eavesdrop effectively enough that I know a lot. Anyway. The medic teams said you fainted at the fancy banquet for the head scientists and that you fell on your face onto your plate. The glass you dropped first shattered, and when you hit the plate, the force of contact popped the glass up, cutting you. So now you have stitches on *both* sides of your face."

I blow out a breath as I take in this new information. I received medical care of some kind. It doesn't hurt, just feels tight, so I decide to turn back to the original question. Before I can voice my concerns about being a specimen here, a new thought strikes. This one is hot, searing like a lightning bolt through my consciousness and leaving a scorching path of anxiety in its wake. "WhataboutEnforceandSecond?" The words run together, spilling out of my mouth in a garbled jumble. One that, apparently, Llama can decipher.

"Oh. They weren't mad actually. I think they wanted to get you away from the scientists and this gave them the perfect out." She drops her voice to a conspiratorial whisper. "I wonder if they actually made you faint."

"What?" I hiss. This seems farfetched. "How would they have done that?"

She picks at her nails before replying. "There are ways. Different smells, things they might have put into your clothes or your food. Do you faint often?"

I shake my head, not willing to commit to that theory. I do have the idea that Llama might be able to help me understand things here—even if she seems unphased by conjecture that Second and Enforce planned my fainting episode. I can't wrap my head around it, so I decide to return to safer territory.

"So, you're a research assistant?" I maintain a neutral tone.

"Yep. And you're on my project." She sits down on the bed next to me.

"So we're going to be working…"

She grins as she responds. "Together, yep."

"On what, exactly?"

"I don't know yet, but we've been doing research in a special library room and setting things up. I think we start tomorrow."

"A library?"

"Yeah, a lot of really, really *old* books. It's pretty weird. It's not usually how things work for research assistants here."

My chest constricts. A library doesn't sound too bad, but this comment begs the question: "How do things usually work?"

Llama's hands have been bunching the fabric of my blanket as she's sat perched on my bed. Her hands still, marking her words as false. "There's a lot more poking, prodding, invasive procedures. But it's all in the name of science. Didn't you help out at the science-y place you were at before they brought you here?"

"Oh, yeah. Yeah, I did."

"Then you know what it's like."

"I guess. But I've never been here."

"Here's not so bad. There's a uniform for research assistants and scientists. There's food in the cafeteria at prescribed times. And we get to help support the heartbeat of Nation." Her voice sounds flat as she says 'the heartbeat of Nation.' I see her body language shift, but I can't decipher what it means.

"Llama." My voice goes dry and it cracks again. "Llama, I d-don't know anything about this place."

"Easy enough. They haven't had a reporting meeting since it's Sunday. You've been unconscious for the other ones. Just follow your arrows when the alarm sounds and you'll get where you need to go."

"What?" I don't know what she means by following *my* arrows.

"Oh, and one more thing." She grins mischievously. "Your uniform is the same as mine."

This comment causes my eyes to wander Llama's body as I take in what she's wearing. My dry mouth becomes even drier. She's beautiful.

*Oh no. Llama. I have to work with her.*

The flare of attraction fires in my brain and I know she sees it because she smirks. Then I realize that my uniform, this white dress-gown thing, will not be nearly as flattering on me as it is on her.

She leaves the room, and I realize that there is no door. There is only a doorframe, made of the same white cinder blocks that have always been the backdrop to my life, creating a place that was both prison and sanctuary. Unease tingles in my spine. I remember Mom's warning to burn the picture of her and Greg. How can I hide something so incriminating when I have no privacy? At least on Compound I had the ability to shut a door and lock out prying eyes. I thought I'd have the same here.

The gentle tap-tap-tap of Llama's footsteps fades away. The silence is gaping, like a black hole, and in the silence I hear my mother's words about her communication devices. She designed it to give the government what it wanted and still be the least intrusive possible.

*I've never had privacy.*

My shoulders slump as my mind unwinds the tangled spool of totalitarian control I've lived—without knowing. The secrets and half-truths have been nothing but lies.

The bed is on the left-hand side of the doorless doorway, and I lie with my head nearest to the door. Or, rather, the not door. On the right-hand side is a small dresser with two drawers and a basin of water on top. There's also a cup sitting next to a metal spigot drilled into the white concrete. A white towel with the emblem of Nation is folded and hanging over the side of the basin. There's a razor and a brush and a canister of shaving cream. My duffle bag from the aircraft sits on the white tile floor at the side of my dresser, zipped closed. Along the top of the back wall, opposite my head, is a long rectangular window that runs nearly the length of the wall. There is no handle or opening mechanism. Heat and tightness stretch across my body as I realize I am trapped and disoriented.

I fight my headache and pull my body up into a seated position before I try to place one foot on the floor. *One foot at a time.* I remember Mom's words about how to always get out of bed, even when struggling. *Just put one foot on the floor.* By the time I do so, I feel woozy. Despite the spinning happening before and behind my eyes, I take a big breath and try to push to standing. As I do, I catch sight of the uniform I'm wearing. It is exactly as Llama said. I groan, embarrassed to wear this garment when my Compound uniform was much more comfortable.

I take a wobbly step as my feet absorb the shocking coldness of the tile. It's too much, but I have to do something. My orange duffel bag is close enough that I think I can unpack without moving around.

I crouch by the bag, pulling the items out one by one. When I get to the deodorant tube, I hesitate, unsure of where to put it. With my back to the nonexistent door, I check the tube and can see the tiniest flash of color along the edge. Either it was disturbed, or it shifted a little during transit. There is no evidence anyone went through anything, so I assume the latter.

Shaking the tube a little, I'm able to tap the edges of the picture out of sight. I put the deodorant on my washstand. The most dangerous thing I have with me in plain sight is not safe, but also probably the last place anyone would look.

Toiletries now dispersed, I open the dresser drawers and discover several more white gowns, some undershirts, and some underwear. There are pairs of socks, but a tag on them reads "optional."

I pull back up to standing and peruse the window. There are no shades and no opening mechanism. The window is at my eye level and shows a wide expanse of blue sky, complete with fluffy white clouds and a stretch of perfectly manicured green grass. In the background are tall buildings, but it's hard to tell how far they are from here. I have no landmarks by which to judge distance.

This exertion has left me exhausted, so I plod back to my bed and fall onto the mattress. I barely tug the covers over my torso before sleep claims me once again.

# 13

A LOUD GONG wakes me this time. My headache is less severe than before, but my eyes throb. The tightness stretching across my cheeks aches.

I scan the room, looking for that girl, *Llama*. She isn't here, and I am annoyed. I'd like to get some real answers.

A woman's voice booms through a speaker. "All capable will report to the cafeteria for morning announcements and scheduling."

I'm up and I'm capable. What was it Llama said about getting around here? *Follow the arrows.* I search for arrows on the walls, but I find none. Frustrated, I step into the hall, where there are no signs of any kind on the walls. Once my feet hit the tile of the corridor, an arrow lights up on the floor. When I step in the indicated direction, another arrow flashes. This pattern continues, slowly at first, but I gather confidence as each time I step, a new arrow takes form just ahead of me. I feel like I'm chasing something, gaining on a goal when each arrow forms.

The further I travel the more people I see, also following arrows. These people aren't watching the arrows with hesitation or even curiosity. I wish I could say the same. They know where they are going and they walk with confident strides. I see one person veer off, yelling over his shoulder, "I forgot my..." Even though he's going against the stream of people, arrows stilllight up in front of him. They just point in the opposite way.

Eventually, I arrive at the cafeteria. A steady stream of people is filing neatly into the space. They form two lines, one for the lab coat-wearing scientists, and one for the people dressed like me, the less-thans. I wonder briefly if I'm the only *specimen* here.

The lines pass by two metal kiosks. A woman scans wrists and presents everyone at the kiosk with a tray. The tray is full of something that looks like food and reminds me instantly of the horrible food Dr. Jog shared with me on the way to Hub.

When I arrive at the kiosk, the woman holds up a hand. I mimic what everyone else has been doing and show her my wrist. She scans it, frowns, and then scans it again. "Name?"

"Err, Reach."

"Reach, Reach, Reach." She frowns. "You new?"

"Yes."

"Why didn't you say so?"

"No one tol—"

"You need a number. I'll print it now." She presses buttons on her scanner and prints a label. She sticks the label to my wrist, scans it, and then hands me the customary plate with the square food. Sharp pain grips my wrist where she stuck the label to my skin. I can't grasp my wrist, but my eyes are drawn to the source of the pain. As I watch, the label disintegrates. The ink bleeds into my skin, carving a barcode into my very flesh. As quickly as the pain began, it subsides. There's only a cool numbness now.

A glance around the room shows the divide. The scientists sit on one side of the room, at tables with cushy-looking chairs. Those dressed like me sit on the other, at long tables with hard plastic stools attached. I murmur a 'thanks' and take the tray to a seat on the side of the cafeteria that I clearly belong in. I slide into the middle seat of a table and begin trying to eat the food. It's not as bad as what Dr. Jog served me, but it's still flavorless. I can tell it's designed to be optimally nutritious; there is nothing enjoyable about it.

A movement catches my eye. A faint smile lands on my lips as I recognize the only person I actually want to see again: that crazy, weird girl, Llama. Llama is deep in a heated discussion with Dr. Jog. She is gesticulating, moving her arms in a wide sweep around her. Dr. Jog's eyes are narrowed and he shrugs at her as she clutches her upper arm.

Buzzing reverberates through the cafeteria. Dr. Jog sits with his scientist comrades while Llama walks to me, plopping down on the stool beside mine. "Hi," she says.

"Hey." I open my mouth to say more when a woman in a navy blue scientist outfit taps a microphone in the center of the cafeteria.

"Good morning, Hub." Her voice is melodious, cool, and pleasant. "We have some new arrivals this week. So I'll start with this. I am the head of Hub. My name is Dr. Quasar. We meet on Monday for our weekly briefing before beginning the work of our great Nation.

"Hub is a place of learning, culture, knowledge, and reform. Here our great Nation joins together to lift our hearts as one. We unite learning, knowledge, and culture to achieve the best possible outcome for our land. We are quiet here, studious. We are the force of Nation's progress. The heart that beats for Nation lives in our breasts, and we—what we do here—is all for the good of Nation!"

Applause breaks out from the scientists. Dr. Quasar smiles graciously before beginning again. "Schedules—we have a new project starting. We are proud to present Global 1 to the docket of our impressive research here at Hub. Projects Roman and Honor will continue. Global 1 team, welcome!"

Polite applause breaks out as every scientist looks at Dr. Jog. He waves and stands.

The woman speaks one more time. "Group leaders, collect your research assistants."

She clicks the microphone off and steps away as a variety of scientists begin circulating the assistant side of the cafeteria and summoning their subordinates away with them. Dr. Jog is stopped many times and shakes hands with each scientist. By the time he makes it to the research assistant side of the room, there are only four of us left. There's me, Llama, and two others who stand when Dr. Jog announces, "Come on, let's get to work."

We file into the hallway, and this time I do not have an individual arrow. Instead I see an arrow on the ground with the text GLOBAL 1 flashing above it. I hear a brief whooshing sound and feel the hair on my neck rise. I turn around and see Llama.

"Are you a pre-Citizen?" She asks it so quietly that I can really only hear her because I'm focused on reading her lips. I'm not sure what that has to do with anything, so I turn the question back on her. "Are you?"

She grimaces. "No."

"I'm not either."

"Those two aren't like us." She jerks her chin in the direction of the other RAs walking behind Dr. Jog.

"Oh?"

"Yeah, they're Citizens. They've been helping get the research rooms ready. I've known them for the past month while we've been preparing."

"You've been preparing for a month?"

"Yeah."

"What did you do before?" I ask curiously.

"Different projects." She's curt and her response sounds final, so I don't bother pressing. Besides, the nerve endings in my body are exploding. I take a big breath, then inhale a second time quickly.

"Why are you here if you're not a Citizen? What does that even mean here?" I ask as we turn down an isolated hall.

She shrugs. "It means I'm a freak, like you."

"What do you know about me?"

"The three of us have been read into certain aspects of what this project is. I know what you *are*."

My eyes widen, but then the person in front of me stops, causing my forehead to collide with their back. "Oof!" I reverberate back like a sound wave off a wall. The person ahead turns around. A man looks at me with narrowed eyes before shaking his head and stepping aside.

I have questions about what *I am* for Llama, but I'm distracted by the fact that this hallway is at its end. We can go no further. I start to turn around, but Dr. Jog puts his hand up, resting his palm against a cinderblock wall. There are no hinges, no doors, nothing that would indicate this is anything except the end of the line. Instead, the wall swings open without a sound. He motions us in, and as I step over the threshold, I find myself in a classroom, lab, and library all in one. It's cavernous. There are no windows, just fluorescent lights illuminating white cement blocks. I know instinctively that this is a secret space, used only in the most confidential of experiments and research. And that I'm the reason for this.

My body stops, my muscles thrumming like a rubber band pulled taut and held still.

Two small doors stand to the left of the entrance we just came through, leading to toilets. I can see shelves of lab equipment—beakers, test tubes, microscopes, and paper. There's a long wooden counter with small lamps placed every six feet, and pen and pencil cups. Other shelves contain electronic equipment. I turn to look back the way we came and discover that there is no entryway. The only thing that gives away where the hidden door is are the two steps that lead to nothing.

A line of clipboards hang from the wall. Dr. Jog passes the clipboards out to the other research assistants.

I take it all in, noticing the people I'm working with. I already saw the one male research assistant, who is probably twenty, when I bumped into him. There's also Llama, and another female research assistant. I can't pinpoint her exact age, but she seems older than Llama.

I step back against the door, leaning an elbow into it as I stand

next to the steps. It's solid. I see nothing assuring me it's still there—
no crack surrounding the frame, no sliver of light creeping in. I push
back a little harder, willing there to be some tremor, some indication
of weakness. There is nothing.

A bead of sweat trickles down my spine.

I am trapped.

# 14

Air whistles out through my teeth as my jaw clenches. I hate enclosed spaces. Some people call it claustrophobia, but I call it common sense.

"Reach." Somewhere, far away, I hear my name. "Reach."

"He looks a little green, sir."

"Reach. Reach. Look up, Reach."

I blink slowly, my eyelashes splashing bars across the image of
the floor, like a prison cell. *That's unhelpful.*

"Reach." The voice is closer now, and so is a shadow. I recognize
the voice, but I can't place it. "Look up at me, Reach."

I try, I really do, but I can't move my neck. A glimmer of movement jerks my eyes away from the floor. A flash of white in my periphery and a cool hand touching my balled-up fists startles my gaze
away from the ground. Llama stands next to me, holding my hand
and offering reassurance in a stalwart way.

My eyes snag hers and she holds my gaze for just a second too
long to be comfortable. I don't know why she's helping or how she
knew what I needed, but I'm grateful.

"Reach." Llama's hand touching mine grounds me. Dr. Jog looks at me, concern written on his brow. "Are you all right?"

Llama's hand squeezes mine gently, and it's like she passed peace into my body with her gesture. I find myself able to look around the room, which is actually many rooms, and not nearly as terrifying as I had first believed. With this boost of confidence, my ability to respond returns.

"Yeah, uh." I clear my throat. "Yes. I don't like small spaces."

"Understandable. If you're ready, we have some things to go over." I nod. He continues. "Good. This space is Sublab. It's an important part of Global 1's process. You've been pulled onto Global 1 for your very specific skill sets, and I'm quite thrilled each of you is here. I spent extensive time reviewing applicant files from the approved pool. Freedom, Hero, you were both selected for this project because of your exemplary contributions to science. Llama, I'm very pleased with the progress reports from your school. Reach…" Dr. Jog trails off and speaks to the group. "I hope that you will all treat each other with the utmost respect and consideration here. You are all working toward a common goal. You are all research assistants in this project. Even if someone tells you otherwise, you *are* research assistants. No matter what you discover, what you are told, what aspects of this project are revealed, you all are here because we need to learn things."

Freedom gives a single head bob of acknowledgment. His mouth is set in a grim line.

"Global 1 is a highly classified project, so we have individual group time in Sublab. This is not typical of Hub's science program, but for reasons we cannot divulge, we have to maintain secrecy. What you learn here is classified and may not be discussed outside of Sublab. Is that understood?"

Freedom and Hero nod in unison, their faces solemn. I can't see Llama's because she's standing next to me. There's silence in the room as three pairs of eyes study Llama and me. Dr. Jog fixes his gaze on our hands pointedly.

"I should warn you that here at Hub, romantic attachment is not permitted until you've been matched. Llama and Reach, you two are academic partners in this endeavor. You are not permitted to engage in romantic activity. You are not permitted to match, and neither of you will be on a list of approved match candidates for the other."

Heat burns down my ears and across my face. Llama drops my hand and steps away, rubbing her fingers. Dr. Jog gives a small nod of approval. "Romantic activity of any kind is not permitted until after matching."

The loss of Llama's hand stings, but Dr. Jog was clearly warning her off. I briefly wonder what *matching* means, but don't have time to ponder because Dr. Jog asks us to introduce ourselves. I despise this question. Meeting new people is one of my least favorite things about *people*. That and, well, most people. I haven't met many I've actually liked.

Freedom goes first. He has sand-colored hair and narrow green eyes. He's tall and not built in a muscular sense, but lean and strong-looking. He gives a small wave with his hand, but he doesn't smile. "Hi. I'm Freedom. I'm a C3 and I'm here to prove my loyalty to Nation. I'll be working with electronics and historic technology on this project."

"Very good," Dr. Jog says. "Hero?"

"Hi." Hero's hair is swept into a long black braid. Her brown eyes are round and she's shorter than I am by several inches. "I'm Hero. I'm a C1. I'm going to transcribe things and help Dr. Jog as a type of personal assistant. I'll be helping with the experiment notes."

"Thank you, Hero." Dr. Jog's eyes flicker over me and land on Llama. "Llama?"

Llama smirks slightly, her blue eyes crinkling in the corners. "I'm Llama. I'm going to be Reach's partner in this project. I'm not sure what that entails yet, but it's not every day you get to work with a half..." She trails off as she studies me. The others turn their eyes to me too.

"Llama..." Dr. Jog grinds out through gritted teeth. "Reach is a research assistant, just like all of you."

I'm overcome with the sudden urge to sink to the floor and lie there until everything goes away. That doesn't seem to be an option, so I step forward and confront the awkwardness head-on. "I'm Reach. I'm new here. I'm not sure how I'll be asked to contribute to this project, but I know what I am—a specimen. And I know you all know too."

Dr. Jog frowns. "Right. Well, Reach, for the sake of this project, you do *not* know anything about your genetic makeup. As I said, you are all research assistants." He dusts his hands on his lab coat and shakes his head, as if to make the frown leave his face. It does.

He turns to each of us with a smile. "Here in Sublab, we are going to be working on thought experiments. In order to prepare you for the next phase of this project, we need to develop high-level thinking and philosophical understanding of ideas. This will be critical in the future in many instances. Sublab has been transformed into a type of library. I will be providing lectures, but also concepts I want you to learn through research. This is not as scientific as what you are perhaps used to in the greater sense of the word, but I assure you this time in Sublab is valuable. We have several months before you join the general population of Hub for coursework and scientific advancement. I regret that I can't tell you more about the future phases, but all will become clear in due time."

Freedom's stance shifts just a little and everyone snaps their attention to him. "Due time?"

Dr. Jog nods and then passes each of us a clipboard. Tacked under the clip is a sheet of paper. "You should all know what to do; it's rather self-explanatory, especially since you three set up the rooms. Reach, I'm sure you'll figure it out in no time. Our lecture will begin in one hour. Until then, I'll be conducting my own research amongst the books." He disappears into a room full of bookshelves, leaving me staring at the clipboard in my hands. I don't know what I expected here at Hub, but it isn't this.

My eyes scan the paper and encounter unfamiliar words. I have no idea what my task is here. The echo of my mother's directive sounds in my mind. *Focus on being excellent at the task in front of you. You have to succeed. We're counting on you.*

There's no one to ask. Dr. Jog has dismissed me without directions, and I've been warned away from the entire female populace of Hub. Freedom does not exude friendliness, and also he's a C3, a third-year Citizen. He's proven his loyalty to Nation to the extent that he's a Citizen. I don't know who I can turn to or who I can trust.

Hero sidles over to me. Her face is drawn, her eyebrows pinched together in suspicion. "What do you know?" she whispers.

"Not much," I mouth back at her, self-deprecatingly.

She smiles, the grin lighting up her face in an unexpected way. "Dr. Jog said we need to treat each other the way we'd treat anyone else here, and you're not what I expected, so I'm going to try this."

Freedom watches her from across the room, his mouth drawn into a thin line.

"I...I appreciate that?" I cock my head to Freedom slightly. "Does he ever smile?"

Hero laughs quietly. "Yeah, sometimes he does." She's soft in her answer, but then straightens up into a more business-like posture. "Would you like me to show you what we're doing here? Dr. Jog didn't give you any directions, did he?"

Llama appears from behind Hero, inserting herself into the conversation before I can answer. "I'll show him. *I'm* his partner." Her tone is surprisingly possessive.

Hero quirks an eyebrow at Llama's words. "Llama, I mean this kindly. Be careful," she whispers before walking away. No one here seems to have any issue with bewildering me.

# 15

Llama does show me what to do, and it's less taxing than I expected. Our days take on a routine that isn't unpleasant. I wake each morning to the sound of a gong and am able to use the restroom before an arrow lights up outside my doorway. Bound by the secrecy of our project, I speak to no one but Llama, Hero, Freedom, and Dr. Jog. That suits me just fine. People are entirely too much.

The arrow leads me to the cafeteria, where I eat a tasteless morning meal and endure some stares and whispers from other research assistants. Then, all of Global 1 heads to Sublab. Every morning, Llama, Hero, and I scurry about the lab library before returning to the cafeteria for a midday meal. After lunch, Dr. Jog begins a lecture in Sublab, usually telling us facts about old philosophers. Llama and I take notes while Hero keeps track of Dr. Jog's notes.

After Dr. Jog's lectures, we sometimes return to our copy work or are free to follow our arrows to dinner. When dinner is over, we are directed to our rooms via an arrow. There's a small male-only common room with a cart full of electronic books, a couch, and a chess board. I'd like to play with someone, but since I'm not supposed to speak to anyone outside of Global 1, I usually grab a book and return to my room. I read until the lights flick out at 10:47 p.m. and am mercifully claimed by sleep. Sometimes I stare out the window with longing for the feel of the sun, or fresh air, or sand. So far my arrow has not directed me outside of the building, and I haven't tried to leave. I'm too busy getting my bearings. The paleness of everyone's skin makes me think most people do not leave Hub for something as trivial as sunlight and fresh air when there is science to be learned.

In the mornings we gather book titles from a checklist on our clipboard, then place them in an orderly stack on a giant wooden counter. Occasionally, there is a book with a word flagged on my list. That means I take it to my personal area of the wooden counter and flag certain keywords based on the index. We each have a notebook in our workspace. Currently, we are defining words. *Metaphysics, thought experiment, logic*…these are some of the words I define. A quick glance at Llama's notebook shows me two things: first, she's left-handed, and second, we're defining the same words. Interesting. I really like the copy work, but I wonder what these words have to do with me.

Since the whole project of Global 1 is about me being half-Martian, I don't feel too conceited about that thought. Still, the twinge of anxiety thrums in my veins as I consider being selfish. Selfish is something I never want to be. It's something that was never an option on Compound and certainly not an option now if I want to protect my mother.

Freedom's role is as an electronics assistant. Dr. Jog asks for something involving technology and Freedom acquires it, sets it up, and puts it away. I see Freedom set up an old machine on a cart. It has a light on top, a mirror, and a glass plate on the bottom. I have never seen anything so primitive in a science lab setting. I would never expect to see such a machine used in Nation Hub, a place that prides itself on its technology, science, and advancements. Although, we're using real books, not just electronic versions.

I pause to wonder why. I'm about to head back to find a new

book by Pluto, but Freedom passes by me with the cart. Something about it piques my interest. I'm not allowed to speak to others, but Freedom is here. Surely I can ask him *what* the cart is.

"Hey, Freedom," I whisper as he wheels it past me. He scowls but slows. I'm not deterred by the scowl because that seems to be his only expression.

"What?" He says it sharply.

"What is that?" I cock my head at the machine on the cart.

Freedom looks enthused for a moment. He glances at Dr. Jog, whose face is hidden behind a large book. He furiously scribbles notes on a tablet with a stylus. Freedom shrugs and seems to accept that Dr. Jog isn't worried about him talking to me or about the machine. I can hardly imagine that this type of machine is a classified secret, but Freedom has been here much longer than I have. I don't know what sort of projects he's worked on in the past, and I don't think he would tell me if I asked.

"It's an old projector!" He really is enthused. He smiles as he studies it, and I realize this is the first time I have ever seen Freedom smile. "It's basically an anthropological artifact at this point. Dr. Jog has a relative who worked for NASA before Nation was Nation and Hub took over science. I guess the NASA relatives couldn't bear to part with such an ingenious machine. I can't believe that they could do so much just by using a simple light and mirror!" A shiny light in Freedom's eyes makes me wonder about him. *Why is he named Freedom? Freedom from what? The past? The present? The future?*

He's past the age of loyalty and is a C3. Most Citizens pick their names when they are eighteen and preparing to enter Nation as adults and full-fledged Citizens.

"Did you pick it?" I ask in a hushed voice before I realize what I just voiced was an extremely personal question. And honestly, a dumb one since I have had exactly one friendly moment with him.

"Pick what?" Freedom says, looking confused.

"Your name."

Freedom's eyes narrow. He sighs. "It's a long story. Yes and no. My parents picked it. The name was fitting, given their beliefs, but it also made me a target… So, I'm here now to show Nation I'm allegiant to freedom by personifying freedom in their service as a research tech when needed." There's a bitterness to his words about Nation. I wouldn't have heard it if I hadn't spent so much time listening to how people talk on Compound. He conceals it well.

I try to process what he's saying. I know some people don't change their names when they turn eighteen. I don't think I would. I've always been *Reach*. I don't want to give up that connection to Mom. Maybe Freedom felt the same.

I was raised by scientists. I know the importance of asking the right questions—and I have a lot of questions. For starters, what things was Freedom a target for? More questions rise in my conscience like bubbles in a pot of boiling water. Why does this top-secret group working with a highly classified half-Martian also include self-proclaimed oddities like Llama and Freedom? Why would anyone's parents name their child something so stupid? Freedom? Really? The government loves freedom, as long as it's carefully orchestrated to follow their schedules and efficiency. Freedom sounds like an ideal, one that could be dangerously close to dissent.

There must be a look on my face that gives away my disgust. It's disgust for Freedom's parents naming him something they knew was dangerous. But then I remember my own parents and my own life. *Did my parents do any better at protecting me?* No, they did not.

Freedom clamps his jaw down tightly and turns away. Before I can explain, Dr. Jog calls for me, summoning me to the stool at his workspace.

"Yes?" I don't know what to call him here. On Compound he was called Jog by the scientists or Doctor. I can't remember what anyone called him here. It's another piece of the impossible puzzle.

"Reach." His voice is calm, quiet. "Not every decision with dangerous consequences is ill-advised."

My eyebrows shoot up. I did not expect that statement. My eyebrows are lost in my hairline as I rashly blurt the question that burns in my heart. "And my parents?"

"Is it ill-advised that you exist?"

"I suppose so."

"And yet, you exist. You, who have no more control over being created than a flower, a tree, or a pair of sunglasses in a factory. The fact that you exist, Reach, *that* says something about consequences. The evidence of your existence points to the opposite of ill-advised."

*Riddles. He speaks in riddles. I can decipher riddles. I can…*

His eyes meet mine, and I find kindness there.

"Sir, err, *Doctor* Jog. I don't understand."

"It's an extrapolation of philosophy. In the Before, a group of people believed in something more than science. This comes from that."

"Oh." I thought I was understanding the philosophers we were studying, but this doesn't make sense.

"I find the past and former great thinkers to be especially clarifying regarding the present and the future. Now, I believe you are still several books away from completing a checklist. Once you've completed the checklist, I'd like you to shelve these books. I'm finished." Dr. Jog points to a haphazard pile of hardcover books leaning precariously against the cinderblock wall at the back edge of the long work table. "Oh and Reach." His tone sounds off-handed, but his gaze is serious. "You know this is top-secret research and you shouldn't discuss it with anyone outside of this room. Those of us in this space are *safe.*" The emphasis on the word *safe* has me perplexed.

"Yes, Dr. Jog." I can't meet his eyes as I say it; there was something too vulnerable about that moment.

I scurry away back toward Llama and the books. I can't decipher Dr. Jog's meaning. *Dr. Jog is happy I exist?* But, logic says, of course he is. He's a scientist, and I'm something interesting to study. Mom regarded him as a type of friend.

*Ally, not friend,* my brain supplies. So, as an ally, he must have known that my existence put Mom in danger. I don't understand anything about human relationships, or friendships, or allyships.

A thought burns as it percolates into my brain tissue.

*I am a lie. I am…nothing more than a specimen here.*

# 16

TIME IS A strange concept. Some thinkers believe it doesn't even exist. After all, it's not a river, but more like a circle. Months pass and the days take on a regularity of routine. Every day I step out of the doorless space that is my room and an arrow directs me to the cafeteria for breakfast. After breakfast, we are directed to our lab, where we do more copy work and research. There's a trip back to the cafeteria for another nearly inedible lunch, and then back to the lab for a lecture by Dr. Jog. I enjoy the lectures. I find my mind stimulated in ways I've never experienced before. I've filled two notebooks so far and begun designing my own thought experiments. If I ever work up the courage, I'll show them to Dr. Jog.

The familiarity of several months of routine is comforting. I almost feel safe.

We've begun filing out of the cafeteria after the morning meal. We stand in the hallway as the rest of our crew arrives. I'm contemplating my thought experiment when I arrive at the dead end, where we wait for Dr. Jog to open the door to the lab. None of us have the clearance to do so. An itchy feeling skitters down my arms. Something is different, but I'm still deep in my own thoughts to figure out what.

When we enter the room, which I am now mercifully not terrified of, I feel it. The word *danger* pulses through my body, and I scan the room for Enforce's bruisers. The men aren't there, and neither is Enforce.

I start to relax before I notice that there are only three clipboards, the door has closed behind us, and Freedom is missing. Llama stands next to me. I feel her tense as she takes in what feels like a gaping hole in our small party.

"Dr. Jog," she says. "Where's Freedom?" Dr. Jog grimaces back in response. "I said, Where. Is. He?"

I'm shocked at her tone. I'd not speak to my superiors this way, but Llama is different from me in so many ways.

Dr. Jog clears his throat and shuffles. "Eleven." He says it quietly.

"Eleven? He's *in* Eleven?" Surprise laces Llama's features.

"Eleven. Llama. You know it. I know it."

"Will he be back?"

"No," Dr. Jog says with a sigh. He runs his hands through his white hair, making the strands stick up awkwardly. Llama looks like she wants to say something, then shrugs and treks back to the library with her clipboard. I wish I understood what Eleven was. Dr. Jog turns his back on us and begins rifling through sheaves of notes. "Hero, you know how to use this machine, right?" He points at something with long cords and a bunch of components.

"Yes…" She hiccups, which is odd for her. I have a lifetime of experience in watching people and reading body language. Over the past months, I developed a suspicion that Hero and Freedom are romantically involved. While in Sublab or the cafeteria, they never say or do anything inappropriate. It's actually the over-properness that drew my attention. The picture of propriety stands out more than any playful, friendly gestures would. The slow glances they gave each other when they thought no one else was watching clued me in to their attraction. They always arrived and left Sublab together.

Hero's voice is wavering, her eyes red-rimmed.

I make the snap decision to ask Llama what she knows. "Psst. Llama," I whisper through the library shelves. Llama holds her clipboard, and I can see her through the books on the other side of the row.

She whispers back playfully, "Psst. Reach. What?"

Dr. Jog does not mind quiet exchanges as we work in the mornings, but it feels like I need to whisper this question. I want to respect Hero's feelings at the very least. She has been kind to me since that first day. I like her, in a friendly way.

"Were...*are*...Hero and Freedom...you know?"

"You know, what?" Her eyes crinkle up in the corners.

"More than just friends?"

"Oh yeah, they're about to be unionized. Didn't you read the signs?" I stare blankly. "You know, the news signs outside the auditorium?"

"Er—I don't know where the auditorium is."

"Oh." She looks crestfallen. "I guess that means you haven't seen much of this place."

I screw my mouth up because...*yeah, I haven't seen anything here because no one has shown me anything.*

"People get unionized here?" I can't imagine anyone getting unionized in this cold-hearted place. Except Second, and maybe Enforce, if she could ever love someone. It's so efficient. They would probably think this was the ideal place for a wedding. No feelings, just cold business, science, work, and schedules. Actually, Dr. Quasar would probably like it too.

"Umm, yes. When approved."

"So if they're getting unionized soon, why is he in *Eleven?*" I cannot figure out why Eleven is so important to all these people.

Llama's mouth quirks up. "Maybe for technology business? I don't know, but sometimes people have to travel."

Hero walks up to me, puts her hand on my chest, and gives a small shove. It's not a friendly gesture, but I sense she isn't angry at me. I'm just the closest thing she can push. Her voice, when she speaks, is venomous. "He's *not* in Eleven, you fools. Dr. Jog is giving you the official story." Llama blinks at her. I do too. "He's in *Pen One.*" Fear, hatred, contempt, and sorrow are all wrapped in her words.

I stand there, dumbstruck, as Llama erupts. She marches down the aisle toward Dr. Jog. Hero and I follow her, her rage boiling over.

"PEN ONE!" she yells in Dr. Jog's face. "You should be honest with us. How can we work when our emotions are muddled by mis-information and…and…*propaganda?*" She spits out the word and saliva lands on Dr. Jog's face. He wipes it away with the back of his hand as his features contort through a myriad of expressions. They land on 'shocked.'

*What is propaganda?*

"Llama," Dr. Jog growls. "Remember your place."

Llama clutches her upper left arm above her elbow, and I can see her fingers shaking.

"Yes, *Doc,* I *remember* it. I think you are the one who has *forgot-ten.*"

No one else seems nearly as confused as I am. I despise informa-tion omission. I already feel in the dark here, but the routine has at least made me comfortable. I'm reminded that I am constantly play-ing catch-up with what everyone else already knows.

"Fine." Dr. Jog sits on his stool with a heavy sigh. His shoulders slump and he talks in a quiet voice. "It's not what you think though. He isn't incarcerated. Reach, do you know anything about the penal system here?"

My mouth goes dry. "I know Enforce," I say.

Dr. Jog doesn't respond, opting to hold his hands in an 'I surren-der' pose. His shoulders sink even lower. "Pen One is a penitentiary. It houses high-security prisoners made up of the Citizens who have committed crimes against the government. It's for those Citizens who have incited rebellion, dissented, or done something to be noticed as a threat to the Three Powers. It's close by, on the outskirts of Hub City. Freedom is not incarcerated. He's there to make a decision."

Hero chokes out a cry. Dr. Jog glances back at her, his face turning a pale shade of red as he continues. "Decision about…family. And trying to prove his Citizenship, to ensure his and Hero's future when they marry. Freedom was already a Citizen when his parents were arrested. But typically the children of…" He glances at Llama and then turns back to me. "The children of those accused lose the right to become a Citizen. Freedom's situation is unusual. His Citizen status is in question, so for now…Litigate insists he acts as a Non. Until he proves his loyalty. Nons and Citizens cannot marry, so Freedom has to take a drastic measure."

Hero's sobs are loud and tears flow freely. Llama's jaw is tense.

"Freedom's parents were arrested for crimes against the government," Dr. Jog explains. "They believe that less government is better and planned a coup two years ago. It went sideways, and they ended up in prison. To maintain Citizenship, Freedom will have to permanently denounce his parents."

Llama's features crackle with indignation. I feel stunned. This new information is a lot more than I bargained for. I can see the pain in Hero welling up and spilling over.

"What does it mean to permanently denounce his parents?" I say it clearly, although I have an inkling of what it might mean.

Hero and Llama look up at me, surprised. Sometimes they seem shocked at the number of things I don't know or understand here. One day I'll take them to Compound and show them what it's like to know nothing.

Dr. Jog butts into my petty thoughts. "It means that he signs their papers." He draws a breath as disgust flits across his face. "As kin, he signs, and then he takes a blood transfusion to express his regret at being related to them. And then his parents are…"

Hero opens her mouth and explains in a harsh whisper, "His parents are executed by the state…and…they will never…" She doesn't stop to wipe her tears, doesn't care that they splotch her white gown.

I stand there, mouth agape, as I realize what Hero is facing. She loves someone—and that person is saddled with two horrible choices: sign death papers for his parents and be with the one he loves, or spare his parents' lives and lose a future with her. It's an impossible choice.

"If he doesn't sign?" I ask quietly, since Hero has now curled herself into a tight ball and is rocking on her heels.

Llama answers, "Never heard of anyone who didn't want to be a Citizen." Her tone is casual, but her gaze sharp. Hero hears her, gasps, bends over, and vomits. Her reaction jars me into full realization. Hero's future in-laws die, or her future husband does.

"Would they…kill…him?" I ask more boldly.

"No one knows," Llama says. "I think he'd be sent to undesirable jobs, but that's just a guess."

Dr. Jog is crouched next to Hero and uses a rag to mop up the mess. "It's a good guess, Llama." He rolls up his sleeves, just above his elbow on his left arm. A dark tattoo, a circle made of small symbols and numbers with one very large black $X$ across it, marks his arm. It means something to Llama because she blanches, grabs her arm again as if she were burned, and stalks to the dark shelves of the library.

I don't see her for the rest of the day.

# 17

My newfound understanding of Nation and its penal system, as Dr. Jog called it, leaves me unsettled. The view out my window is inky black, broken by the lights of the buildings in the distance. I can't see the moon from my window, and I don't ever see the sun rise or set. I know I face either north or south, but that information is useless. I'm staring at the buildings, trying to process all the information I've been given about Nation in the few months I've been here in Hub.

I know I'm intelligent. I know Mom said my aptitude test scores were great, and that she raised me in such a way to encourage—the word still feels strange in my brain—*dissent*. I have fallen into a comfortable routine the past six months, and I am ashamed. It's so easy to follow along, to lose sight of what I'm doing here. I started here with the intent of using game theory to disrupt whatever evils they could dream up. I haven't done anything except follow an arrow they provide.

The ache of missing Mom is too much. It's all too much. I don't know if there are cameras observing me in here, but I need something familiar. I stand at my washstand with my back to the door. I lay a towel out over the edge of the counter, then open the drawer just below it. The towel should obscure any overhead images of what I'm about to do while my back blocks prying eyes from the hallway. I fumble a bit in the drawer as I draw the photograph out of my deodorant tube. It maintains its curl from being in the tube for so long, but I manage to unroll it enough to see Mom's face. I miss her face. I miss *her*.

Serving Nation in a scientific capacity trumps family ties, according to the government. I had known this to some extent, but Freedom's situation drives the point home in a way that leaves me restless. I had held on to a glimmer of hope I would be able to see Mom again, or at least talk to her. After today, I understand that is not an option. I'll have to cling to the memories, which shift like sand through an hourglass as I study her face, noting the genuine happiness splayed across it. It hurts to think of her.

I slam the drawer shut, unable to bear it any longer.

I need a distraction until lights out. Anger at this regime courses through me. I stomp out of the room, heading to the male common room. I walk through the door frame and find three other males inside. One lounges on the couch with his feet propped up on the arm, legs casually crossed at the ankle. He watches as another bounces a purple ball on the tile floor, angling it to hit the wall with a thwack, then catches it. The third is idly standing near the small table with a chess board.

My mouth goes dry, but I think of my mother and her words about rebelling in small ways and then large ones. Tonight I'll break a rule, even if it's not my natural inclination to talk to people. The draw of the chessboard and the ache of losing my mom can't be offset by common sense.

"Do you play?" The words spill out, directed at the male research assistant by the chess board. The ball thwacks and then comes to a halt. I feel three pairs of eyes staring at me.

"You *talk*." The boy by the chess board recovers the quickest. His hair is dark brown, and there's a light dusting of freckles on his nose. The freckles make me curious if he's been outside recently.

I nod in response, then jerk my chin to the board, wondering if he'll answer my question about chess.

"I know a little," the boy replies. He has to be a little older than I am—probably sixteen.

"Want to play?" I ask. I'm so desperate for a distraction that playing with a complete stranger who knows *a little* about chess sounds like a good idea.

His forehead creases and he shifts his weight from side to side as he glances at the other two males in the common room. I follow his gaze. Each of the others shrug, the one with the ball in his hands looking nearly identical to the person I'm speaking with. The ball begins its rhythmic thumping again. "Ok," he says.

I sit down, taking the black pieces aside. White goes first, which is an advantage. He doesn't seem confident, and I could use the challenge. "I'm Reach," I say once I've arranged my pieces properly.

"Mitch," he says as he positions his pieces on the board. He's misplaced the bishop and the knight. "That's El." He points to the research assistant on the couch. "And that's my twin brother, Cyto." He indicates the research assistant bouncing the ball. They do look identical, right down to the dusting of freckles.

I clench my jaw because my usual reaction to introductions is to grimace. I manage to give my hand a wave in their general direction before turning back to the board. "Your bishop and your knights are switched," I murmur, keeping my eyes downcast.

Mitch doesn't say anything, just switches the two pieces. "Ready?" he asks, and then makes his first move.

There's a thrill to playing again after so long. I make short work of Mitch's game, checkmating him in only eight moves.

"Are you a savant?" He stares at the board in disbelief.

I smirk just a little, because it's nice to be good at something. "No," I say. "But I've been playing for a long time."

El and Cyto wander over to the board. El is older by a few years; he might be close to being a Citizen. He's broad-shouldered and tall.

"Rematch," Cyto states. "But with *me*. I'm better than he is."

"That's not a *rematch*, Cyto," El drawls. His voice is smooth and impossibly deep. He sits down on the floor to watch.

"Whatever, we share the same DNA," Cyto quips.

Mitch vacates the chair and sits next to El. Cyto is better than Mitch, but not by much. I beat him in twelve moves. He grunts and then looks at El. "You want to try?"

"Actually," El says smoothly, "I would like to know more about Reach here."

My jaw tightens and a pit of dread pools in my stomach. This was a bad idea. I can feel the stupidity of what I've done pulsating through the air. I have to answer questions now. I am an idiot.

"So, Reach…on the classified Global 1," Cyto starts.

I nod, because this isn't exactly secret information. Dr. Quasar announced that Global 1 was starting the day I arrived. It doesn't take a genius to understand that I'm on that project based on who leaves the cafeteria with whom.

"Can you talk about it?" he asks.

My response is to shrug and shake my head. Cyto looks disappointed.

"So are you a research assistant or something else?" Mitch asks. I'm surprised at the astute guess.

I gesture to my clothes. "Research assistant, same as you."

"Where were you before?" El grills.

I pause. I don't know what to say, or what I'm allowed to say. I land on, "I can't say." It's not a total lie.

"Interesting. You show up and Global 1 begins. You're freakishly good at chess. You don't talk to us for months and then decide to talk today. What's up with that? It's weird." Cyto seems the most brash of the three, and his words confirm it.

"I was told not to talk about work, but I misunderstood it to mean don't talk to anyone except the RAs on the project." As I say it, I realize it's true. I had self-imposed a no-talking-to-anyone rule. "Do you ever go outside?"

Six eyes blink in unison as the three of them chortle. I stay stock still as they laugh at my expense. My hands begin shaking, but I place them under the table to hide the tremors.

El recovers. "No. I've been an RA for two years and am preparing for Citizenship this year. When you're an RA, your contract states that you don't leave the Hub building unless required by your project. Didn't you read the contract?"

*No. I have no contract.* "What happens if you leave?" I realize how that sounds and try to recover. "What would happen if an RA left? Went outside without permission?"

Mitch quietly stands and says, "You lose everything. I'm going to bed. Lights are almost out."

With those cryptic words, my three new acquaintances file out of the common room, leaving me to stare at the chessboard, alone.

# 18

MITCH'S WORDS BOUNCE around my skull after lights out. I lie there in the dark, my mind whirling so fast I can hear the thoughts as they spin past. I wonder if they watch things in the specimens' quarters at night. Tonight is the night I'm going to find out. Pushing a boundary isn't the smartest thing, but I think about the contract that El, Mitch, and Cyto signed, Freedom and papers, blood and death, and…I just have to get out of here.

*What will happen if I refuse to follow the stupid arrow?* The thought of a small act of rebellion gives me a sense of power.

I step out of my room. The arrow immediately lights up and points back into my room. I've never left my room during the lights-out period. *How do these arrows even work?* I'm amazed that the simplest form of freedom has been removed, without my notice. I ignore the arrow and take a step in the opposite direction. It flashes in front of me, pointing back the way I came. I take another step and the arrow moves, still pointing opposite the direction I'm going, but nothing else happens. No alarms, no voices, no yelling.

As I move down the hall, it dawns on me: Freedom's parents are literally incarcerated, but the research assistants here have their own type of prison.

I continue down the hall, in the opposite direction from what I take each morning for work. I've never been down this part of the hall. I keep to my room, the male bathroom and the male common room. Everything is strictly separated into male and female at Hub. I make my way further down and find the door labeled 'female bathroom.' The fact that none of the rooms except the bathrooms have doors has always bothered me, but at this moment I'm glad for the lack of privacy. I'm looking for Llama. I sense she holds more answers. I know I'm invading privacy as I peer into each room, internally cringing as I see sleeping forms, but I press on.

Twelve rooms later, I find her. She is sitting, awake, on her bed, her foot swinging like a pendulum. A faint glow makes its way into her room from the window. It's just enough to see her in the shadows. I don't want to scare her and make her scream, but I also don't want to stand in the hallway with an arrow pointing me back to my prison cell of a room.

I cough quietly.

Llama jerks her head up. "Reach?" she whispers, her expression bewildered. "Look at you being all *rebellious*."

"Hey, Llama," I say as I step inside her room. The arrow disappears from the hall. "What happens to the arrows when I—when someone—doesn't listen?"

"This is really your first time not following directions?"

"Err. Yeah?"

"Hmmm," she hums.

"Llama, you know things."

She smirks in response. "Yeah, I guess I do."

"What do you know about *me*?"

"Narcissist much, Reach?"

I let loose a sigh. "Llama. I know only what little information I've picked up from my time here and what my mom told me on Compound. It's really hard to do anything other than follow along when

I don't understand the big picture here. You're practically a Citizen, but you push the limits at times. You work on a super classified project. You are unique, but they wanted you to be my research partner here for a reason. You know I am the experiment because you're on Global 1. No matter what Dr. Jog says about me being treated like an RA and needing to be seen as one by others, I don't understand why I'm being used as a research assistant and treated like a student here."

"You really don't know? Reach?" She says it with consternation in her eyes. "You don't know anything about me?"

"I know you are respected here. I know you know something about Eleven, but I still don't know what Eleven is. I literally lived under a rock. Well, not literally. Metaphorically. Literally, I lived in a seventy-mile circumference of sand, populated entirely with scientists who always treated me like an experiment because I'm half—"

"Martian?" she supplies. I nod. "So you really are? Halfsies?" she asks.

I don't know what to say to her. I'm not half anything. I settle on the most truthful statement I can think of. "I'm just all me, all Reach."

"I like that, Reach," she says back, biting her lip. She's considering something, but then she drops a mask over her face. With a calm that can only be described as eerie, she says, "Reach. I'm not a Citizen, not even close. I'm here because money buys most everything and pain buys the rest."

I stare. I try to muddle out that statement because it feels profound and volatile. "Pain?" Also, money? On Compound there was a small amount of currency, but all the major needs were met. Llama's experience must have been different.

"Pain. It buys things. Like Freedom's cooperation."

"So what happens to people who defy the…system?"

"They die," she says calmly.

"So…Freedom can't win. He can't have Hero and his parents, can he?" I ask, but I already know the answer.

"You can't outsmart the government. Trust me, I know all about it."

I sigh. "This conversation feels wrong. Are they…listening?" I haven't seen anything that indicates our rooms are bugged. I haven't seen anyone other than research assistants in the wing.

Llama shakes her head and smiles. "Hubris. But also, they are kind of right. The research assistants are here to do the work of the Three Powers and have been vetted to such an extent that unwanted activity isn't much of a threat. The arrows keep most people in line at all times with a dopamine rush, and they are confident enough in that system not to bother with detailed security in our rooms. There's not much that anyone could get up to here. We work, eat, sleep, and have our days mapped out by the arrows. They care much more about the Citizens who aren't inside Science Hub."

Pride. The weakness of the government. I hadn't considered that before. "Llama, if they aren't listening—"

"They aren't. Not in here anyway."

"Ok, then would you tell me what I don't know about *Eleven*? It keeps coming up and I feel really confused."

A shadow crosses her face as she frowns at the floor. She closes her eyes and tips her head backward. "Yeah. I'll tell you," she whispers. "I think that, given our final mission, you should probably know."

I blink in surprise. "You know what our mission is?"

She blinks in turn. "You don't?"

"I thought maybe a space mission, but I'm not sure. No one has said anything, and we're just *learning* about thinking. So that's not a real clue."

"Space. Mission. Yes. With me." She shakes her head. "Anyway, about Eleven. Eleven is a Ward. It's a hotbed of contention. The Nons are broken into Wards, and Eleven was mine. I think there are thirty Wards, but no one knows the exact number. Anyway, they don't want the Nons to have complete information about how many of them there are. Being overthrown is every government's greatest fear, right?" I nod in agreement. She continues. "My parents were very active in a coup movement before I was born. In every Ward, there are agents of the government who live 'underground.' They're spies. One spy found their way into the defector group led by my mother. The spy passed every test, every precaution, and eventually took the second-in-command leadership position. She worked right below my mother in the organization and they became friends. This spy was trusted for *years*."

She exhales sharply, a shrill whistle of air filling the space between us. "My father was one of only a few people who did not trust the woman. By the time my mother was eight months pregnant with me, he confronted the spy. Told her he had suspicions about her motives. She laughed, then told him he was the smartest of the group because he was correct. She *wasn't* a Non. The government was already in the area and making arrests." She sighs heavily. When I open my mouth to ask why they didn't run, she anticipates my question. "There was nowhere to go. In the Wards, the exits are controlled by guards, and the spy knew too much about the organization for safehouses to be effective. My father resisted arrest and was killed. My mother was sentenced to life in Pen One. Which is where I was born." Her voice cracks, but she purses her lips and continues. Her expression of determination makes me want to give her a hug. I don't, but I want to.

"The government took me back to Ward Eleven to be raised 'care of the state,' in a home for children with imprisoned or otherwise absent parents. When I reached school age, the teachers discovered that I had an excellent academic aptitude. I owe the teachers and house parents who believed in me in Ward Eleven everything. I graduated last year, at fifteen, and then came here because the government wanted to keep an eye on me, and it made the people at the state school look good. When I'm eighteen, I'll have the same choice to make as Freedom." The sarcasm placed on the word *choice* is unmistakable. "But the government also wants you to have a partner in the space mission since you're not fully human." She gives me a knowing look. Somehow, she's learned my secret: I'm not half-Martian.

"I'm here because I can be useful to Nation," she says, "and I owe that to them, but they also want to keep me contained. They know that the pain of severing family bonds is the surest way to minimize risk. I'm sure it works, usually."

"What do you mean, usually?" I ask.

"I have enough awareness to understand what they're doing. I have the emotional pain and the mental pain of having to serve them, knowing that they are holding my mother over me. Knowing that I can't win, but that they are psychologically abusing me. But by putting me here on this project, I have to see you. You are the result of stepping outside government-approved policies. I'm sure they've figured out by now you're not a Martian, but it's a good cover story. They are just weaving our loose ends together." Llama grits her teeth. "We are risks. Daughter and son of rebellious acts. The difference is that my parents got caught. Your mom is a space mission hero, right?"

I nod.

"She was really high profile before she served, so she can't be caught yet, or else it will make them look bad." She keeps going, voice shaking at the unjustness of life. "We're in similar positions here. Forced to consider where we come from, and who we serve, and *why*, every moment of the day. Most people just serve blindly." She takes a big breath. "And they didn't account for all the risks I pose to them. They didn't realize that I have something stronger than pain to fight with."

I like the idea of fighting. I really like the idea of fighting with her. I shouldn't ask. I do anyway. "What is stronger than pain, Llama?"

Llama's eyes flash. "Vengeance." It's a feeling I understand.

"How do you know they aren't listening?" I whisper, because she's talking about *fighting* the government. And I've seen Enforce in action. I do not want to experience her wrath.

"I've been here for a year. I've yelled *things* at the top of my lungs in this room. No one has said anything. My favorite was when I yelled 'down with Leader!' If that didn't get their attention, there's nothing in this room."

"Hey, Llama. How do you know…about me?"

She grins. "I've watched you every day since you arrived. I've read anything about you I could get my hands on—which is easy, since I'm on your project and they want me to know about you before our space mission. The data, in small pieces, is difficult to decipher, especially when some of it has been falsified. I'm guessing Dr. Jog did that."

"Mom." The word slips out and I realize I shouldn't have said it.

Llama's face brightens in understanding. "That makes sense. She was protecting you?"

I nod, nervous, but since I can't rescind my words, I have to choose to trust her with this. She already knows the worst—that I have supposed half Martian genetics. This is a fact that the scientists all seem to know, but it has been classified information kept from the Research Assistants.

"I should get back," I say as I feel anxiety roaring its way up my chest. "But before I go, how do the arrows work?"

"Oh." She blinks in surprise. "You did ask that earlier. I forgot you didn't have the same entrance to Hub as the rest of us. They take samples of your DNA, usually skin, when you arrive at HUB and upload them into a server. There's a scheduler who attaches your DNA codes to where you're supposed to be in the building. The floor tiles have special DNA sensors that are linked to your profile. That's why RAs don't wear shoes; the floor can sense the DNA through the special socks, but not through shoes."

I remember Dr. Jog scraping the bottoms of my feet when I was with Sty.

"But do they *watch*?" I whisper.

"No, I don't think so. That would be really inefficient when they have all the safeguards in place here anyway. They have enough to keep an eye on in the Wards and the Cities. But they can pull data on any person at any time and see how compliant you've been, I'd suppose."

My head spins. I have to get out of here. I'm leaving a trail of rebellion. "What if they find out? That someone didn't listen to their arrow? In big things?"

Llama shrugs. "That person would probably become a Non and be dismissed. Forced to live in the Wards where you never have *enough* to feel safe, only *enough* to survive. If you're really a threat, they just make your family agree to kill you. I can't think of anything they'd do to you though. You're already here against your will, right?"

I swallow. She *is* right.

"Yes," I growl. She lifts her chin and surveys me in a way that makes me know she hears my own anger and respects it. The scrutiny in her gaze is too much, even in the gloom of the night.

"Hey, Reach." I look at her, my own eyes meeting hers in the dark. "Goodnight. We're ok. I promise."

I step into the hall, where the soft luminescence of my arrow greets me. As I trudge back to my room, I wonder about Llama. I've gotten to know her, become friendly with her over the past few months, but she's always seemed guarded. Her history is surprising, but there's something else. And then I realize what it is.

Llama is going to fight back. Llama is going to seek revenge—and whether I want it or not, I'm part of her plan.

I guess it's a good thing that I want revenge too.

# 19

I MAKE MY way to Sublab the next morning, mulling over my new status as a government conspirator. After my visit with Llama, I realized I already was planning to foil them, but my survival isn't what's really at stake. I want to take down Enforce and Leader, Legislate, Litigate, Pen One, and the whole Citizen-Noncitizen disparity. Above all, I want information. How can progress truly happen when people only have a teaspoon of truth?

I've been treading carefully for months, but my visit to Llama was reckless. I need to understand more before I can make a plan. Hub feels comfortable, but I am learning more and more about the secrets of the government. And the more I learn, the more I see gaping holes in the logic of what I've always been taught. Llama said hubris was their weakness. I can see that. I have a feeling that Dr. Jog is leading us to find more flaws, too, with these philosophy lectures and thought experiments. I decide that, for now, the best thing is to continue what I'm doing: gathering information and better understanding my opponent.

I round the corner and stop outside the nonexistent door. Dr. Jog is facing me, but he is in a conversation with someone else. I can only see her back, but I know her—I'd know her anywhere. Enforce.

I stand quietly on my arrow as we wait for the others to arrive. Hero, then Llama, appear behind me. I study Enforce's profile as she talks to Dr. Jog. I overhear the words "Phase 1, move to Phase 2," and "updated schedule." Dr. Jog does not look pleased.

I shift and observe Hero's and Llama's reactions to seeing Enforce. Hero's face registers a flicker of dislike, but it passes in less than a second with a narrowed eye and flare of nostrils. Her face returns to passive, and if I hadn't been watching her, I wouldn't have seen her reaction.

Llama's reaction is less discreet. Her mouth screws up in a twisted smirk, eyes narrow and widen, cheeks flush, and a hardness settles in her gaze as she stares at Enforce with a palpable hatred. I can understand. Enforce is in charge of the penal system here, so she's the one with the whole sign the papers, execute your parents, and become a Citizen spiel. Llama makes no effort to conceal her contempt.

Dr. Jog opens the room and we all step in. Enforce stands so that each of us must pass her on our way in. I hope that she doesn't come in, a hope that is dashed moments later when I register the clickety-clicks of her pointy shoes behind me. She claims a stool and sits down, observing all of us with interest.

Dr. Jog is surprised, evidenced by his slightly agape mouth. He must not have expected Enforce to remain in Sublab. He clears his throat and begins to make a speech. This is nothing like how we usually start our days.

"Ahem," he says. We look at him in unison. I choose a place to stand where I can appear to be looking at Dr. Jog but surreptitiously watch Enforce. "We have with us today a representative of our illustrious government. Enforce is here to check on our progress. As you know, we have been in Phase 1 of Global 1 for the past few months. Enforce has brought it to my attention that we will be moving into Phase 2 next week. We will need to increase our learning this week. Phase 2 will be substantially different from Phase 1, so be sure to follow the dietary guidelines of your schedule. Back to work."

I notice Enforce's eyes quickly flick over to Hero, bore into me, and then land on Llama, where they stay. All morning we retrieve books, write notes, and return books. Enforce has settled in on her stool, watching Llama. Llama is flustered. She's graceless and clumsy. Several times she drops something, stumbles, or breaks her pencil tip. It's not hard to see why Llama is unnerved. Enforce is staring at her with the same expression a lion has when it is tracking prey. It's unsettling.

I take pity on the girl I think of as a friend and now as an ally. Enforce is a terrible person. She is clearly taking pleasure in Llama's discomfort. Her focus is so lasered that I pull the bottom book out of a particularly haphazard stack. The laws of physics mean the books come crashing down in a tumult of noise. Enforce jumps on her stool and averts her eyes from Llama. They are angry when they land on me.

"Sorry," I say.

"Be quieter! Next time..." She glares and then turns back to Llama. But by this time, Llama has disappeared into the stacks. I grab books to be reshelved and escape into the dim aisles, where I catch up to her. She's leaning against the back wall, breaths coming shallow and fast.

"Hey, are you ok?"

"Reach, I hate her."

"Yeah. But you can't let her get to you. You can just do your work and she might go away. You could ignore her."

Llama smiles sadly. "I doubt it." She mutters the words under her breath.

The rest of the day slowly passes. A heavy tension builds in our group. Hero keeps her head down and stays quiet. Dr. Jog doesn't lecture, choosing to hand us more research lists. Llama spends most of her time out of sight in the stacks. I try to ignore Enforce, which goes against all of my primal instincts.

When the work for the day is over, Hero and Dr. Jog stride past Enforce without giving her a second glance as they leave the room. She doesn't notice. Her gaze is zeroed in on Llama. Dr. Jog slows and

Hero continues down the hall alone. I don't want to leave Llama alone with Enforce, so I'm standing on the stairs that lead out of Sublab like a deer in the headlights.

Dr. Jog gives a quick jerk of his head to indicate I need to come with him. I shake my head. His eyes narrow, and it's as if he telecommunicates with me. I swear I feel him say, "I know, come on," even though he never opens his mouth.

I have to trust him a little. He fudged data with my mom. He's the one who's protected me from more invasive experiments. I drag my feet and slowly make my way over to him. Llama has stepped out and is in the hallway with Enforce. She moves to get past her, but Enforce blocks the way.

Dr. Jog grabs my arm and propels me around a corner, where he stops. He's waiting, just out of sight, and listening to whatever is happening between Enforce and Llama.

"Oh little Llama," Enforce calls out, her tone mocking. Llama stops and turns. "So nice of you to recognize me." Llama says nothing. "Come, come now, Llama. You and I both know that this will get you nothing. You have one choice, and only one."

Llama sarcastically spits the words back. "Is it a choice if there's only one?"

*Bad idea, Llama!* I draw in a sharp breath as Dr. Jog does the same beside me.

"Too much philosophy. Tut tut." Enforce clicks her tongue in indignation. "You know, Llama, your mother wrote a legal document that named *me* as your guardian."

Llama utters a curse word and I am shocked by her vehemence. The implications of what Enforce just said slide into focus, and I suddenly understand why Llama hates Enforce with more passion than anyone else I've ever met. I crumple to the ground as the air leaves my body with the realization that Enforce betrayed Llama's parents. Dr. Jog pulls me up by the armpits.

"Don't make it harder for her. She needs us," he whispers urgently.

I lean against the wall and listen.

"...I couldn't take you on and jeopardize my career, but I am at the point where I could flex my schedule and *care* for you."

Llama responds with more profanity. "Thank you, but I am gainfully employed here helping the heartbeat of Nation. Scientific progress is more my style than betraying trust."

"Llama, Llama," Enforce mocks. "I think you know that loyalty and trust belong to one entity only. Your parents certainly didn't think that, although I do have to thank them. Without them, I never would have risen so far. Bringing them down took a certain amount of savvy. I showed Leader what she needed to see, and I got noticed." She gives an airy laugh.

Llama takes three steps before a rustling sound and a shout accost my ears. "Does this mean *anything* to you?"

Enforce laughs coldly. "No. Should it?" She snorts. "It actually means I'm the best at my job. My service to the government is unparalleled. Shame that people are manipulated when you give them just a little bit of trust."

Llama's voice drops and I have to strain to hear it. "You know, there are some beliefs people once had. After death, a person is required to answer to a higher power. Higher than you, higher than Leader, higher than anything or anyone. They have to answer for everything they did in life. It's called reckoning. I like it. I *believe* it. Enforce, you'll spend the afterlife answering for what you did in Eleven and what you're doing now. Justice might not be served in this life, but it will be served in the next."

"What next life are you talking about, Llama?" Enforce's voice drips with scorn. "These books and old thoughts are foolish. You might need them when you encounter other beings, but they aren't real. It's primitive. You're so much smarter than that. I know, I've seen all your aptitude tests. How could the education system fail you so badly?"

"Did it fail me? Or did it teach me to think for myself? I'm *independent*. I'm not some puppet on a string like yo—"

Enforce smacks Llama across the face. I start to move, but Dr. Jog pulls me back.

"Not yet, son," he hisses.

Moments later the stiletto click-click-click of Enforce's shoes passes by us. She turns down the other corridor and doesn't spot her eavesdroppers.

Dr. Jog and I rush back to Llama, who now sports an angry red handprint on one of her cheeks. Enforce's rings have left her with several cuts. The blood stands out against her pale skin.

"Llama?" I stop. There is nothing more to say. The glimmer of tears in her eyes is mixed with pure and unadulterated hatred.

Dr. Jog places his hands on her forearms and speaks quietly. "Come on, Llama. She's not pleasant to people she respects; she's brutal to her enemies. We will get you away from her. Trust me."

Llama glances at me, shame clouding her features, and then at Dr. Jog. "Ok."

Dr. Jog puts his arm around her shoulders and begins leading her down the hallway. I stay put. It is rare to see a scientist display any affection, let alone say something against a government official. I don't understand what's happening with Dr. Jog and Llama.

"Reach," Dr. Jog calls over his shoulder. I race to catch up to them, my sock-clad feet sliding on the tile. Dr. Jog goes past the cafeteria and through a labyrinth of corridors. I stare at my feet, noticing Llama and I have our arrows pointing back away from us, but Dr. Jog does not. We reach a silver door with the number fifty-one on it. Dr. Jog flashes his wrist at the door, and it slides open. The normal act of opening a door makes me want to cry. A firm hand claps my shoulder, and Dr. Jog meets my watering eyes with a small shake of his head. I understand. He means *no*, don't be emotional.

I shove my feelings deep into the recesses of my mind and focus on Llama.

# 20

ONCE WE HAVE all crossed the threshold, the door slides closed. A pleasant light flickers on when Dr. Jog reaches above a coat tree and illuminates apartment-style living quarters. There are multiple rooms, carpet, furnishings, and interior *doors*. Scientists get privacy here, apparently.

"Welcome to my home," Dr. Jog states with ironic emphasis on the word *home*. "The two of you. I might as well just tell you both. You're in a lot of danger."

I shrug, having already known that I was in danger since the moment I was extracted from Compound. Llama grimaces as she scans the apartment. Dr. Jog gestures to a verdant, velvet-green couch. I sit. Llama continues to stand and rub her thumb and forefinger along the hem of her white uniform. Dr. Jog sinks into the armchair across from the couch.

The chair squeaks as Dr. Jog begins speaking. "Reach, I know you have been kept in the dark about a lot of things, and truly that was for your protection. It seems my hand has been forced, and I have to share some information with you. Llama, I think you know that in Eleven, you develop a supreme distrust of the government. And rebellion is ingrained in us from the very air we breathe."

Llama's eyes flash as she looks from me to Dr. Jog. "Are we really doing this? Here? Now?"

"It's the only way," Dr. Jog says quietly. Llama shrugs, then sits next to me. "Enforce is what used to be called a sadist. She…she enjoys inflicting pain on others. She's effective at her job because of it. She's ruthless, and I think you know—"

"That she waited until my mother had named her as my legal guardian before she made her move to bring down the Resistance movement. That I'm just a *game* to her, and that I always have been," Llama says.

"Right," Dr. Jog says. "Right. You are a game to her. I'm doing my best to protect you. I haven't forgotten." He rolls up his sleeve and shows Llama the strange tattoo around his inner elbow.

She looks at him with teary eyes. "Thank you," she breathes.

"Alright, Reach." He directs his words toward me. "You are going to be training for a space mission. You are allowed to know this now. Your mother and I both suspected that would be the case. Officially, you'll be training for a trip to Station 51. Since I'm the only person who has ever returned from that deep in space alive, they've assigned me to your training. You will undergo extreme physical fitness tests, mental tests, and emotional profiles. Llama will be training with you.

"Hero will continue to assist you and me in various capacities. You have a battery of new scientists that will be teaching you skills. Some are *friendly*. Make *friends*. But only with some of them. Your survival, and the survival of your mother, myself, and Llama, depends on your compliance. Do not manipulate your data. Be completely honest about your knowledge and capabilities. But all you know is that you're training for a space mission. You don't know you're half-Martian, and you don't know what your mission will ultimately be, just that it's a wonderful opportunity to further Nation's progress. Got it?"

I blink, digesting the words. This is the most frank conversation anyone has had with me about life here in Hub. My eyes aren't focused on anything in particular as I try to commit the words to memory. I start returning my vision to Dr. Jog's face, but I catch the red handprint that still blazes on Llama's face. It has to sting and burn, but she hasn't even touched it. I stare at her, entranced, as she rolls up her sleeve and treads lightly to Dr. Jog. She bends her arm and lines up her strange tattoo with Dr. Jog's. They form an optical illusion, swirling and spinning together as they stand arm to arm. He startles at first, then looks her in the eyes and says, "Yes, I promise."

I am unable to hold it in. "What is it with the tattoos?" I blurt out with frustration.

Llama turns and lets a laugh loose and returns to the couch.

Dr. Jog adopts his teaching posture: shoulders back, chin up, hands clasped in his lap, but ready to gesticulate. "Reach, I realize this is confusing for you. Your whole life has been wrapped up in half-truths and secrecy. Your time on Compound was meant to protect you, and it really did. Llama and I are both from Ward Eleven, which has its own hazards. Llama and I also both graduated from the Ward of the State School in Eleven. It's for—"

"Children who have incarcerated parents," I say. Dr. Jog looks startled. "Llama told me that."

"Yes, that's true. When you graduate from the Ward of the State School in Eleven, you are given the opportunity to receive a tattoo. Since you don't have any real family, the tattoos mark the family you take on as your own. The tattooists developed a technique that causes the tattoos to interact when they are aligned. When Llama lined her tattoo with mine, she was showing me that I'm her family."

"But I saw Enforce has a tattoo too. Did she graduate from the school?"

"No!" Llama cuts in. "She was a spy for the government. Her tattoo is from the rebel group my parents led. It doesn't interact the same way Dr. Jog's and mine do."

"So, 51," Dr. Jog says. "It sounds like you know enough about

Llama's history that mine might be of interest. When Enforce was infiltrating Llama's parents' group, I was in space. I graduated in the top ten of my class at the school and was offered Citizenship because of my extreme athletic ability in endurance running. The government figured that an endurance runner would have what it took to go to Station 51, and if I died, as every other space mission candidate for 51 had, then it was no real loss to them. And if I returned a hero, even better. I was just a boy with aptitude they could use."

"I don't understand." My brow crinkles.

Llama and Dr. Jog look bemusedly at me.

"Reach, what do you know about *game theory?*" Dr. Jog asks quietly.

*Game theory.* My plan. The plan I spoke about with my mom before I was taken off Compound.

My face flickers with recognition and Dr. Jog smiles slowly, deliberately. "Reach, we have a common enemy here. And we're going to use game theory to upset the order of things."

Llama places her hand in mine. It feels cool and warm and soft all at the same time, and I am amazed at the way my stomach drops when she touches me. "The reason we're going to succeed isn't just for ourselves. We're going to make things better for people here. We can be like Dr. Jog when we return. We can make ripples that grow into waves, and waves that turn into tsunamis."

"Game theory. I know game theory," I say.

For the first time, a well of hope that I don't have to figure this out alone wells up inside me. Dr. Jog is showing his allyship. He called me *son.* A sense of belonging fills my being with purpose.

I clear my throat. "What now?"

PART 2

# 21

Dr. Jog, Llama, and I spend hours discussing a plan for space mission training. Llama and Dr. Jog have motives to make big waves of change. Dr. Jog explained that I have to be an experiment for any of this to work. Also, I've been part of the insurgent scientist movement since I was conceived. I didn't know that my mother was part of the movement, but I do now.

Llama's connection to the insurgent movement is more obvious. Her mother awaits execution in Pen One. Apparently it's a miserable place, high security, and makes people so uncomfortable that they would "do anything to get out of there" when they are forced to visit. Llama has been forced to visit three times in her life.

Ultimately, the plan we come up with is for Llama and I simply to wait, bide our time, and learn as much as we can. Dr. Jog assures us that other things will be set in motion. He briefly mentions Enforce. "I don't trust her. She's up to something. I need to figure out what," he says. "For now, you two need to learn everything you can in order to survive space. That needs to be your focus. Next year will be intense academics, and they will be real. Succeed, because if you fail, this will all fail."

*This* being our little group of insurrectionists. Except I've realized there is a much bigger movement at stake. I remember Mom's words about Greg and his people—*a place where they give people respect not just because of what they do, but because of who they are.* I can't even imagine what that would be like.

The next year is entirely focused on academics. Llama and I take courses together and learn theoretical math, calculus, quantum physics, geometry, and statistics. I'm surprised to find Cyto and Mitch in some of my classes. El is older, so he is in Citizen prep courses. Cyto and Mitch are studying different components of cell structures, with a focus on bioengineering in the future. We overlap in statistics lectures.

The first day of statistics, I follow my arrow through Hub into a new classroom. Several other research assistants are already in the room, their chatter making a low buzz in the background. Since I dislike meeting new people in general, I sit by myself, as close to the door as I can. When Llama walks in a few moments later, the room goes completely silent. My mouth goes dry. Llama is definitely more womanly than when I first met her. I can't help but notice she's shapely, in a very, very good way. I'm a guy, she's attractive, and the sudden silence in the room indicates that I'm not the only one who thinks so. I'm also not very suave, so I think she knows I like her and is just being kind in her gentle teasing. Also, romantic involvement is *very* much against the rules.

Llama gives a little wave in acknowledgment of the stares and then slips into the seat next to me. When Cyto and Mitch walk through the door, my face breaks into a grin. Their eyes skip past me and land on Llama. The identical twins turn to one another with broad smiles and sidle over to take the chairs on the other side of Llama. A burning sensation bubbles in my gut as they start talking to her. She smiles, but doesn't engage much until the twins call my name.

"Reach. Chess again?"

I flash a polite smile. "Sure." I'm trying to look at them, but my gaze keeps drifting to Llama. She bends over in her chair to retrieve a pencil she dropped. Mitch catches my attention as he mouths, "Sorry. We won't get in the way of your matching."

My mouth twitches as I think of some response. I can't match with Llama, but I don't want anyone to know that. I feel protective and surprisingly possessive. She *is* my partner in research, after all. The timely arrival of our instructor saves me from having to reply. The next two hours pass in a blur of statistics before we disperse in a myriad of arrows.

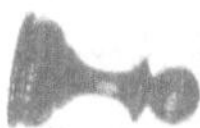

Over the next year, Mitch, Cyto, and El are friendly. We play chess together in the male common room at least twice a week, when our studies allow. Dr. Jog's emphasis on philosophy is surprisingly helpful. It makes it easier to think logically; math proofs are really just philosophy with numbers attached. I'm asked to create a new theoretical chemistry experiment each week. Although I never complete the experiment, I write the proposal and what I suspect the results will be—it's a thought experiment.

When our academic Phase 2 began, Llama, Dr. Jog, and I were summoned to a meeting in Sublab. In this meeting, Dr. Quasar read us a long list of rules and explained our 'next steps' for Global 1. According to Hub, we are training for a space mission to deep space. Llama is training as my partner because she has a significant aptitude for foreign languages, and they suspect there may be intelligent life forms (Martians) out there. No one mentions my genetics, but I find myself being taken to a medical lab every week where Hero and Dr. Jog oversee a few RAs who tell me to spit into a dish, collect strands of my hair, and draw my blood. I consent to nothing because I'm never once asked. Dr. Jog's advice was one word: *cooperate*. I trust him, so I do, but his hair is graying and thinning faster than I would have thought. He looks thin and drawn, and I overhear him telling Hero to "add .001 of the H solution to the isolating solution, then reseal it." He's manipulating my data just the smallest bit, and Hero's helping him.

Nearly a year after embarking on the most intense academic studies of my life, my arrow directs me to a new classroom, where I find Llama. She's sitting at a table in the center of the room. There are two stools on either side, and on the upper shelves of the cabinets behind the table are stacks of games—board games, puzzles, decks of cards, and a chess set. Llama sits and stares at the boxes glumly.

"Whatcha doing, Llama?" I tease. "Most people like *games*."

"I'm no good at games," she whispers as tears form in her eyes. "And the directions say our assignment is to play games."

She's right—she's not great at games. Our clandestine conversations with Dr. Jog over the past year have always consisted of him telling us, 'Wait, the game theory will show us the next move,' and Llama insisting it was time for more action. So we still wait, and she still grumbles about game theory because she doesn't understand the premise. I get it—she's impulsive, but impulsivity can get results.

I'm taken aback at the tears in her eyes. Llama's emotional range doesn't seem to include sadness. The last time I saw her near tears, they were ones of anger. These ones look sad. I want to touch her, offer her some form of comfort, but I don't know how to do it. I opt to sit on the stool across from her and smile. "I can teach you one. It's all about *game theory*."

She rolls her eyes at my emphasis on game theory. "Which one? I don't know any of them. Fun isn't a priority at…where I'm from."

"It's not a priority where I'm from either," I say. "I only know because my mom taught me. She liked learning about old things."

"Which one is it, then?" Llama asks dejectedly.

"Chess!" I say.

"Chest?" Llama's eyes flare wide and she crosses her arms over her chest in response.

I start to stare but drag my eyes away from her arms and back to her face. She's almost eighteen now, and it shows in every womanly way. *Not helping, Reach. Not helping.*

"Chess. The greatest strategy and thinking game of all time. It's ancient. Mom and I played on Compound."

Sublab is extremely secure. Dr. Jog explained that security measures are so intense that there is no way for them to listen or watch us in there, short of them visiting. Because he's such a high-ranking doctor, they trust him with reports of our progress and time in the room. Whenever we are directed away from Sublab for an activity, we know that we're being observed.

"There are a lot of rules to chess, so I should write them out on the board," I say. "Could you get the box down?"

Llama stands and huffs over to the cabinet as I grab a piece of chalk and begin listing the names of the pieces and their abilities.

"Hey, Llama?" I want to begin explaining the game to her, but she's not in her seat. She's on her tiptoes by the cabinet, her fingers just barely grazing the box, but she grabs it. I dust my hands off and come up behind her.

"Reach, could you—"

"Reach it for you?" I ask in a husky voice that I didn't even know I possessed. She steps back and bumps into me as she turns around, losing her footing. My hands find her hips and steady her instinctively, keeping her from crashing to the floor. We stare at each other for a heated moment, and something like an electric shock passes through me. I begin to lean in. I swear she begins to lean toward me, the spark of desire in her eyes, until she draws back abruptly.

"Reach! You can't! You…you can't do that!" She gestures to my hands, which are still on her hips.

I drop them sheepishly. "I know. I'm sorry."

"That's that, then." She walks back to her seat and I retrieve the game. There's a tension between us from my stupidity. "Observations," she says simply.

A glimmer of hope flares in my chest that maybe she finds me attractive too. There have been a few times I've wondered if she might like me, and the look in her eyes hints that she does. I catalog her behavior, trying to figure her out. She only ever sits by me in our classes. She doesn't interact much with any other male RAs, like Cyto and Mitch. She's hard to read, but most of the RAs who've noticed her have noticed *me*.

She breaks me out of my thoughts. "Teach me this game, teach me chessssss." She hisses out the *s*, sounding like a snake.

Despite my embarrassment, I laugh, and the tension dissolves.

"You really don't want to call it 'chest' again, do you?" I say.

"No, I do not want to. Now, what do all these crazy things do?" She waves a knight in the air. "What does a horse have to do with a game?"

Several hours pass, and Llama still hasn't gotten the gist of the game. She is beyond frustrated and has gotten snappy. I try to reassure her with a friendly smile.

"It's ok," I say. "It takes people years to learn how to play. It's really complicated."

"Ugh," she says. "This game is the *worst*. Who thought this up? The rules are so stupid. Why can this guy only move in an *L*-shape? And this one can only move diagonally? And this one only in a straight line? And this one can only go two spaces at first, but then only one after that? And don't get me started on this castle-y thing! It's just all about power."

I stare at her for a moment. "Castle-y thing? It's called a rook." She screws her face up at me and I laugh because, despite being terrible at this game, she did actually manage to learn the way the pieces moved. "Hey, Llama, it's ok. You learned how the pieces move today. *Game theory* is about understanding how the pieces move in relationship to power."

Her blue eyes meet mine, narrowed. "I should have known," she says. She reaches across the table and touches my hand. She rarely initiates contact with me; it makes every touch all the more potent. "Reach, I wish I understood this stuff as well as you do. I'm happy you're my friend."

I open my mouth to speak but remember they are watching, so I shove the retort about friendship down and manage to say, "I'm happy you're my friend too."

We clean up the game, put it back in the cupboard, and follow our arrows to the research assistant quarters.

"Goodnight, Reach," she says softly as we pass my room. She places a soft hand on my arm and walks away, leaving me staring after her and desperately wishing I could show her how she's so much more than a friend.

# 22

THE MORNING AFTER our game evening brings an abrupt change to my schedule. Instead of directing me to a classroom, the arrow takes me to the administration wing. In the past eighteen months, I have become adept at following the arrow and observing my surroundings. I've never been to the administration wing before, so I find myself marveling at how much of Hub I haven't seen as I take in unfamiliar territory.

Honestly, I explored a little once I realized my arrow wasn't a total leash and I could defy it, but I avoided the administration wing because it reminded me of the administration of this government. Who, you know, regularly forces people to make life-and-death choices about their family and hides the fact that a sadist will come after you if you are a threat to its power. Enforce, Leader, Litigate, Legislate, Second—these people represent something vile, something I want to fight against. Something, I remind myself, that I *am* going to fight against. The balance of power makes me think of Freedom and his impossible choices. I always think of Freedom before meeting with new people at Hub. It grounds me.

No one has mentioned Freedom to me since the day Dr. Jog told us he was visiting Pen One. Hero isn't distraught, so I suspect she knows something. I choose not to ask because sometimes it's better not to have answers.

My arrow has led me to a door marked AC-III. Administrative Center, Unit Three. The arrow slides under the door, and I reach to knock on the heavy wooden door, but it swings open before I make contact.

"Welcome, Reach." The voice comes from a woman sitting behind a curved desk. She doesn't look at me, focusing her attention on stamping papers and placing them crisply into different trays. "You can continue down the hallway to the third door on your left. AC 3-112."

"Eh, thanks?" I mean to sound confident, but it comes out as a question. I really hate meeting new people; that part of my anxiety will probably never change.

I scan the placards on the wall as I look for the room. When I find it, the door is ajar. I step inside. A large man sits behind a small desk. The white walls are covered with pictures from telescopes, real pictures of space. Behind his desk is a line of photographs of men and women in spacesuits, each holding their helmets under their arms.

"Reach!" He stands up and exclaims my name with great gusto as he maneuvers around the desk and grabs my hand. His teeth are so white they must glow in the dark. His curly dark hair and jet-black eyes only make them look brighter. His hand is warm and large and reminds me of a sausage as it grips mine with so much force I am certain my arm is in danger of detaching from the socket.

"H-h-hello," I stutter.

"It's so good to have you here at last," he says. "Please, sit, sit, sit." He indicates a chair and returns to his seat, the chair groaning under his heavy frame. "You are here because you finished Module A, academics. This is wonderful, wonderful, wonderful."

I stare and wonder if he always repeats his ending words three times.

"So Reach, the next modules are underway after this meeting. Dr. Jog is still your immediate project supervisor, but I am the official Administrator dedicated to space mission training. I receive all reports about your progress and handle getting you physically ready for space from a paper perspective." He chuckles. I continue to stare, since no response is necessary. "You're here to be presented with your new uniform! You're officially approved to train for a space mission since you've passed the academic aptitude requirements."

"I don't have to wear this anymore?" I say, gesturing to the hospital gown garment that has been my attire since I arrived.

"No. You can wear *these*." In dramatic fashion, he reaches below his desk and draws out an orange package, which contains my clothing, folded into a perfect square. I shake it out. It's a nylon orange zippered jacket with elastic sleeves around the cuff, a cotton t-shirt with short sleeves, and matching orange nylon sweatpants. The sweatpants taper and have a cuff around the ankles.

I stare in shock at the significantly more comfortable clothing I now get to wear.

"Do you like it?" the man asks. I still don't know his name.

"It's an improvement from…this." I gesture at my white gown and he beams.

He hands me a pair of shoes. "These will still allow you access to your arrow for scheduling ease."

The word *scheduling* makes me think of Llama. She's been with me in all my classes. "Is Llama changing schedules too?"

He looks up at me in surprise. "I suppose you want to know because she is your…"

I grimace as I realize my error. Matching hasn't been explained to me, but I know that's the only way to have a relationship here. And I also know I can't match with Llama. I dig deep into my gut and pull out the best lie I can find. "We've been in our classes together and have worked on assignments together to understand our strengths and weaknesses, so we can be successful in space." It's not why I'm asking, but it's close enough.

The man seems to accept my reasoning. "Her training program will be different from yours. She will be training a female body, which will require specific things you will not need. Not at all, all, all. You will have some overlap, but you won't be at every training together. This is where your individual strengths are honed for the mission, for the good of Nation!" He glances at a clock on the wall. "Look at the time! You'll be late on the first day. That just won't do, do, do. You need to get to the gym. Goodbye, Reach. And good luck."

I know when I'm dismissed, so I step out of the room and wander back to the front of the Administrative Wing, still holding my clothes. When I pass through the door and into the hallway, my arrow lights up, with the word *gymnasium* above it. There's nothing left for me to do but follow the path laid out for me.

THE GYMNASIUM IS on the opposite side of Hub as the Administration Wing. I've passed by it a few times but have never actually been inside. Large circles and strange markings cover the polished wood floor and the walls. There are also various nets placed around the room, a giant rope suspended from the ceiling, and what I recognize as dumbbells from the gym at the school on Compound. No one is here.

"Hello?" I call out. My voice is the only one I hear as it bounces back off the walls.

"Hey!" A younger man wearing a bright blue zippered jacket and blue pants that look exactly like the ones I was just given strides out from a door in the corner of the gym. He looks at me and frowns. "You need to get changed before we can start. Locker room is here." He starts off toward another door, then pushes it open, and I step inside. "This is your locker. You have extra clothes, shower stuff, and swimming day materials. You have two minutes to change out of that." He gestures at my hospital gown and then lowers his voice so low that I almost don't hear his comment. "So I can burn it."

I stare.

"Two minutes. Meet me in the center." He strides out of the room, but I'm so shocked I haven't moved. He turns. "Go on, then!"

Two minutes isn't much time, but I manage to change into the new clothes. The locker room is white. A row of green lockers lines the back wall. One of the lockers says REACH in bold script. When it creaks open, I see an array of clothing and supplies, just like the guy said.

I don't want to be late, so I ball the research assistant uniform gown into my fist and dash to the center of the gym.

"I see you can't wait to get started!" the guy in the blue says. His eyes crinkle up in humor at the corners.

"For your fire," I gasp between breaths. I hold out the white gown. He raises his eyebrows.

"You heard that?" I nod. He grins. "I much prefer this uniform, don't you?" Again, I nod. "So, Reach, I'm Lift. I'm going to get you in space shape." He looks me up and down. I'm panting from my sprint. I haven't had any real exercise since I arrived at Hub. "It looks like we have a lot of work to do."

I grimace. I'm well aware that I'm gangly and not muscular. My body is too thin and lacks substance. This guy has his work cut out for him.

Lift unzips his blue jacket and shrugs out of it. Biceps the size of footballs work along his arms, and his body has zero fat. His sandy blond hair is cut to standard regulations, but above his left eye he has a circle tattoo with three $x$'s on the circumference.

"Today's training is about establishing a baseline. It's a test you'll become familiar with, because we'll be doing it regularly. Once you have established a proper foundation, we can move on to more complex exercises. I think you'll enjoy our time together. Most people do." He's not cocky when he says it. Lift has a confidence I can only dream of. I like him. It helps that I'm not experiencing the typical sense of doom I usually am privy to when I meet Hub strangers.

By the end of the training session, I realize I was wrong about

Lift. He does, in fact, inspire dread. He is brutal. His test is relentless. I run, jump, row, throw heavy balls at markings on a wall, and climb the giant rope before he calls time.

"That's all for today, Reach. We have a lot of work to do, but now I can plan our sessions to build your strength and endurance. Hit the showers, then head to what's next on your schedule."

He walks away while I am doubled over, palms on my knees. I did not know knees and elbows could sweat. I take several deep breaths, but the air won't go into my lungs.

Lift turns back to me and looks at me with pity. I've been looked at with scorn, but I decide at that moment pity is my least favorite of all the looks I've ever received.

"Hands over your head," he says. "It will help."

I try, gulping at the effort.

Lift frowns. "You've had no physical training since you got here, have you?" The most I can do is shake my head. Lift swears. "Physical fitness is the most important thing you must have before space. Your body will be under extreme conditions, and you have to be prepared. Having a body in optimal condition is like having a machine that has passed every diagnostic test before being put into orbit. You have to understand that your body is your number one asset in space. If your body fails, you fail." He mutters under his breath, "What are they playing at?"

My breaths slowly start evening out.

"Looks like you can shower now, kid," he says. "Also, eat every bite of food in your portion. It's designed to work with our training program."

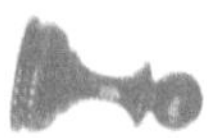

I shower in the locker room before I am directed to the cafeteria for lunch. I stand in the typical line for rations, holding out my wrist to the same woman I have since my first day. She frowns when the scanner angrily buzzes. "Space Plan, Diet A. They really moved you along, then." She hikes a thumb over her shoulder to a small purple kiosk that has never had food on it before. "Your food is over there from now on. You can just press your finger on the square and it will register that you've taken it."

"Thanks," I say before making my way over to what actually might be an appetizing meal. The kiosk contains two trays. The trays hold a bowl of leafy greens, a brown powder, a carton of milk, a hardboiled egg, and a portion of meat. There's even a tiny bit of pudding. The research assistants and I had been given scientifically designed food that would meet every nutrient need. Efficiency in all things here. Apparently, removing the distraction of taste made our digestion more efficient.

I'm trying to savor the delight that is *taste* when Llama sits next to me at my table. She's wearing the same orange outfit I am. I don't mean it to sound like I'm flirting, but something decidedly flirty comes out of my mouth. "Awww. Llama, you don't have to dress like me to make me notice you."

She shoves me. "Reach!" Her hand lingers on my shoulder for a fraction of a second longer than it needs to. I grin. "Ok, but really," she says. "What did you do this morning? It was weird not seeing you in the classrooms today."

It was weird not being there. I shrug. "I went and got these clothes and then met..." I pause for dramatic effect. "Lift."

"Lift?" She raises her eyebrows. "Who is Lift?"

"Lift is a madman. A torturer, a...personal trainer."

"Oh." Understanding dawns on her face. "That bad?"

"Yes. It was rough. I'll be sore for the rest of my life. He's going to make me into a machine for space."

"Part machine too now?" she teases in a whisper. I roll my eyes. She brightens. "Is *he* handsome? Do I get to train with him too?"

Jealousy wraps its tentacles around my core, but I answer as nonchalantly as I can. "He's ok, I guess. You'll train with someone, but I don't know if it'll be him."

She taps her foot twice on the floor, and instead of an arrow, a list pops up. "Did you see this new thing we can do with our arrows?" she asks.

"Nope."

"It's our schedules," she says. "Now we can see what we're supposed to do all day."

"Nice." I stand and tap my foot twice. A list appears. It is the first time since I've been here that anyone has bothered to share my schedule with me.

"What's next for you?" Llama asks, peering over my shoulder.

"Cartography lecture," I say. "I like maps. I think this sounds good. What about you?"

"Errr—a nap?" She squints at the floor. "Then at two, I have training."

"What did you do this morning?" I ask as I scan my list. I see no line item directing me to nap. *Figures.*

"Oh, I had short lectures on foreign languages and machinist repairs in zero-g." She grabs the spoon from my tray and begins to eat her pudding. "Reach." She drops her voice to a low whisper. It's not necessary since we're the only two at our table. "Reach, I liked it. I think I like this. Maybe I could make Eleven proud." She finishes the pudding and tosses the spoon onto my tray.

I shrug. "I'm sure you will, Llama." I throw the spoon back at her, which she bats away. "Have fun napping."

The arrow appears once I step into the hall. I obediently follow it to cartography, thinking about how I like this phase of training too. There's a niggling worry in the back of my brain about game theory, but I shove it down, whistling as I walk.

# 24

Cartography instruction is amazing. I love it. The man in charge of my instruction, a Dr. Geography, gives me a basic refresher but quickly realizes that I have a rudimentary understanding of maps from Compound's Educational Facility. After a week in the classroom, my arrow leads me to a new space.

Dr. Geography smiles broadly when he sees me. "Hey, Reach. This is my personal lab for geoscience studies. I had us moved here since you're ahead of schedule. Great job, it's like skipping ahead in a *game*."

My eye twitches as I fix him with a look. The word *game* has been a codeword of sorts. It could just be how he talks, but there's the slightest emphasis on the word. I don't know what it means. My best guess is that Dr. Geography is in his mid-twenties. On Compound, the leading scientists were all above thirty, but things seem different at Hub.

"So, Reach," he continues. "I had our instruction space moved here so we can move on to more advanced subject matter. I need to tell you, they were worried because I have access to classified information here, but that's on me to make sure you don't see it. So, don't worry. But just to cover my own tracks, let's keep our session specifics confidential, ok?"

I shrug in agreement.

He grins, his olive-green eyes turning up at the corners as he shakes his shaggy brown hair, complemented by a short brown beard. Hair, which I note, is not cut to standard regulations. He shifts some of the wavy hair out of his eyes, and I catch a glimpse of a small tattoo. His eyebrow nearly hides it, but it's still there.

"So, let me show you around." Dr. Geography leads me around the impressive lab. There are computer screens, files of old paper maps, and an impressive database of electronic maps. Both historic and current maps are available on a disk drive that can be plugged into a tablet. He's more relaxed in the lab, seems less stilted.

Dr. Geography has me making and reading practice maps using different techniques for the majority of our learning time together. We fall into a comfortable rhythm. He insists I call him "Dr. Geo" when we're in the lab together. He isn't trying to change me, he's giving me the opportunity to learn a skill I enjoy, to learn something that will be beneficial to others one day. I like feeling useful. After the first day, my cartography lessons have always fallen after my training sessions with Lift. We've been working together for weeks, and I'm excited to begin a new unit on charting a course in space. I arrive at Dr. Geo's lab, still damp from a particularly brutal training session. Dr. Geo greets me with a "Looking buff, Reach," and then cuffs my arm. There actually is a hint of muscle there, which makes me grin.

I shrug. "I guess I can make stronger maps, then."

He guffaws, laughter bouncing around the room. Then he glances around and quiets, suddenly serious. "I was talking with your supervisor, and it's time to show you something. We'll have to go into the archives." He's vague, but I'm intrigued. "Dr. Jog would like to have an update on your progress. He needs to understand where you're at on the deep space course charting. The *theory* of it can be made into a kind of game."

The first time I met Dr. Geo, he emphasized the word *game*. It struck me as odd, but since I wasn't sure how he naturally talked, I didn't want to read into it. The words 'theory' and 'game' in the same sentence suddenly make it clear: Dr. Geo is part of the insurgent movement. Dr. Jog is passing information to me through him.

Dr. Geo heads into a small archive room. It's always been locked, but today it stands open. He shuts the door and pulls a crumpled paper map from a drawer before he spreads it out and lays it on the floor. It looks like a child's drawing of a mitten but with relief shading marking precise details. It's a hodgepodge of information, crude and yet precise.

"What do you think?" he asks.

"What is it?" I can't make sense of it, but it must be important.

"That's not a fair question. I want to know what you think," Dr. Geo says.

"It looks like a mitten," I say. "Is it a map of a mitten? Is it cartography gone wrong?"

Dr. Geo snorts at that, his smile disappearing into his facial hair. "Dr. Jog thinks that it's time to show you some images. The game isn't moving at the pace we thought it would, so we're making a move."

I'm embarrassed, and Dr. Geo sees it. He steps around the map and puts his hands on my shoulders. "Reach," he says. "Reach. It's not easy to be in your position. You need to understand the past so you can understand the future. This place is designed to make you only focus on the present."

I sigh. I had gotten comfortable again. I'd even allowed myself to think of what would happen if I returned from the space mission, what I'd do. Obviously, I'd become a master cartographer and work with maps. I'd conveniently failed to consider who would be benefitting from my cartography skills.

He continues, "It's hard to keep sight of the ultimate goal when you don't know what it is. That changes—soon. And it starts with a history lesson."

Dr. Geo steps away from me and stands back at the top of the map. I stare down at it, fascinated. "This is a map of a place from before the Scientific Revolution. It's a place called Michigan. It's easily identifiable from space, because the inland seas still border it. Today, it isn't called Michigan; today, it's called Ward Eleven."

I gasp, my mouth open wide. "Llama's from there?"

"Yes," he says. "And Dr. Jog too. And it's important because it's one of the few places that didn't suffer major geological damage in the catastrophic events before the Scientific Revolution. Geography can make a nation. And it can break one just as easily."

"Is that why this is classified?"

He gives a tight-lipped smile. "Yes. Remember this shape. It's important." Then, he pulls out another map in similar disarray and lays it out over the map of Ward Eleven on the floor. This map looks like the cartoon drawings of an apatosaurus, with only two legs and no tail. He points to it. "This is the shape of our continent before the Scientific Revolution. Sea level rises, earthquakes along fault lines, and other natural disasters caused significant changes to the shape over a three-hundred-year period. Three hundred years is long in human time, but short in geologic time. A major shift in geography led to the upheaval of the economic and political structure of the nation that was here before us.

"Previously, the political and economic structure of that nation was tied to the geographical placement of people. The people believed they should be responsible for selecting their leaders. It was a strange system, and it was driven by economics. The society of before valued goods and currency over science and knowledge. Knowledge wasn't seen as desirable. Accumulating currency and things was the pinnacle of success. Do you follow, Reach?"

I nod. I have been hanging on his every word. This is highly classified information. I knew that maps were considered dangerous, which was why I was given practice maps to work with. Pre-Scientific Revolution history is vague at best. On Compound, questions about the past were always met with evasive answering techniques, and no one asked many questions unless we were studying history. I can still hear my teachers: '*We're so much more civilized; the past isn't as important as the present.*'

"Good. I know it's a lot of information. Just before the Scientific Revolution, a woman named Hannah received her doctorate from a university. Hannah's field of study was anthropology, the development of human societies and systems. She was overcome by the sense that there was about to be an inevitable downfall of the current system. A group of people supported her ideas—ideas that framed knowledge and science as the supreme goods—and the Scientific Revolution was born.

"Hannah's ideas gained traction, especially as the previous system was crumbling. She had spent her academic time learning how societies broke apart, and she knew what weaknesses to exploit to help the process along. She also knew what resources were essential for life and determined that if one central figure was responsible for the good of the people, they would be loyal, so long as their needs were met. Hannah became the first Leader when the old system finally fell."

I sit in rapt attention as Dr. Geo speaks. History is a 'fluff' subject on Compound; science, technology, engineering, math…that's the focus. What little history is taught is usually squeezed into small blocks of time where something more meaningful can't fit. I've picked up bits and pieces over the years, but no one has ever started at the beginning. The basics of history, according to Compound, are pre-Scientific Revolution: very bad, uncivilized, awful people. Post-Scientific Revolution: our great society was built, and we continue to pursue greatness in knowledge and advancement, so let's get back to work.

Dr. Geo slides the Michigan map on top of the continental one. "This region was important in the development of the new society. It provided salt, fresh water, iron ore, and wood, and was a manufacturing hub for automotives. These industries, though important, did not necessarily further the ultimate goal of a science-focused economy. The people who worked in this industry were considered heroes at first, but eventually the focus on science led to the people of this area being relegated to a type of second-class Citizen. Their jobs, and therefore their contributions to Nation, were not as prestigious or recognized as science.

"Even though Hannah hailed from this area, and even though this region was important in the development of the new order, Hannah selected a more central location for the government, here…" Dr. Geo taps a point on the map. "This was once called Saint Louis, Missouri. Once she moved the government, a sister city to Saint Louis was created just to the west. Its name—Hub City."

I look hard at the map. It's strange to see where we are in relation to Nation's previous shape and borders. An unmistakable sense of guilt washes over me. I've seen what can't be unseen.

"The government broke the surrounding areas into numbered regions," Dr. Geo says. "The regions were numbered by order. Each region had one major city, which was the center of scientific progress in that area. By the time several Leaders had reigned, those persons who were not contributing to Nation's progress were given a Noncitizen status and forced to live in the area surrounding the Cities. This was the start of the Ward system. Ward Eleven has always had a reputation as a troublesome Ward, because it was where the first attempted coup was staged. It failed, but it nearly didn't. In fact, it almost toppled the regime that Hannah and the Leaders after her worked to build.

"Maps are considered highly classified in Nation. The geography of the Wards, the Cities, the Compounds, and Hub make Hub extremely vulnerable to renegade action. By keeping the people of Nation in the dark about their own geography, the Nation is protecting its own power. There are small rebellions all over, but Eleven, with its many resources, has never forgotten how it supported the beginning of Nation and was passed over in favor of what was newer, shinier, and deemed better."

I sink to my knees and study the map. I have a question, and I know that once I ask, Dr. Geo will be implicated in rebellious activity if they ever find out. Although, we're in a small dark room full of files that are classified anyway, and he just told me more about my own Nation's history. I have to be brave. I have to ask. "Do you have a map of Nation now?"

Dr. Geo smiles. "That is highly classified, so I can't share that with you *yet*. But I have found a loophole in our training. I could show you these as part of the *game* and because they are paper. Current maps are digitally tracked, so I can't just show them to you. What I can do, and what we're going to do, is to learn how to make real-time data observations in the official GIS survey of Nation, which gives you backdoor access to the most accurate maps of Nation, if you know how to read them. And, Reach, since you'll be adding observations, you'll know this system inside and out."

"Ok," I say. "Dr. Geo, you are…" My words fade. I don't know what he *is* exactly here.

"An ally," he says. "Maybe even a friend. Someone who you could play a *game* with." He rolls up the old maps, flipping the locks on the filing cabinets into the active position as he shuts the drawer. He ushers me out of the room and begins a lecture on the masterpiece that is Nation's official GIS system and how I can use elements from this system on my space mission to chart uncharted territory. He's talking like nothing is different, like he didn't just share classified history and maps with me, but I can't help seeing him in a new light.

He's an insurgent too.

*How many layers deep does this place go?*

# 25

Llama and I have regular progress meetings with Dr. Jog through-out our training modules. These are in Sublab, because our mission is considered highly classified, and although our uniforms make us stand out as people who are training for a space mission, the details of such a mission are not something we can share with people outside of our approved contacts. My approved contacts are Hero, Llama, Dr. Jog, Dr. Geo, Lift, and the other instructors assigned to my body and mind. Dr. Jog reminds us to follow the protocol to the letter, and only to speak to each other about this mission when in Sublab.

Llama, Dr. Jog, and I are in Sublab giving our progress reports for the week. Each week, Dr. Jog writes up an overview report to be handed in to the Space Program Administrator. In turn, he keeps the Three Powers briefed on what's happening with the space mission progress. Dr. Jog is given information from our instructors, but he says he wants to encourage us to learn how to improve our own learning, so we self-report too.

"Anything to share this week, Reach?" he asks.

"Yes. I learned history with Dr. Geo this week," I say.

Llama's eyes widen. Dr. Jog nods encouragingly.

"Why can't you just tell us?" I whisper.

"Tell you what?" Dr. Jog replies, frowning hard.

"Who is working against…them," I say.

"Reach, it's not that simple. You know this. Think it through. I often don't even know who I can trust until certain precautions have been taken. I can't give you a *list*. But you seem to have picked up on the clues he left for you."

"Will it always be coded clues?" I ask back.

Llama opens and closes her mouth. "I haven't had any clues that any of my instructors are…" she says.

"That's because they aren't," Dr. Jog says calmly.

"But Reach's are?" she asks bitterly.

"Just the one," he replies. "So, Reach, you learned history. Anything else?"

"I'm starting to learn Nation's official GIS system so I can input real observations. But how would I do that when all I observe is inside Hub?"

Dr. Jog grins. "Well, I was able to convince the Space Mission Administrator that you need practice charting uncharted territory on a terrestrial level before you try to do it extraterrestrially."

Llama's quicker than I am at the language stuff. I'm still trying to figure out what he means by 'terrestrial.' She blurts out, "You mean that he's going to be charting a place that Nation doesn't have data about here? In Nation? He gets to go *outside*?"

The bitterness in her tone would be comical if I didn't know exactly how jealous I would be if she was leaving here. I haven't left Hub since I arrived. It's been clinical tiles, fluorescent lights, and no fresh air. At night, I've longed for the feeling of sand grits on my face. Which is something I never thought I would miss.

"Actually," Dr. Jog says, "we're all going."

"What?" Llama and I both exclaim.

"The final phase of your training module is a space test. But it's not possible to put you into space for a test, so the next best thing is a cave. It will help you understand the implications of spending years in space on the mission. It's two weeks of exploring a cave system in an understudied region of Nation. The government has data about the cave system from above ground but wants to know more about it from below ground. You're the perfect candidates to serve them in this way."

"When?" I ask excitedly. I can already taste the air, feel the sun on my cheeks, and imagine scooping up a handful of sand.

"Not until you've passed your studies. It really is the last phase of training. You'll be moving onto more advanced subject matters now. Remember, this is all part of a game. Our opponent is not making many moves right now, but we are slowly gathering information and laying the groundwork. A functioning city can't be built in a day. The infrastructure is important." Dr. Jog fixes me with a deliberate look as he says this. "And Llama"—it's her turn to be glared at—"the language you are learning is just as important." She puffs up a little, obviously proud to be contributing something. "Also, I have some news that might interest you, about Freedom."

That gets both of our attention locked on him faster than if he'd said, 'Your space mission is tomorrow.'

"Freedom has chosen to become a Non. He evaded security at Pen One. He's currently in a Ward and working on that infrastructure. Hero is staying here, because she can't join him safely without jeopardizing your safety and his. Your approved contacts are safe, but remember this: where talking takes place is important."

Dr. Jog dismisses us and begins writing memos on official Hub paper. I stop for a moment and study the logo watermarked on the body of the sheets. It's double helixes, wrapped around hands, palms open. It's meant to be a symbol of the way we receive the knowledge science gives us, but from my vantage point, the double helixes look like chains.

# 26

Lift is an effective trainer. He's crazy, insane, psychotic, delusional...I typically think of as many insulting adjectives to describe him as I can during our sessions together. It's unfortunate because he's also fun, and I enjoy being around him. His intensity for physical fitness showcases a dedication to his craft, which is the exact mindset expected of a person at Hub. I know Dr. Jog, Llama, and Dr. Geo are part of the *game*, but Lift never indicates his loyalties. I don't press, I just train, begrudgingly. And think of rude words to call Lift that I never actually say, because the truth is, I like him as a person.

Dr. Jog was right: our subjects have become much more rigorous. Lift's physical fitness sessions have been no exception. I've put on muscle, and the times I catch a glimpse of myself, I'm amazed at how I've transformed from a scrawny teen to a muscular almost-man.

I enter the gym, mentally preparing myself for whatever punishment Lift is going to mete out today, but stop short when I find Lift and twelve people I've never seen gathered around the circle in the center of the gym floor.

"Hey, Reach!" Lift calls as I approach slowly. "Everyone, this is Reach. I'm training him. I got approval to let you all meet him. He's going to observe our training for the Hub Tri's and join us for one. I think next year." Lift turns to me. "These are the professional athletes Hub City is sending to the Nation triathlon. Six men and six women from each city compete in the tri. It's a lot of fun. Winners get to choose where they train for the next four-year cycle." I eye each newcomer with curiosity. Lift just shared new information with me. I'm trying to sort out what it means and why it feels important when a dark-skinned man in the same blue outfit as Lift holds out a fist.

"Hey, man."

I knock it with my own. "Hey." It's always disconcerting. I don't know who knows *what* about me. Some people know me as a specimen, others know me as a person, and few as a piece in the long game that's happening here and around Nation. I say as little as possible as a rule. Too many secrets, too many lies, too many trusts— that's a sure way to get someone killed.

"So, you're really going to space?" a woman with fiery red hair in a long braid down her back asks. Her tone is full of disbelief.

"Britta…" Lift says harshly. "He's doing great."

"Let's see it, then. Let's see the best Nation has to send to freaking space."

Lift sighs. "He's supposed to be watching us. As a psychologically motivating tactic. It's part of his *training*."

"Yeah, and he will," Britta says. "But first I want to see what he can do."

"We need to do our training, and only *then* can I show off my protegee." Lift speaks in a tone that brooks no argument. Britta scowls, but begins stretching along with the other athletes. "Reach, you can be the official timer for us." Lift hands me a stopwatch.

For the next hour, I observe these people. They are clearly just as enthused with fitness as Lift. They run a mile to warm up, then they run a mile at 'race pace', sprint, dash to various marks on the floor, and then lift weights. It becomes glaringly apparent how Lift got his name. For each exercise, Lift's weights are by far the heaviest. He also completes the most reps of any athlete before I call time. The athletes are dripping sweat, but Lift looks fresh. There's barely a sheen of perspiration on his face.

*Lunatic, madman, insane, freak…*

"Time!" I yell out. The athletes slam their weights down, but Lift just shrugs and lowers his gently to the floor.

Britta wipes her hand across her brow and smirks. "Now can I have *my* psychologically motivating show?" She's mocking me, and I hate it. Although I can definitely see why she's mocking me. I might be impressed with my changing physique, but I am scrawny compared to these professional athletes. They're grown men and women, and I'm just a teen.

"Fine. Reach, let's show them the medicine ball routine."

*Ugh.* This one is Lift's favorite and my least favorite. The only thing that makes it bearable is that I have gotten pretty good at it.

I shake off my orange jacket in preparation and make my way to a line painted on the floor. An assortment of colored shapes is scattered over the wall nearest to the line. Lift will call out a color and shape and expect me to hurl a heavy medicine ball at the proper mark. It takes immense concentration to listen to his words as a twenty-pound ball ricochets off the wall and returns to my face. I have no idea how I'll manage to do this with an audience, especially if that Britta woman is a heckler. She sounds like she is.

I pick up the medicine ball and Lift begins to call out shapes and colors, slowly at first, and then increases the tempo. I'm good at focusing on one thing, so I try to block out any distractions. He's calling faster now—faster than he's ever called. I hurl the ball at the purple star on the wall. It hits with a satisfying thunk just as Lift yells out, "Time!"

The gym is silent, and I look up for a moment just to see the athletes' reactions, especially Britta's. Unfortunately, I forgot that I lobbed a medicine ball at a wall and that physics dictates an equal and opposite reaction. The ball hitting the wall results in the ball returning to me. With speed. And force. And…vigor.

My eyes scan the room for some sign of approval when the side of my head and nose is walloped with a crunch. I crash to the floor, a puddle of sweat and blood forming around my body. I'm dazed, but conscious.

"Reach?" Lift bends next to me, assessing my situation. I catch a glimpse of red hair. Britta kneels over me too. She shoves something white up my nose.

"How many fingers am I holding?" Lift asks me with concern.

"Seven?" There might actually be thirteen fingers, but there are only ten on hands, so I take my best guess.

I hear a bark of laughter from the other athletes, but Britta's voice cuts through, surprisingly tender. "Lift, he needs to go to the hospital wing."

"Yeah, Britta. I'll take him." Lift sighs and hoists me to my feet.

"He's really good. He's gonna make it. You're doing great. Just like we always knew you would." Britta's talking in front of me, and I can't see very well, but I can hear. I wonder what these words mean.

*Make what?*

"Thanks, Britta," Lift says. Then he ushers me off to the hospital wing.

By the time we reach the hospital wing, my vision is slowly coming back into focus. I'm a mess, so the doctors keep me for several hours, mostly so they can clean up my bloody face. I'm excused from my regular learning sessions for the rest of the day, which is the first unexpected day off I've ever had. When I'm released from the hospital wing, my arrow just spins in a circle, like I actually have *choices* about where to go and what to do. It's a program malfunction, but I curse the stupid arrow and the way I depend on it. Truthfully, without it, I'm lost.

I trudge back to my room and sleep. I sleep so soundly that I miss dinner.

# 27

My schedule is back to normal the following morning. Lift waits for me in the gym, concern and guilt clouding his eyes. "Hey," he says. "I'm really sorry, man."

I shrug. "It's ok. I got to sleep extra."

He gives a small smile. "I thought of something that would make you happy. We weren't going to do this for a while, but I owe you one."

"What?" He doesn't owe me anything.

"You know, your girl," he says.

"What girl?" I say.

In return, Lift rolls his eyes to the ceiling and mutters something nearly unintelligible, but might be the word "idiot."

As if on cue, Llama walks out of the locker room. My mouth drops open.

"Dude…" Lift says. "Close. Your. Mouth." I close my mouth and swallow. My head hurts again. "You two are going to be training together now. It will help you both improve in your areas of weakness. And I owe you one, because I know you *like* her."

"How?" I ask quietly. Llama is still walking toward us with a wary expression.

"Because I'm *not* an idiot," Lift says. "I saw you throw a spoon at her the other day in the cafeteria. It wasn't that long ago that I was a teenager too. A hint: don't throw things at the girl you like. You need to match with the girl. And *I know* she's off limits. But I'm bending the rules, just a little. I'm here training you. And you need a push. But mostly, *she* needs a push to get space-ready. Competition is the best way to do that."

Llama arrives and stands off to the side, her eyes flitting back and forth between Lift and me. Lift smiles warmly and waves her closer.

"Great!" he says as she stands next to me. "So, you two need to get space-ready from a physical standpoint, and conveniently you each have different physical strengths and weaknesses. Due to Reach's accident yesterday"—he glances at me sheepishly—"we are going to take a lighter workout today: core-focused strength building."

He motions to the three mats lying on the gym floor and begins to lead us through a series of breathing exercises. We move and twist our bodies in unfamiliar positions. I had no idea that core would be so punishing. When we finish the workout, Llama dashes to the locker room. There's only one, so I let her shower and head to the hallway with Lift. I'll rinse off in the bathroom near my quarters. I should be able to make it to my geography lecture with Dr. Geo in plenty of time if I hurry.

Lift and I step into the hallway. Out of habit I glance at the ground to see my arrow, but I'm surprised when another arrow lights up next to mine. I haven't seen Dr. Jog with an arrow, or Enforce, but I've never been in the hallway with Lift.

"You have one too?" I whisper.

"Yep," Lift replies brusquely, popping the *p*, and there's an undercurrent of anger in his voice. "I have a meeting with the nutritional team. I need to help you and Llama bulk up for space. You lose a lot of muscle mass in zero-g. It's complicated to get it just right." The anger is gone, but I know I heard it. I can't stop unhearing the things people say without their words. It's ingrained apparently. I wonder if Lift is everything he seems.

"Hey," I say. "Thanks for letting Llama and I train together."

Lift grins, his tattoo wrinkling around his eye. "Anytime. But it really is self-preservation for all of us. She isn't progressing the way I need her to. She's got to be space-ready, and she doesn't respond to training with a natural athletic inclination. Some people need competition to improve."

I shrug. "Works for me."

Lift laughs and turns away from the cafeteria doors as I step inside. Lift might not be part of the plan, but he's turning into a friend. A crazy, insane maniac, but a friend just the same.

# 28

The GIS program Nation uses is geological perfection. Dr. Geo has been teaching me the finer points, but he's also teaching me the software code. A small device takes observations that are manually inputted by a scientist and creates an immersive relief map. It's fascinating and fun to use.

"Reach!" Dr. Geo calls out from behind one of the devices we use for GIS practice. "We have to adjust your schedule a little for the next few weeks, so don't get comfortable today."

"Oh?" This is unprecedented. My arrow pointed me to Dr. Geo's lab, just like it has every day after lunch.

"Yeah…" He lets his voice trail off and grimaces. "It's, uh…I wish someone had told me, so I'll tell you, but you don't know anything, ok?" His words rush together in an uncharacteristic display of nervousness. "It's mensmanners."

"What?" I say.

"Men's Manners," he whispers. An involuntary shudder escapes him.

"What is 'Men's Manners'?" I whisper back.

"It's a secret class that men have to take before becoming Citizens."

"I'm a half—"

"Half-Citizen, I know. But you'll be a space hero, and they need to make sure you understand how to behave around women you have…amorous feelings toward."

The words *amorous feelings* make me think of Llama, and the device slips. I catch it, but Dr. Geo's eyes tell me he noticed.

"I know how to behave around women." The words sound more biting than I intended.

He shakes his head but doesn't respond to that. "I'm going to walk you over there. Dr. Etiquette changed the schedule, and you don't say no to her. It's not in the official arrow software yet, so you won't be able to find it unless you know where you're going." He steps out of the lab and into the hallway. Dr. Geo does not have an arrow, and mine is still pointing at the Geo lab.

Dr. Geo presses his lips together tightly while walking down several hallways. He knocks once on the open door's frame and then steps inside. His voice sounds strained. "Hello, Dr. Etiquette. I brought Reach here as you requested."

"Thank you, Rex." A woman sits on a tall stool behind a podium. She has curly white hair, large, muscular arms Lift would be proud of, and no trace of humor anywhere on her face.

Dr. Geo looks at me and mouths 'good luck.' Then he's gone, more quickly than I'd have thought possible.

"Well, sit," the woman commands.

I turn my head and find that I'm not the only male here. There are others, all in their research assistant uniforms. A cursory glance reveals Cyto and Mitch sitting together in the farthest row. Among the sea of white, my orange outfit stands out. I'm subjected to stares and snarls as I make my way to the only open desk, the one right in front of the woman.

"Welcome to Men's Manners," the woman says in a clipped and rough voice. "Here at Hub, you are serving Nation in a pre-Citizen capacity. In order to fully appreciate the genius of this system, you need to be initiated into certain protocols. In Nation, we value Female Leadership. Female Leadership is one of the keystones our Nation was founded upon. It is the feminine that makes us great, and as men, you are *not* feminine. I'm here to teach you about your natural role in this society."

I sense a prickling in the guys sitting behind me.

"Shouldn't we be learning about our roles from a *man?*" someone shouts out. I am tempted to turn and see who said it, but Dr. Etiquette's face stops me.

"As a woman, I am the perfect person to teach you your role here. I am superior. You are inferior." A hiss sounds behind me. She shrugs. "You cannot become Citizens without understanding this basic fact. Women are meant to lead. You are meant to follow."

The murmurs behind me give rise to an arrogant voice.

"What if we don't want to follow?" The voice is cocky, the kind of voice that comes from someone who is self-assured and convinced *they* are better than anyone else. I know this voice. *Why do I know this voice?*

My mind flashes back to Compound, to the cadence of the voices there. To all the voices that sounded like *this.* There were a few, the children of scientists who didn't so much want to learn as they wanted to ride their parents' achievements into the halls of fame and glory.

"Sit. Cyto, I appreciate the attempt at humor by being volatile, but really, it's immature." I didn't peg Cyto for a troublemaker, but maybe it's a good thing I'm not sitting by my friends. Dr. Etiquette's tone is dry, but the way her eyebrow arches indicates that she does *not* appreciate the attempt at humor. "As Cyto has asked an inappropriate question, I suspect you males will want to know the answer. I will tell you, but first, a history lesson."

She presses a remote in her crepe-thin hand. The lights dim, and a screen lowers from the ceiling at the front of the room. I have the benefit of seeing the screen perfectly, with the exception of Dr. Etiquette standing to the side and casting a shadow. The same cannot be said for the research assistant behind me. He's shifting around and finally taps me on the shoulder.

"Hey, man," he says. "Could you, like, crouch down or something? I can't see."

This is how I end up slouched over on my desk, my cheek pressed to the laminate wood surface, and watching the video sideways. Perhaps it's my posture, or perhaps it's the content, but something about this movie strikes me as very definitely *not right*.

A female announcer's voice fills the room as still images slide rapidly across the projector screen.

"Long ago, before Nation was born, there was a society rooted in power. Men, physically stronger than women, forcibly took leadership positions. These men subsequently forced women into subservient positions in the social hierarchy. A caste was born where women were the underlings. Abuse was rampant [image of a man's shoe stomping on a sidewalk].

"Despite this abuse, there were heroic women who escaped the shackles of this social order [image of woman with chains sliding off her wrists and running into a field] and attained great scientific progress [images of female scientists].

"Despite this progress, no woman was ever quite able to shake the pervading belief that men should lead and women should follow [images of men wagging their fingers in a 'no' gesture].

"In the *before*, no woman attained the highest office of leadership, then called *president* [image of men sitting behind a gigantic desk; the man changes in a timelapse form, but the desk doesn't].

"Men, as would be expected, led that country into ruin. It was women who rose up and devised a new system [image of a phoenix rising from ashes]. Our first illustrious leader was a woman named Hannah [image of a stern woman in a tan-colored pantsuit shaking her fist at a crowd]. Hannah, a scientist, understood ancient cities and civilizations. She understood their ruin and how to build a new one [images of historic cities in ruins, replaced by images of structures being built].

"First Leader Hannah was practical. She eliminated the terminology that was no longer useful. She developed the functional naming system—a system that is now used everywhere in Nation [image of a woman at a desk, writing things on a piece of paper]. First Leader understood that there was a common element in the ruin of all the societies of the past: men in the position of supreme authority [image of a man bowing before a woman].

"The key tenant of Nation is Female Leadership. Hannah showed us the way forward; the way to scientific progress could not be led by males. Males have achieved positions of power in our society, but a woman always oversees them. Nation is a place where men and women live together in harmony, for the good of learning, for the good of knowledge, for the good of the future [image of woman shaking a man's hand, fading into the flag of Nation waving and snapping in the wind].

Dr. Etiquette flips on the lights. "Any questions?" she asks in a tone that makes it obvious we should not have questions.

I sit up and turn my aching neck.

"Yes, you in the front." She points at me, and I realize I've just placed my hand on my head in an attempt to work out the tightness in my muscles. She misconstrued my motion as a hand raising.

"Err—" I say.

"Err," she says mockingly. I can see now why Dr. Geo was nervous. This woman is mean. "As Reach so eloquently put it, this video is a lot of information to take in." "Why didn't we learn about that until now?" a different voice calls out from behind me. I can't tell if the guy that I spent all the movie with a crick in my neck for is taking pity on me or actually wants to know, but I'm grateful that Dr. Etiquette's attention is off of me for now.

Dr. Etiquette approaches the desks, which means she's right in front of me. She's staring down at the student behind me, but I'm caught in the crossfire of her glare. It's terrifying. "There are certain finer points of Citizenship that your brains are not developed enough to understand. This course will prepare you to know your place in

the natural order, but also instruct you in how to appropriately behave around the superior sex." The students' murmuring builds, like
the buzzing of an insect coming closer to your ear, but she cuts it off.
"Now, your biological deficiencies are not your fault, exactly, but
how you choose to approach these shortcomings is up to you. You
will have to temper your natural inclination toward power. You cannot be successful if you do not learn how to behave. Women understand that you must be taught how to be the best version of yourself.
There are men in positions of honor in our society. These men have
learned how to treat women with the respect they deserve and con-
tributed to Nation's scientific progress in valuable ways. Women are
fair-minded. This seminar will teach you to harness your weaknesses
so that the mistakes of the past are not repeated.

"The next few months will endeavor to teach you the appropriate etiquette of a man in a female-led society. You will come to see
the benevolence of female power and understand the regulations you
are required to follow. This is not only what is best for Nation and
its pursuit of knowledge, but also for yourselves. Dismissed."

# 29

THERE'S AN ANGRY hum as the research assistants in the room digest Dr. Etiquette's words. Dr. Etiquette leaves the classroom, simply ignoring the pulsating discontent. I don't participate; if this is all game theory, then I've just been given new information, and I need time to process it.

I duck through the doorway and find the comforting glow of my arrow lighting the way on the cool tile. The abrupt schedule change must have been recorded in the software because the arrow points me back to Dr. Geo. I am relieved.

Dr. Geo's lab door is open, but I still knock before entering. He looks up from a planimeter, then sets it down sheepishly. There are digital tools that are more accurate than the analog old-fashioned ones, but he likes to use the old-fashioned tools sometimes.

"Reach," he says, relieved.

"You didn't tell me," I spit as I slam the door shut in frustration. Omitting information is manipulative. I hate being used.

"I couldn't," he says.

"Who said you couldn't? Dr. Jog, or *them*?"

"Valid question. It's best sometimes to not give too much information to a student at once. They would get overwhelmed in the *game*."

His words cool my ire. I suppose that makes sense. I think about trying to teach Llama chess. We've had a few other evenings where we were directed to play games. She's still terrible at it, but she has improved. Giving her too much information at first was a disaster. When we asked Dr. Jog why we were playing games in a random classroom, he said playing the games in a typical classroom was a way to observe our team dynamics. I'm grateful to Dr. Geo for moving our instruction out of the classrooms and into his private lab. The classrooms are all hooked into an observation feed, but according to Dr. Jog, the private labs are not. The scientists who work here are all so closely in line with the government that there's no need to spy. For now.

I prepare to ask a question, but he surprises me and talks first.

"What did you think about the propaganda?" he asks in a whisper.

"Propa—propa, what?" I ask in low tones. There might not be video observation feeds, but I'm still cautious. I have heard that word—propaganda—before, but I can't think of where.

"Propaganda. Purposefully misleading information. Men's Manners is where I first realized that I wasn't as invested in Nation's progress as the others. Dr. Etiquette started me on a path of discovery about the true workings of Nation."

I stare. "But you're here, and obviously have really high clearance..."

"Yes. But, I had a mentor who helped me make sense of what was happening, what *is* happening. Reach, you have to understand that this entire system is going to fall, and there are cracks at the foundations already. I have an aptitude for maps, mapmaking, and geographical studies. By using this aptitude to obtain classified information, I help the cause—*our* cause."

I pick up the planimeter, twirling it around as I think, buying time to digest this information. Dr. Geo *is* part of the Resistance. "Is she this intimidating every day?" I ask him.

"Yes." He nods emphatically. "I'll tell you what my mentor told me years ago. Do not cross her. Keep your head down and do what she says. It's only a few weeks."

"Everyone was pretty mad by the time it was over."

"Yeah," he says. "But what happens is that everyone finds a Citizen they trust to complain to. From there, each pre-Citizen is told to follow along because the punishment for not completing the seminar is to not achieve Citizenship, to become a Non, and to not have any status or glory. It's a play on vanity, and it usually works."

"Usually?" My eyes flick over Dr. Geo's face as I understand what he means. "How many times do people find a mentor like yours?"

"That, I can't say. But some mentors watch the aptitude tests and consider the best ways to widen the foundational cracks in the system. They find the students as much as the students find the mentors."

"Does Llama have a mentor?" I ask.

"I don't know. I know my mission. I know that I'm committed to helping *you*. I know that I'm committed to *mentoring* you. We have the same end goal. Now, let's get to our maps."

I nod in agreement, which is probably foolish because I don't know what the actual end goal he's talking about is. Maybe my goal has been shortsighted. Maybe I'm being selfish, with the whole wanting-to-survive mindset. Maybe my goal should be the same as his goal, which sounds a lot like making cracks in the system.

A new thought comes, unbidden, creeping through my conscience: *What if I'm not making cracks? What if I'm the one who takes it down?*

"Oh, and Reach," Dr. Geo continues, interrupting me from my own thoughts. "Your cave training mission date has been scheduled. You've been excelling, and they want you to head to space as soon as possible. It's a good look for them; they haven't sent anyone on a space mission in years, and it's a good thing for us too. So, good job—and we've got work to do."

He tosses me the GIS system device and a bunch of handwritten observations. I key in the code and get to work adding the fictitious observations to my practice map sets. Tension fills my body as I remember my mother telling me that I can't fail. Dr. Jog said the same thing. I didn't realize it, but this entire time I've been scared of failing. Dr. Geo's words mean I'm not failing.

I'm doing exactly what I'm supposed to be doing.

# 30

Llama, Dr. Jog, and I are meeting for our weekly progress meeting in Sublab. Hero is here too.

"Anything to report this week, Reach?" Dr. Jog questions.

"Men's Manners is new," I reply tersely. I've dealt with Dr. Etiquette every day this week, and I do not like it. I do not like *her*.

Dr. Jog has the decency to look sheepish. Llama looks amused.

"You didn't tell him about it?" Llama says.

"Too much information at once," Dr. Jog says.

"But still…" Llama trails off as she sees my stormy expression.

"You could have warned me," I say bitterly.

"Reach, you know that I can't tell you everything." Dr. Jog says. He's calm, and I hate it.

"Yes, but that woman is teaching us…" I pull in a shaky breath and try to still my fidgeting hands. "It's a class full of prop—"

Llama tilts her head to the side and raises an eyebrow, listening to my weak argument with interest.

Dr. Jog cuts me off. "Yes. It is. But it's required. So it's a horrible hour every day. You'll be fine. Do what she says, learn how to treat women, and then come back to do the real work."

Something Llama said niggles my mind, and I blurt out, "Llama knew about it?"

Llama and Dr. Jog both snap their heads toward me. I feel the flush of anger creeping down my face, and like a too-hot shower, it burns my skin.

Dr. Jog starts to speak, but Llama interrupts. "Yes, there is a difference in female and male instruction here, so we know about it. As soon as I got to Hub and before I began work as a research assistant, I had an orientation. I learned what to do if any male research assistant intimidated me."

"Nice of them to tell us about these high stakes," I mutter.

"Reach, is it really *that* important?" Llama asks.

I hate her patronizing tone because it *is* important to me. I'm here, surrounded by a government that thinks I'm half-Martian and has paraded me through a room of scientists like a prize toy. I've already had to deal with the effects of that. Now I have to deal with the consequences of being male. It's too hard, too heavy, too frustrating, too much. I want to explode, but something on Llama's face stops me from yelling. Yes, her tone was patronizing, but her eyes held an understanding light.

A memory of Llama yelling the word *propaganda* at Dr. Jog surfaces in the back of my mind. She knows exactly how I feel. I can't articulate it, but she knows. The thought is comforting, if baffling.

Dr. Jog watches our exchange with narrowed eyes. A flicker of concern passes over his face as Llama and I stare at each other. "Reach, we need to get you to your space mission, so you need to pass that seminar. End of discussion. Llama, what do you have to report this week?"

Llama launches into her week, then drops her voice and leans closer to Dr. Jog, effectively pushing me out of the conversation. This is the first time I've felt dismissed by Dr. Jog about the workings of Hub. I don't like it, and I don't understand it. Hero has been quietly writing notes in the corner. When she's at these meetings, she takes on the role of scribe, writing down notes for Dr. Jog's official reports. I catch her eyes, finding something like sorrow there as she places the pencil back on the clipboard. The private conversation between Llama and Dr. Jog allows her to stand and walk to me.

She sinks down beside me and slings her arm around my shoulder in a gesture that is entirely new and also comforting. I'm not sure what to make of it. "I know it's a lot, Reach," she says. "But it's part of the system." Her voice is venomous. "It's what *we* are all fighting against. And sometimes the best way to fight your enemy is to know it."

"How do we not *become* the enemy? It's too easy to become what they want," she murmurs in agreement. "But that's just it. You can choose easy, and you'll have chosen their way. You can choose the harder thing, and you'll be choosing to be free from their mind games, you'll have—"

"Freedom?" I venture.

Hero removes her arm from my shoulder and stares into my eyes, hers filled with tears. "Yes," she says softly. "Freedom."

I understand. She misses him, but there's something bigger happening here. Since Freedom left, I have avoided talking about him out of respect for Hero.

"Where is he?"

"I can't say," she says.

"Are you going to see him soon?" I ask.

"Not so soon. I have to help *you* here," she says.

"Once I'm extraterrestrial?" I ask. Her head moves in an almost imperceptible nod. "It's about *me*?" I prod. Again, the tiny nod. "You can't make a move until I'm off the board?"

She shakes her head. "That's not what I'm implying. Anyway, Reach, I'm going to be helping you with your research experiments and data and journal keeping. We're going to be working together more, and I'm happy about that because I get to work with a friend. I don't have more information than you, but I do understand what you're going through. Freedom and I will be together when we can, but this *here* is what I can do to contribute. Please, just do the best you can. It matters more than you might think."

Men's Manners continues. It's been weeks of Dr. Etiquette's lectures about how men lack the proper qualities to lead and therefore must be taught how to maintain appropriate posture toward women in every aspect of our lives. We've learned how to stand deferentially, how to speak calmly and measuredly, how to not interrupt and wait patiently, and how to leave the appropriate amount of space between the male and female body.

Today Dr. Etiquette stands in front of the room, tapping her foot and wiggling her fingers. The door shuts, and she begins the seminar at exactly ten. "Today is practice for your final exam. Being a male Citizen means that you are going to experience a level of attraction to a woman at some point. It is imperative that you know how to approach a woman in a romantic context. So, you are going to use all the knowledge I have so graciously and effectively given you to ask a woman on a romantic date. I will be playing this woman."

There isn't even a low buzz of any sound behind me anymore. That murmur of discontent, frustration, confusion, and fear has been replaced by acceptance. Complete and total acceptance.

"Reach!" she barks. "You'll go first. Come up here."

I walk to the front of the room, feeling all the eyes on me. The phrase "choose the harder thing" bounces around my skull like the rubber ball Lift sometimes has us throw and chase around the gym.

I stop four feet from Dr. Etiquette and say as clearly as I can, "Excuse me, Dr. Etiquette, would you accompany me to the cafeteria today? I would like to spend more time with you, if you are amenable."

Her eyebrows disappear into her bluish-white hair. Her fingers stop tapping and she frowns. Her narrowed eyes bore into my own. "Thank you, Reach," she says. "However, as your instructor, that would be most inappropriate." Her lips curl up in a snarl, and it's clear she wants everyone to laugh at my expense. The conforming class behind me obliges, and laughter fills the room. I catch sight of

Cyto and Mitch. They're frowning. I played chess with them last night. It's nice to see that my friends at least don't appreciate this.

She smirks. "That wasn't terrible. But as your instructor, I will provide you with this feedback. You delivered your statement with clarity, so that was good. The verbiage you used was not entirely correct. You should have said"—she adopts a falsetto low voice that is meant to mock me—"*I would like to spend more time with you, but only if you are amenable.*" She returns to her normal voice. "I take it you have never requested a woman's presence on a romantic date."

I nod; the only submissive gesture I can think of is nonverbal agreement. Even saying the word 'no' seems brazen. I'm supposed to play nice, but that doesn't mean giving in and giving up. Something these *males* behind me haven't figured out.

Dr. Etiquette frowns but marks something down on a sheet of paper after studying my face for a fraction of a second too long. She calls up the next male. No one escapes unscathed, the brutal humiliation she metes out being taken in turns with compliance.

The session is almost over when Mitch is called. "Mitochondria."

He stomps heavily down the aisle to the front of the room. His sock-clad feet manage to make as much of a thump as heavy boots. Dr. Etiquette's lips press into thin lines that are so narrow they nearly become invisible on her wrinkled, pale skin.

Mitch turns to everyone in the class. "What's the point of this?" he shouts. "Why are you all ok with her doing this?" He waves his hands wildly and scrubs them through his hair. "She's shaming us for being *male*! This is absurd—"

Dr. Etiquette taps Mitch once and smiles—a terrible, slow smile. She taps a button on her tablet, then grabs him by the arms, yanking them behind his back. His wrists are caught in her hands and pinned against his back at an awkward angle. Though old, it's obvious she is strong.

Mitch cries out in pain. "Stop! Stop! I'm sorry. I shouldn't have done that. I'm sorry. I'm sor—" Tears stream down his face and he howls in pain. Mitch is my friend, but I can't move as I watch his pleas. I've never witnessed someone begging nor seen the perverse pleasure on someone's face as they ignore any opportunity for mercy.

Cyto stands from his seat, a look of abject horror on his face as his twin breaks down.

I'm an idiot. "STOP!" The words pour out of my own mouth.

Dr. Etiquette startles and drops Mitch's wrists. She eyes me expectantly. I open my mouth, but before I find words, two men walk through the classroom door. "You have been revoked," one says. The other places cuffs on Mitch's wrists, and then both haul him out of the room by his armpits, his feet dragging against the floor.

The door snaps shut. "Well, that was fun." Dr. Etiquette surveys the class. "Cytoplasm? Sit."

Cyto sits, but his eyes shift from side to side constantly.

"Males, listen up." She says it in her commanding voice, and we all look at her as one. "Your final is next week. You will remember that if you cannot pass this final, you will not pass this seminar, which means you are not fit to be a Citizen of Nation."

"What happened to him?" Cyto speaks out of turn. Interrupting Dr. Etiquette is a bad idea.

Dr. Etiquette's beady eyes sweep the room, landing on Cyto. "He has lost his status here. He will become a Non. You're welcome to join him if you like."

I swallow, tensing all my muscles, trying to force the rage from pressurizing and being let out. Becoming a Non means I'll never see Mitch again. Cyto and Mitch have done everything together; will he ever see his twin again?

She narrows her eyes and waits for his response. When one doesn't come, she continues. "Your assignment is to find a woman and appropriately ask her to join us at our final class. This woman must be of your age and a pre-Citizen or a level one Citizen. No one who has been a Citizen for over five years is permitted. You'll need to remember the feedback I have provided and note that the woman's interactions with you during class will be part of your final score. If your final goes well, you and the woman will be considered appropriate possible matches. So, choose wisely, because this is the easiest way to be matched."

The murmur that has been absent for weeks is suddenly back. Matching means long-term commitment…marrying, having babies. My palms begin to sweat. We're not even eighteen.

I close my eyes and try to school my features, but it takes a moment, because in the darkness of my eyelids, I have a vision of Llama and me, matched. A double inhale lowers my pulse, and I feel the muscles in my face return to a neutral position before I raise my hand tentatively.

Dr. Etiquette looks at me with one eyebrow raised. I haven't ventured a question if I could help it this entire seminar.

"Yes, Reach." She points at me while saying my name.

"Dr. Etiquette, I do not understand what you mean by matching." I keep my voice even and calm. I understand what matching is, I just don't understand the full picture. Yet another thing I've only been given a piece of.

*When will I ever see how it all fits together?*

"Will you males ever learn?" she says with condescension. "Matching is how Nation provides the greatest of progeny to continue our forward progress into the next generations. In order to match, you typically need to submit applications. It's a formal process overseen by the Matchmaking Department. Just because you match with a woman doesn't mean you'll be unionized, but it does mean that when *she* feels ready, you will be able to pursue a more romantic relationship and, ultimately, a union. From the union, children will take up the mantle of Nation and continue our path to knowledge and scientific growth. Each male is listed on a woman's potential matchboard. Passing this final will allow you to skip the application process and be listed on her potential match board immediately after. Only after you've been listed on a potential match board can you consider pursuing romantic activities. Your classmate Mitochondria showed you what happens if you fail. If you can't at least be seen as a potential romantic partner for a woman in Nation, you're not fit for Citizenship."

She looks at me again. I want to say something dripping in sarcasm to her, but Hero's voice—*'it matters more than you think'*—pounds its way down my throat, keeping the sarcasm at bay.

I nod in understanding.

"Dismissed," she says and turns her back on all of us males.

# 31

I FOLLOW MY arrow mindlessly as I contemplate who I should ask out to the final for Men's Manners. I have two choices: Llama, who I'd actually like to ask because I'd like to pursue a romantic relationship with her one day, or Hero, who is in love with Freedom. But Freedom escaped, and somehow Hero has managed to not be incriminated by his defection. And also, Llama and I aren't allowed to have romantic interest in each other. That was made very clear.

I haven't talked to any other female research assistants. They've ignored me, and I've ignored them. I'm not good with people, having been a loner for so much of my childhood.

Cyto runs through the hall, bumping into me. I crash to the ground.

"Hey!" I yell out. He turns and sees me on the ground.

"I don't know what to do," Cyto says. "I can't let him…we need each other. We're twins. We can't be separated. We've never been…" He looks dangerously close to tears.

"Try to find out where they took him?" I suggest. "I'll try to find out too."

Cyto's relief is palpable. Then he's off running, shoving past people in the hall.

I decide that this is the sort of thing a mentor is supposed to help with. It's tricky, because while Dr. Geo hinted he was my mentor, he made it clear he doesn't always see the full picture. We're working together on the same puzzle, but he only sees the pieces in one section, and I only see three or four pieces. I'm not sure *who* is holding the design, but at least now I understand *why*.

I duck inside Dr. Geo's personal lab and smile. It smells like maps. Like paper and ink and color, old and new all mixed together. Dr. Geo writes something at his desk. He looks up. "Hey, Reach. Almost done with Men's Manners now, right?"

"Yeah," I say. "Um, something happened today, and I don't know who to ask for the final."

There's understanding in his eyes. "It's not that difficult. Most girls are nice."

"No, it's not that," I say with a pointed look at the floor. "It's the *game*. I know who I want to ask, but I don't know who I *should*. And the other thing: I don't know what to do."

"Oh." He looks perplexed. "Maybe you could explain further? I don't know if I can help with this."

"My friend Mitch was revoked today."

Dr. Geo hisses through his teeth. "I'm sorry, Reach. That's always a frightening thing to witness."

"But his twin brother is here. And he doesn't know what to do. He's running around and confused and I don't understand what happened."

Dr. Geo frowns. "The twins?" I nod. "Why was he revoked?"

"He kind of just…snapped during the practice with Dr. Etiquette. He shouted at us about why we were letting her do this to us and then two men came in and dragged him away after telling him he was revoked. Cyto was confused, and Dr. Etiquette said he would be a Non and that if I don't pass the final, I would be too."

Dr. Geo holds up a hand to stop my rambling. "One problem at a time. You had a friend harmed by powerful people in Nation today. It happens. It's not something you can deal with. It's not something you can fix. Yet. I see what you want, but I don't know if anything can be done. You have to get used to the fact that people you care about will be hurt. And people you care about can hurt you. You have to function in that space of pain."

His words sound like defeat. I ball up my fist and throw a punch at the solid wall. It does nothing but make my knuckles bleed.

"Feel better?" he asks wryly. "Look, the twins were on a project with a friend. I'll see what I can find out. I don't know if anything can help them, but maybe their supervising scientist has some sway. Now, on to the other problem?"

I don't know how he can switch topics so quickly. I can't. I take a moment.

"The problem with the final for Men's Manners?" he prompts.

"Llama and I can't be involved together. The rules. They said that a *lot* when they read us the space mission rules. They said we couldn't match. Ever. But-I-like-her."

"Come again?" he says.

"But I like her. I like Llama. And I'd like to be…"

"Reach, that sounds like a distraction," he says.

"It's not that, it's just that we have to bring someone we could potentially be matched with, and I don't know—it's confusing. I'm playing by the rules, but I don't know the game." Dr. Geo nods in understanding. "Who did you bring?"

He reddens. "Do you have an alternative guest to bring?" I guess he doesn't want to talk about his experience or his matches.

"Yeah, the RA assigned to our group, H—"

"Hero," he says. "Yes, bring Hero. That would be the best way to help everything along."

"What do you mean?" I ask. "Help *everything* along?"

"Hero seems like a good choice. She has clearance, and she's been connected to that Citizen who went missing, right?"

"Connec—? They were matched and preparing to be unionized."

"And that's been a big problem for Hero since Freedom disappeared. They won't leave her alone until they know she's got nothing to do with him, and her loyalty is in question every day until then. Freedom gave up his Citizenship when he disappeared. Since she was matched and preparing for a union, she's under extreme suspicion."

"What aren't you telling me, Dr. Geo?" I'm blunt because it's been a long day and I am frustrated with everything.

He sighs. "I'm saying what you already know. That there are lots of pieces moving in this machine. You only know a small part, and your role is important, critical even. But there are other roles, just as important. Hero's role overlaps with yours, which makes her a good person to bring, and a good person to be allowed to get close to in the future. Llama is useful, but not in the way you might think. Just…as your mentor and *friend*, please ask Hero. That's the right *move*."

I bite my lip and look at the ground.

"I know that's not what you wanted to hear, and I'm sorry. But we have work to do today." He unfurls a piece of paper and tacks it to the wall. "This is an old map of aquifers from before the Scientific Revolution. I'd like you to read the map and write out a detailed report of your understanding after studying the map."

I begin my work in quiet, and it stays that way for our entire time together. The laughing, easygoing friendship I had with Dr. Geo is replaced with a tension I don't understand. But it has something to do with Men's Manners, Mitch and Cyto, Llama and Hero. I debate ignoring Dr. Geo's advice and just asking Llama to the final, but after writing out 'samtode' instead of 'sandstone' for the tenth time, I realize that thinking about Llama is a distraction. I make up my mind to ask Hero and write the rest of my report without spelling errors. I'm rewarded for my decision by bumping into Hero in the hallway.

"Hero!" I call out. She stops, her arrow flashing in the opposite direction as mine.

"Reach?" she questions. We've never spoken in the hallway.

"We're friends, right?" I ask.

"Yes…?" She trails off in a question.

"I'm supposed to ask for you to come to my final at Men's Manners with me," I whisper-blurt.

She blanches. "Men's Manners?" Her voice is an octave higher than normal, and her face stark white.

"Yeah. Please, as a friend?" I'm begging and I know it.

"That's how Freedom and I…" She pauses and inhales, her hand on her collarbone.

"I know you don't have romantic feelings for me, and I don't for you, but I need to pass the class…and…Dr…G—"

"Ok," she interrupts, looking around with alarm. "As a *friend*. But I probably need to look interested in you." She shudders slightly as I sigh in relief. "But I think you need to ask me again, in a more proper way, and in a more public place. This is the end of the seminar, right?" I nod. "You're going to the cafeteria for lunch? We have overlapping dinner times and then some experiment time after dinner. Ask me at dinner. Where. They. Can. See." She hisses.

I see her point; I need to make this look real, not so much for my benefit but for hers. I don't exactly know her role, but I like her as a friend, and I'd like her to have what she wants. What she wants is Freedom. Maybe in some convoluted way, I can help.

I ask Hero to accompany me to the final in a quiet moment during dinner. I make sure to ask her where the kiosk lady can hear us. Hero accepts with fake enthusiasm in her voice, but I'm not offended. She puts her hand on my shoulder and squeezes.

Llama watches us with narrowed eyes and pursed lips. She stands up and throws her trash away when we approach with our food. The stench of jealousy clings to her as she walks away without a word. *Interesting.*

"I think you'd better explain to Llama," Hero says quietly to my right. "Also, you're still staring after her…"

I turn my head back and look at Hero. "Sorry. It's just…you…I can't—"

"I know the rules. I was read into this project too," she interjects with surprising gentleness. "We have to do this right to achieve the outcome. Llama's caught in the middle. She'll understand when you explain."

But Llama never gives me a chance to explain. She's cold and distant for the next few days. One bright side: during our training sessions with Lift, Llama participates with unforeseen vigor. I catch her glancing at me when she's in between sets.

Lift corners me after a session. "I don't know what you did to her, man. But she's mad. She needs to stay mad to get in shape. But it's probably not good to have your space mission partner ice you."

I nod and walk off to the RA quarters to shower. Llama has the locker room as long as we train together. I am a gentleman, after all.

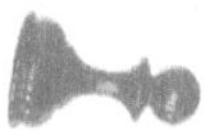

The day of the final, Hero accompanies me to Dr. Etiquette's classroom. I open the door and allow Hero to step through first, then follow her to the seat she chooses. The room is set up like a small cafeteria. The desks have been pushed into pairs of two. Dr. Etiquette looks at Hero with some suspicion.

"How long have you been a Citizen?" she barks at Hero.

"Three years," Hero responds with a small smile. "I'm a C1." Then she turns back to me and places a hand on my arm. Dr. Etiquette makes a note.

The other males have brought women, some looking pleased and some appearing bored out of their minds. Cyto isn't there. We spend the session chatting with our dates and pouring small carafes of coffee into cups and sharing them. Dr. Etiquette wanders around making notes and asking questions.

At the end of the session, she hands the couples pieces of paper with the word MATCH on them. I've passed the final, but something about this paper feels incendiary. I don't know why I have a feeling of dread as I leave the room behind Hero, holding my piece of paper gingerly between my fingers like it's a bomb.

# 32

Our weekly progress report meeting is missing Llama. She's never missed a meeting. Dr. Jog doesn't acknowledge the gaping hole in our group when he gets started. "Great, Reach. You passed Men's Manners. Thank you, Hero. I know that was hard for you, but you did help the cause."

He takes a breath, then turns to face me. "Your cave mission is next week. I've secured permission to accompany you and Llama. They want to send me into space with you two. Since you're both pre-Citizens, Leader suggested a former space mission member join you. Hero, you'll stay here and prepare for the return. When we return, you'll be inputting Reach's scientific data into experimental periodicals. It won't be long after the return that the actual space mission is scheduled."

Hero shudders. "Thanks for pulling me off the near sentients project."

My head swivels left and right, looking for wherever Llama might be lurking. I can't take it anymore. "Where is she?"

Dr. Jog looks up, concern etched on his features. "Llama?" he says. "She's doing something on her own this evening. I think the rules of the game are difficult for her. She has a lot of things to consider. You'll be spending an entire week with her underground. I'm sure you two will be able to figure out whatever the problem is. Give her space for now, and prepare for the cavenaut in the meantime." He stands and disappears into the back of the Sublab, clearly dismissing us.

Hero's eyes are full of sympathy as she meets my stony gaze. "We will need to pack your approved scientific experiment equipment. You leave next week. I think we should make a list. I'll help you gather materials and pack and everything."

Hero and I work well together and spend the next few evenings gathering materials and reading the approved scientific experiments. We both have to understand the experiments so that we can interpret the setup, the procedure, and the meaning of the results.

Llama avoids us.

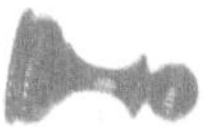

The day we are scheduled to leave on our cavenaut mission dawns with a hum of excitement in my ears. I haven't been outside in years—since the morning I woke up in my doorless quarters. Now, I'm going to be outside exploring a geographical and geological phenomenon. One of my scientific experiments is simply collecting data regarding the cave. Tracking coordinates underground is shockingly similar to charting courses in space. I'll be subterranean, but I won't be *here*. How could I not be excited?

But the excitement is replaced by the punch of fear that lands in my gut as I consider Dr. Geo's warning when I picked up the live GIS system device I'd need on the training mission. "Reach," he'd said. "You know that there is no choice here. You cannot fail. It's your life. But it's not just yours. You have to give them what they need to keep you alive. To keep *everything* alive."

Those words root themselves in my brain. Occasionally, I forget that this government regularly executes people. My mother warned me about this process, and Freedom's choices and escape showed me its reality, but I've never been put on the spot where I would be eliminated if I wasn't useful. Dr. Geo's words hit home in a way that no others have. His meaning is clear: I can't forget.

I take a moment to unfurl the picture from my deodorant tube, standing, as always, with my back to the door. I have a habit of looking at it every so often, especially when things feel big. I miss Mom. If things were normal, she'd be so proud. She is a scientist, and I'm off on a scientific mission. I'm going to space. I'm following in her footsteps. I'm learning skills from the brightest and the best.

I scan the picture, letting my eyes travel over Mom's smiling face. I imagine she's smiling at me. I wish I could talk to her. I wish I could tell her everything. I don't have much time, so I roll the picture back into the tube and toss it into my drawer. A quick shove of the drawer and I'm ready to leave my quarters.

I'm still thinking about Mom when I step into the hallway and observe my arrow leading me to the cafeteria for breakfast. I know from packing that the rations used in space and the cave mission are similar, and that this will likely be the last good meal I get for the next week.

I push through the glass doors and discover Llama sitting sullenly at the table we used to occupy together. Hero sits next to her, her tray of rations the unappetizing lumps that Llama and I were served in the first module of training. Llama picks at her food and pointedly ignores Hero.

I retrieve my rations and sit on the other side of the table, facing both Hero and Llama. "Hey," I say. Llama twists her head away from me in a gesture of scorn. Hero rolls her eyes. "I'd like to talk, when you're ready." I say the words in Llama's general direction, but it's hard to tell if she hears them because she acknowledges nothing.

Hero puts her fork down. "So, Reach," she says. "Everything is all packed. I can't go with you to the loading bay, but you need to put everything into the cargo hold in order of reverse importance.

You'll all be under strict timing protocols when you arrive at your location, so getting the most important equipment off first is the best move. It should be like that in space too."

I nod, still looking at Llama. Llama turns slightly, sees me staring, and stomps off, her food mostly uneaten.

Hero watches her go with a sigh.

"She doesn't understand *games*." I grimace.

"I wish I could at least have eaten her food," Hero says with a bit of dramatic flair.

"Hero, this whole thing with Llama started after Men's Manners. What exactly is going on with her?"

"She's jealous."

"Jealous of what?" I ask.

"You're a better actor than you think you are," she says.

"But I was supposed to act like *we* were interested…"

"And you did a good job of it," she interrupts. "Llama won't listen to us try to explain what happened because she feels hurt. She wanted to be chosen."

Hero's explanation makes sense. What we had to do, what we were *mentored* to do with the Men's Manners final, feels like the heat of a knife slicing through my skin when I consider how it impacted Llama and me. I would really have liked to ask Llama. I wonder if maybe our mentors steered us wrong with that.

Thinking of mentors brings me back to Dr. Geo and his evasive answers when I asked him about his experiences. An idea pops into my head.

"Hero," I say slowly. "I don't know how old you are or how old Dr. Geo is, but do you know what happened to him at his Men's Manners final?"

"Dr. Geo?" She thinks for a moment. "Rex?"

I shrug. "I only know him as Dr. Geo."

"He's in charge of all the cartography stuff now, right? He's got super high clearance. I know him because we were only three years apart at our school in Hub City. Rex changed his name to Geography when he became a Citizen." She taps her fingers on her chin for a moment, her eyes brightening in understanding and then dimming with sadness. "He really is a very nice person. But he was never good at speaking while nervous. He stuttered. When I arrived here at Hub, I had an orientation led by Dr. Etiquette. She showed us something she found hilarious, a type of hand drawn map, as an unacceptable way for a male to request our romantic attention. She detailed the way that a male had tried to indicate romantic interest with a map and how he would have failed the Male Manners seminar if it wasn't for the insistence that higher-ups make sure his aptitude be utilized in the best way. I knew it was Rex because I *knew* him from school, and his signature was on the bottom corner. He always had a unique signature, and since his work was always being displayed in the halls, I saw it plenty of times. He didn't fail the class, but…" She lets loose a long sigh. "He isn't allowed to match with anyone, even if they both want to match. He's off limits."

I frown. I can imagine the humiliation he suffered at the hands of Dr. Etiquette. Not only with a stutter, but with being creative and being mocked. His feelings about Nation and its systems make more sense—I can understand his motives.

It's time for me to head to the aircraft hangar. I scoop up my tray, then impulsively drop it down on the table. I lean over and give Hero a quick hug. "Thanks," I say. "I'll see you when we get back. And I'll talk to Llama. I'll make her see…what we were doing."

Hero nods with a sad smile on her face. "I'll miss you, Reach. You've been a good friend."

"It's only two weeks," I say with a wave. "I'll be back, and you'll have to decipher my chicken scratch before you know it."

She laughs, remembering all the times she's had to ask me what I wrote on my notes.

I throw my garbage away and begin the trek to the hangar. As I go, I think of Dr. Geo, of Llama, of me. I can't help but notice that Dr. Etiquette seems prone to burning down relationships instead of building them.

THE AIRCRAFT HANGAR is a hive of activity. Crews of people use various tools to clean, sweep, and load items. I spy my orange gear bags, neatly labeled with numbers so I can retrieve the most important ones first. Llama's gear bags are purple. A crew of loaders toss her bags in as she looks on, shoulders slumped.

A female voice rings out over the hubbub. "Gather 'round."

Llama's head snaps around. The voice belongs to Second, and where Second is… Enforce is usually close behind. I spy Enforce slowly creeping her way through the throng toward Llama as everyone turns their attention to Second.

There's an interesting grouping that happens in the moments of gathering. The tech support group stands in one area, the supply task group in another, and the gear group in another. There is space for Llama, myself, Dr. Jog, and the aircraft pilot at the front. Enforce slides in next to Llama. I watch as Llama stiffens, her eyes fastened on Second.

"Excellent," says Second. She doesn't smile. "Excellent. Very well. You all know what you are doing here. Captain Loyal, here is the sealed envelope of your coordinates. You will not open until airborne and secure. It is crucial the trainees do not have any clues prior to the mission.

"Trainees. You are headed on a two-week space simulation mission. This mission will be subterranean in nature. These are your watches. You'll find that your ability to be scheduled will be your greatest asset in space and underground." She procures three wristwatches and hands them to us. They are lighter than the communication device we were assigned on Compound.

"Should you fail, you will not be sent out on the space mission that you have been trained for. That would be a pity, and you would then owe Nation a great debt for the education you have received and the training facilities you have prepared at. Success will result in a continued education at Hub until such a time as Leader deems fit to send you on your mission. Enforce."

Enforce steps forward, grinning ear to ear. Llama has inched slowly backward but is now frozen in place as Enforce fixes her with a glare. Enforce speaks in a cadence, sing-song, clearly enjoying her power. "You all have your assignments and duties here. They are all confidential. Breaching that confidence will result in certain…*penalties*." Her smile grows even wider as she scans the space, taking in all the eyes locked on her. She swings her focus to our group. "What occurs on this mission is confidential as well. You have a research assistant at Hub who will assist you with your reports after you return, but other than that, the details of this mission are to remain classified. Consider anyone outside of your group a hostile being until otherwise informed by a high-ranking official."

She steps away from the center of the circle and toward Llama, but one of her bruisers comes bustling over, leaning into her ear to whisper something. She clicks her tongue, narrows her eyes at Llama, and stalks off on her pointed heels. When she disappears through the doors of the hangar, Llama exhales.

The crews back away and Captain Loyal signals for us to board. When we climb aboard, Llama tries to walk away from me, but Dr.

Jog stops her. "Work it out," he says, then continues to a different pod of tables.

She bites her lip, then sinks into the closest orange chair, turning her face to look out the window. I sit next to her, self-conscious and nervous I'll mess up. The irony that I'm more nervous about this conversation than I would have been thanks to Men's Manners is not lost on me.

"Hey, Llama," I say softly. She continues to look out the window. "I wanted to ask you."

Her head turns toward me slowly. "You didn't though."

"Yeah, I was *advised* to ask Hero."

"But why? Why *her*?" she says.

"The rules. Following the rules…gets us…closer. She and I were *acting*. You know she loves Freedom. She was under suspicion when Freedom disappeared. The only way to get her safe was to make it appear as if she was truly done with him."

Llama scrubs a hand down her face. "I'm an idiot."

"No. You were…" I stall, searching for the right way to express my thoughts. I need it to be neutral; I don't know if the aircraft is being observed. "You weren't given all the information. I hate when information is deliberately withheld."

She nods. "I know. I can see why now."

"Can we be…good? Again?" I ask.

She doesn't say anything, just slips her hand into mine and smiles a small, sad smile. She closes her eyes and drifts to sleep. We sit there, hands clasped, as I catch sight of Nation through the window. I can tell from the position of the sun and the time that we are zooming rapidly west. Eventually, tall peaks rise into the sky. They are rocky, brown, and covered in dirt, with sparse vegetation. The craft maneuvers between two peaks and comes to rest on a plateau. Dust swirls around, obscuring the view as we touch down.

Captain Loyal comes out of the cockpit, holding his envelope. "Alright, folks," he says in a warm baritone. "You'll need to use your GPS settings on the watches to hike to this location. This is as close as I can get with the craft, since this can't go underground." He pats the wall of the aircraft. Then he passes around a small machine that spits out two labels after we press our thumbs down on the pad. One label is written in red ink, the other black. The labels have coordinates on them. Llama looks perplexed as she stares at the numbers. "The black coordinates are this location. I'll pick you up from here in two weeks at 10:16 a.m. The red coordinates are your subterranean target location; the entrance to the target location is just to the west. You have thirty minutes before the detonation, which begins"—he checks his watch—"now."

"Detonation?" Llama whispers.

Dr. Jog is already up and beginning to disembark. "We have to go. Quickly, let's get the gear and get moving." He isn't exactly shouting, but he's not the picture of calm either.

"There's an explosion." She's still not moving.

"Yes, they are sealing us in the cave so that we can't be influenced by any outside events. There will be three detonations. We have to get our stuff inside, and we have to be inside, a safe distance from the blasts, or else we will *fail*." Dr. Jog runs down the exit stairs and into the open cargo hold. I follow, my pace jarring Llama from her stupor. She sprints after me. Dr. Jog has lifted two of his bags and is running toward a clump of boulders to the west. It's hard to see if it's a shadow or a cave opening, but when Dr. Jog disappears inside of it, I have my answer.

He sprints back to the cargo hold, passing me as he does. "That's it, Reach!" he says.

I run into the cave and deposit my bags before turning and running out again. Llama is close behind. We scurry back and forth across the plateau for twenty-seven minutes. When my last bag is inside the cave entrance, I slump down, breathing hard. Llama deposits her bags, then looks down at the number, panic rising on her face. We have three minutes, but we also need to be deeper in the cave before the explosions. Dr. Jog finds his helmet, clicks on the headlamp, and disappears down a tunnel-like shaft.

Llama looks back at the aircraft, then bolts out across the plain. I'm stunned. She has to be here. If she fails, *we* fail. There's no time to think; the clock is a ticking bomb. I launch into a sprint, following her. She disappears into the cargo hold when I'm halfway across the plain. Llama is fast, but I'm faster and stronger. We know that from our training sessions with Lift. I hear a hiss on the wind; Captain Loyal must have lit the fuses. I see a spark in my periphery running along the fuse cord on the ground.

Llama barrels toward me, her purple bag in her arms. I can't overthink this. I stand still, turning my body so that I can grab her. She comes closer. I don't think, I just do. I hold out my arms and she jumps into them, securing her bag to her chest with her arms. I'm already running. I can hear the crackle and sizzle of the fuse line just behind me. We don't have much time. I've never run so fast in my life.

I dart into the cave entrance and throw Llama as far away from me as I can before I sprawl on the floor with my hands covering my head. A cacophony of falling rocks sounds as soon as I slam my body onto the ground. Shrapnel zips past my body, rocks and grit sting my back, and something sharp slices my ear. Sticky blood oozes down onto my hands as a tremor follows a gigantic crash.

Everything goes black.

# 34

"Reach." The sound of flesh hitting flesh and a burning sensation in my cheek registers.

"Reach?"

I blink open my eyes. Everything is fuzzy in a hazy pinprick of light coming from above. Slowly I begin to regain my focus. Dr. Jog sits near my head. Llama's right next to me. I begin the slow process of taking inventory of my body, wiggling fingers and toes and reminding myself that I'm alive.

"Think you can sit up?" Dr. Jog asks quietly. I don't bother answering, I just push onto my elbows in an attempt to. Llama puts her arms under my torso and helps lift me up. I manage to lean against the wall.

"Here, Reach," she says. She passes me a canteen and I gulp down water. Dr. Jog pours a fizzing liquid on my ear and then presses a bandage to the cut. I feel better immediately.

"I think I'm better now. I just need a minute." I sip some more and feel the tightness around my forehead, the aches and pains of hitting the ground, but also the general joy that I am actually alive. "Llama? Are you ok?"

Llama swallows. "Y-yes."

I've regained enough awareness to ask my next question. "What's in the bag?"

Even in the dim light of Dr. Jog's headlamp, I can see Llama's coloring flush to an embarrassed rose color. I see her shame. "Never mind…" I start.

"My experiment equipment," she mumbles. "I know we ordered and loaded everything in importance, but I don't know how bag five got shoved to the back of the hold. I must have made a mistake loading." She hangs her head and I feel something in me cracking. Yeah, I'm the one bleeding on the ground, but she looks so lost.

"It's ok," I say. "It was a mistake." To clarify, this is not a mistake. This is a colossal error in judgment and protocol. In space, mistakes are lethal. But we have the equipment she needs to do her experiments, and we can continue with the mission. I'm only minorly harmed. We need to move on. "We needed it, and we're a team," I say in a tone that brooks no argument, but her head still hangs in shame.

Dr. Jog stands, peering down a sloping tunnel. He passes Llama a hardhat with a lantern attached, then hands one to me. "We need to get set up. We will need to go deeper in to set up our campsite and begin routines and experiments."

Llama and I follow him, carrying our survival gear bags and leaving our other bags in a cache closer to the entrance. As we descend, the sound of flowing water reaches my ears. The shaft slopes like a hallway, and webs of other tunnels branch off. We stay on the main one, which seems most likely to end in a space large enough for the three of us to camp in.

The tunnel spits us into a cavern, where a steady stream of water gushes down from one side of the cave wall and flows into a pool along a channel. There's an echo, making it feel like a much bigger waterfall. There is a flat, smooth surface along the pool, reminding me of the pool deck that Lift has us swim in during some of the training sessions.

"Reach! Look!" Llama grabs my hand and points with the other. The wall of the cavern opposite the tiny waterfall contains what can only be described as niches. Some are elevated off the ground while others are near the cave floor. "Think we should sleep in those?" she asks above the roar of the water.

Dr. Jog stares at the water, one eyebrow raised as he focuses intently on something.

"I think we should check them out," I say as I let go of her hand and stride over to the wall. I have some free climbing skills thanks to Lift, and I'm able to climb to one of the niches. The rock is damp, but not wet. It doesn't crumble under my pressure, so I know it's strong.

I shine my lantern into the niche and discover it's too small for me to stand up in, but it's plenty deep. I back out and grapple along the wall to another niche. Again, it's probably tall enough for Llama to stand in, but not me or Dr. Jog.

"It's tight, but I think it will work really well for sleeping," Llama calls as I begin to climb down. She has been exploring a niche only a few inches off the cave floor.

I settle on the cave floor and look over at Dr. Jog, who holds rolls of reflective tape on his wrists like bracelets as he paces around the pool. "I agree. I'm not sure if he can climb, though."

I jerk my head in Dr. Jog's general direction. I don't want to offend him, but he's never indicated any interest in or ability to climb when we've discussed our training.

"He could take this one," Llama says. She steps aside and I peer in. It looks adequate for him. It is only two weeks. In space, we'll have years of tight quarters. This is fine, really.

I shrug. "I guess we should tell him and see what he's doing."

Dr. Jog is now bent over and marking pieces of tape on the floor every few steps. He's moving methodically, so we catch up to him quickly.

"Oh good, you're here. Did you find what you were looking

for?" he asks from a crouched position, sticking the tape down and not looking at either of us.

"Yeah, the niches in the stone are good sleeping quarters. So, we'll use those," I say.

"I can't climb," Dr. Jog says, confirming my suspicion. He stands and paces a few more steps, then begins crouching down and peeling more tape off the roll again.

"There's one that's only a few inches off the ground. It will work for you, if you're good with it," Llama supplies.

"Sure. But this is important." Dr. Jog gestures at the tape markings. "I'm worried that this pool might flood. I want to take precautions. Reach, what sort of rock is this?"

"Sandstone, I think," I say as I look around the cavern. "The niches could have been carved by higher water events. But there's no way to know for sure. It wasn't soggy when I climbed it, so high water events could have happened centuries ago."

"We should still consider the possibility." Dr. Jog thrusts a roll of tape at Llama and then another at me. "I'm marking the perimeter of the pool at five feet. Llama, you do a ten-foot perimeter, and Reach, you can do fifteen."

Llama looks concerned as she grabs a tape measure and lays it out five feet away but parallel from Dr. Jog's mark. "You study this stuff, right?" she asks as she fidgets with the end of the tape roll.

"Yep," I say, wanting to reassure her. "The rock is sandstone, which means it's extremely porous. I suspect the pool here is the top layer of an underground reservoir. The water from above probably seeps into the cave through an underground spring, which fills the reservoir. Then the water seeps even further into the sandstone until it meets a more resistant material. It's probably a really big aquifer, with runoff from the mountains we passed feeding it."

"But flooding." She draws out the suffix. "Let's talk about the likelihood of flooding."

"It's dark in here, so it would take a long time for the sandstone to dry. Since the stone I climbed isn't wet—it's more just damp from being underground and being near a pool of water—I can guess it doesn't flood often. Besides, these marks will help us keep an eye on it. It's just a precaution."

"Just a precaution," she mutters darkly.

We work in companionable silence, returning to our starting points. Llama stands up, arches her back, and holds out her hand. I assume she wants me to give her the tape measure, so I reach into my pants pocket and place it in her palm. She rolls her eyes, pockets the tape measure, and grabs my hand. Her fingers curl coolly around my own. We've touched before, but this gesture feels decidedly romantic as she leaves her hand in mine. It's intentional, and there's no one here to witness it. Dr. Jog has disappeared.

I don't understand women, despite Men's Manners trying to teach me the mysterious ways of the female. But I do know Llama. I've been her friend, studied beside her for years. I know she was jealous when I asked Hero to the Men's Manners final, and I know that, while Llama is impulsive, she is neither innocent nor naive.

"Reach," she whispers. "I like you. I know it's against the rules, but for the next two weeks, we don't have to deal with *them*."

I don't know what to say because I like Llama too, but she brought up the rules. I squeeze her hand in response, and she squeezes back.

"Ok," I say quietly. Llama gazes up at me with a look of adoration. I find myself staring into her blue eyes, rifling through my vocabulary to see if I can find any words to describe the color. I cannot.

"Reach," she murmurs. I stare. "This is a good time to hug me." Her words jar me from my adjective search, and I circle her body with my arms. She feels perfect, her head just under my chin, her arms around my neck. I've never hugged anyone like this before. It feels significant, it feels whole, and also lacking all at once. I'm searching for what's missing when I realize that I want to kiss her— and she would like me to kiss her too.

Dr. Jog chooses this exact moment to clear his throat. "Ahem," he says. Llama and I spring apart, but he isn't fooled. The man is not an idiot; he is a highly knowledgeable scientist. "You two are playing with fire. This doesn't end well for anyone. And you cannot get caught before you go to space."

I hang my head, ashamed, but before I lower my gaze to the ground, I catch sight of Llama's eyes. They are snapping with anger as she bursts out, "Why shouldn't we have some *freedom* here? We will in space. They can't control everything we do all the time! Why are *feelings* such a problem!"

Dr. Jog sighs. I know he heard her emphasis on the word *freedom*. I know it's not a coincidence. "Freedom was able to…manage…a relationship with Hero while working for the greater good, yes. But his role was very different from yours. And it ended up being a mess to sort out anyway. If he really cared for Hero, he should have left her out of it, knowing what he knew."

I feel the corner of my mouth pull down in a frown. *What does he mean?* I'm distracted from my thoughts when Llama drops my hand and strides over to Dr. Jog. She shoves her sleeve up and waves her tattoo in his face, her eyes wide. "Tell us the truth. Tell us *all* of it."

"And what happened to Cyto and Mitch?" I add.

Dr. Jog swallows, then his jaw ticks. "Fine. This is one of the reasons I petitioned to accompany you on this task: they can't listen in underground. There's too much interference from the structure itself. We can tell them the narrative we choose to tell them. That's important. We always have a choice."

"What if it's just *one*?" Llama spits out bitterly. "Then it's not a choice at all."

"That's true," Dr. Jog agrees, shaking his head. "Maybe we should sit for this." He gestures to the area I now mentally call the deck as he sinks cross-legged to the ground. I obediently follow, Llama lagging behind. I sit against the wall of the cavern and Llama plops down next to me. She leans into my shoulder, and while contact isn't unwelcome, it's just new and thrilling. And also uncomfortable because it's in front of Dr. Jog, who disapproves.

He clenches his jaw, but begins to speak. "Reach, Cyto found

Mitch in the holding area and demanded they keep him with his twin. They were each sent to one of the Wards to live a life of hard labor. They separated them, despite Cyto's demands. Do you understand why they did that?" The image of Cyto's stricken face as he ran through the hall after Mitch was removed from Men's Manners, paired with the emotional cruelty of Nation, makes me want to vomit.

Dr. Jog shifts his weight. Llama's shoulders slump. We all know who was behind that decision. "Back to the other things you'd like to know. Freedom was faced with some difficult choices. His Citizenship status made his situation unusual. When he saw that the two choices offered to him by the government were not acceptable, he made a third, very dangerous choice. We've been cleaning it up ever since. Thank you also, Reach, for helping with Hero. It reduced suspicions of her."

"Enough. What happened to Freedom?" Llama's face is red, her gaze steely. Her body is still pressed up against mine, but she's rigid.

"He went…" Dr. Jog lowers his voice to the barest of whispers, which seems unnecessary because he just assured us no one could hear us here. "He went off grid."

Llama stiffens.

Words of wonder slip from my mouth. "People go off grid?"

"No, people do not. Fighters do," Dr. Jog replies.

"Fighters?" I ask.

He nods. "Fighters—there's more than you might think."

"How big is this…" I struggle to think of the right word.

"The movement is large. It's been gaining strength for years. Reach, your mother wasn't part of the movement when she went to space, but she was as soon as she returned and had you. You're the culmination of what we need to move forward with the ultimate plan. It's been the plan since she returned from space, ready to give us what we needed."

"Ultimate. Plan." I enunciate the words slowly. "What exactly is the ultimate plan? Everyone has been vague so far. And *what* is it, exactly, that I'm doing?"

"You know what you're doing, Reach. You're undermining the government. You're playing their own game and beating them at it."

I stand, causing Llama to shift off me and startle. "I don't know what their game is!" I yell.

"It's politics, Reach!" Dr. Jog yells back. "It's power. It's chess, and coups, and rights, and freedoms, and controlling people until there are no choices. It's manipulating people into service for an ideal that doesn't exist."

"So what?" Llama ventures. Dr. Jog's eyes drag toward hers. "So what if they manipulate? So what if there are no choices? What if no one cares?"

"You care, Llama. You know what the alternative is. You know what letting them win does. In the end, they can't win."

There's silence in the cavern except for the trickle of water behind us.

"Llama," Dr. Jog starts, "you're the closest thing to family that I have ever, or will ever, have. We've worked together for so long. Sometimes you can't see the forest for the trees, and I promise you, both of you, that is the case right now too. We're in amongst the trees, but all will become clear enough by the time it needs to be."

I clench my hands into fists, tight balls of sinew and fingers hanging at my side. "So then tell us. Tell us what will become clear."

"I can't tell you more. I can't jeopardize lives like they don't mean anything to me. Lives mean something to me, and I know lives mean something to you two. Reach, your mother's involvement in the movement is on account of your life. Llama, your mother is wasting her life away in a prison cell for the movement. You both know what *life* really means." His tone holds both a warning and pent-up anger.

I'm full of dread. *My mother…has always been in perilous danger, because of me.*

With that sobering thought, I hoist my survival gear bag onto my back and abandon my team as I climb to my niche. I lay out my bag and curl into myself as I envision my mother's face. Thoughts haunt me.

*Will I ever see her again?*
*Does she miss me?*
*Does she know I'm doing well?*
*Does she know that Dr. Jog became more than an ally at some point?*
That last thought makes me freeze over.
"Ally, not friend," I mutter.
What game am I even playing? I'm not sure anymore.

# 35

LLAMA AND DR. Jog talk in hushed tones, the noise of the waterfall keeping their words unintelligible. I close my eyes, but I can't sleep.

Soon a light scuffling sound reverberates around my niche. Llama isn't as good at climbing as I am, but she manages to make her way to my niche. She scoots inside, places her helmet on the ground, and looks down at me, her blue eyes filled with concern.

"Reach. I…" she starts. "I don't know what to say. I forgot about your mother. I'm sorry."

My cheek presses against the cool fabric of the sleeping bag. I close my eyes and wrench the words out that make me hate myself. "I forgot about her too. But now I remember."

"Reach, you can't blame yourself. They design it that way. The experiment, the protocols, all of it is so you don't have family to turn to. Family bonds are difficult to overcome."

"Why is everything about me a lie?"

"What do you mean, Reach?"

"I mean, my mom. She lied about everything about me. She told them I'm half-Martian, so I wouldn't be killed as the child of an unpermitted union. My parents met in space. My father is a legacy defector. I have a picture of them," I mumble into my sleeping bag. I'm vulnerable and sad. In all the excitement about the cave mission, the training, everything, I forgot about what I promised my mother. That I would work to undermine the system she used to love but had turned against.

Llama sits down near my head, reaches out her hand, and softly strokes my cheek with her palm. "Reach. You didn't forget her. You might have been blindsided by the fact that you're surviving. Which is probably the most important part of the plan, right? You can't do anything if you're dead." Her words are soothing, her touch calming. Suddenly I'm very aware of her comforting me in another way. I feel weak. I don't want to feel weak.

I sit up and wrap my arms around her shoulders. She leans in, and I don't want to feel alone, or weak, or feel anything at all. My lips claim hers, and she claims mine. Our kiss deepens in the dark, and I feel pleasant heat coursing all over my body. Nothing else is in my mind, nothing except *more*—more kissing, more of her. I have to get closer to her.

I shift her toward me, her hands tugging at my hair. My hands slide over her back, cursing the stupid fabric between us, when she stiffens and pushes away. She hunches over, her breathing ragged.

"Reach," she says, "Reach, I like you so much. I've liked you for such a long time. I want to… But we *can't*."

I stare at her in the pale glow of her lantern. Her white skin is pearly in the eerie light, and I don't understand why we *can't* when we just *were*. Someone has severed my arteries and exsanguinated me. My throat is dry. I remember why we *can't*. The rules. Also, I'm the perfect example of what happens when the rules are broken.

"Curse the rules," I growl.

Llama smiles at my gravelly tone, but the corners of her mouth dip down. "We *can*, but only when we get back from…" She trails off and tilts her head back, and I see her swollen lips glistening. She's looking at the ceiling of my niche, but I know she means from our space mission. She nudges my shoulder. "So, a picture, really?"

I swallow hard, pushing down all my thoughts about that kiss. "Yeah. I keep it hidden in my quarters. When we get back, then—is that a promise?" I hear the vulnerability in my voice, and the tremor I'm trying to hold in escapes me. I shiver.

"Reach, I think…" Llama breathes deeply as she slips away from the niche. "It's a wish." Something in her tone cuts deeper than the abrupt end to our kiss, but I can't understand why there's an undercurrent of guilt in her voice.

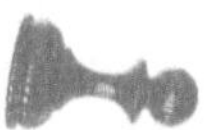

The government-issued alarm clock I wear when I sleep buzzes, jolting me into consciousness. The rules of the mission dictate that we have to follow a wake-up and sleep schedule for optimal productivity. Since there's no light in the cave, we need devices to help us stay on schedule.

I pack up my nighttime gear and begin descending the stone wall. The cave is bigger than I'd thought at first. Since sandstone is porous, we know that there are holes letting in an airflow. I survey the space more easily now that my eyes have adjusted. There are actually pinpricks of light coming from above, which is good. It means more air. The large cavern is easily ten stories high, but the ceiling forms a type of dome. There are stalactites overhead. It's oddly peaceful.

Dr. Jog sits away from his niche holding a cup in one hand while writing on a tablet he's balanced on his knees with the other. Llama is not up yet; as a woman, she is allotted more sleep than Dr. Jog or me. I don't know how much sleep time Dr. Jog gets, but I'm certain it's less than me.

"Morning, Reach," he says in a gruff voice. "Rations." He points to a zippered bag stamped with the word RATIONS in bright red.

I lean over, select a bar, and then begin the arduous task of eating it. I pull a water-purifying tablet out and prepare a cup using the trickle of water from the cave. The water doesn't taste quite right, but it's better than the bar. We sit in an uncomfortable silence.

Dr. Jog sighs. "I need to talk with you about…things." My eyebrows arch at his ominous tone. "You have more of an aptitude for this than she does. And you need to keep this information to yourself. Your romantic feelings for each other complicate things. That's why there are so many rules against it, on both sides. I suppose that you wouldn't be *you* if you cared about the rules."

"Dr. Jog," I interrupt. "You're talking in philosophy again."

He grins, sheepish. "Sorry. It's just that I don't know how to say this. I don't trust people, and I can't trust Llama with this. Enforce is too interested in her. I have to put my trust somewhere in order to be what I am to the movement. Our ultimate goal, the one that we need *your* help with, is to acquire help from your father's colony and to destroy the system here."

"How am I supposed to do that?"

"You have to make contact with the colony and use what you know about family and power and technology, and everything. Your job is to convince them to return to Earth and join the fighters."

"I thought no one knows where the colony is and that no one has made contact since my Mother."

Dr. Jog nods. "That's all true. But we have some ideas of where they might be. It's closer than 51. I think you need to understand your role here in the movement."

"I'm listening." I sit up, training my gaze on him. I can sense these next words will be important.

"Reach, you *are* the movement. When your mother returned from space, she developed a plan that would use you to bring back the colonists. The way of life described to her by your father was something monumental. There have always been fringe movements against Nation, but your mother and Greg gave us something to believe in, something to fight for. Everyone in the movement is working tirelessly to make this type of system, the colony's, a reality. The government wants to send you to 51. Our lies about you being half-Martian have worked at keeping you alive as a science experiment—but 51 isn't your destination. You're the only hope we have of getting to Greg and bringing them back. We can't contact them. We've tried every method we could think of. We have to have *you*. And *you* are the only one who can convince them that we're ready for their return to Earth. The truth is that we probably can't defeat the Three Powers without outside help, and Greg's colony doesn't want to be found."

The question I was about to ask dies on my lips and a new one forms. "So *I've* always been the plan?"

"Yes."

"In a way that's more than just undermining the government, right? I mean you're talking about a full-fledged rebellion, like the Scientific Revolution, and you want *me* to put it in motion?"

"No, Reach. It's already in motion. It's just that on our chess board, you're more than a pawn."

I roll my eyes and chew my lip. "So now what?"

"You do what you have to: you keep playing the game. You get to space, make changes, and usher in the start of a new era here on Earth."

"What does Llama know?" I jerk my chin toward the niches. "I don't want to keep secrets from her."

"I'm sure in most romances that's very admirable. But Reach, you are not most people. You can't tell her everything. She doesn't need to know. And also, Enforce has a way of breaking people. Llama has been her special target for years, and I wouldn't trust Enforce. The movement has lasted this long because it's been operating on a need-to-know basis. Every cog in the machine only knows what its job is and pertinent information to the cogs around it."

"What are you, then?" I retort. Llama's loyalty being called into question has me feeling protective.

"There are a few of us who know the full..." He considers his next word carefully. "Scope of the project."

"Is my mother one of them?"

"Yes. She and I and a few others."

"Can you talk to her? Do you talk to her?"

Dr. Jog shakes his head. "No. That would be precarious, given the situation. Our interactions were always brief, and we kept a lengthy distance from each other."

I frown. There's an ache deep within me that maybe speaking with my mother would have healed. "How many people are in the *movement?*"

"Thousands. It's always growing, spreading. Reach, you going to space will be the sign that we're ready to initiate a new phase. And Reach, telling the wrong person even *one* piece of information could bring the entire thing down. It would kill hundreds, maybe thousands of people, and it would be because of you."

I stare, slack-jawed at him. *Killed, because of me.* The weight of his words settles on my chest, and I realize I can't tell Llama things. I can't be with her romantically. I can't have anything of my own because my life was already dedicated to a cause before I was born. According to Dr. Jog, I am the cause. My entire body feels itchy, like I'll never succeed in scratching the surface area.

I ball my hands into fists to stop from scratching the overactive nerve endings. I know it's anxiety, but it doesn't make the sensation any less real.

"Dr. Jog," I ask. "You and my mother are—"

"Allies, not friends," he responds.

"She said that about you before we left Compound for here. What does it mean?"

"It means, don't let people in. Don't let them see that someone is important to you. Don't expose the chinks in the armor. Relationships, family ties—those are always the chinks. I'd suggest you let Llama be an ally and nothing more, but it's too late for that." He says it dryly, but there's a tiny bit of humor as he gazes toward the niches.

My brain fizzes as it absorbs all this new information. I follow Dr. Jog's gaze and see why I sensed humor in his tones. Llama is awake but moving as if through sludge as she trudges over to us.

"So, Llama," Dr. Jog says. "You're not a morning person, are you?"

She grunts. "Coffee."

I frown. "Will there be coffee in space?"

"No," Dr. Jog responds, just as Llama says, "Yes." The two look at each other, Dr. Jog grinning and Llama with a death stare.

"Cof-fee." Llama enunciates the word into two syllables. "COF-FEE." A showdown is happening between the two of them that I do not understand.

Dr. Jog backs away, his palms up, still grinning. "Fine, Llama. You win. You can have your fix today, but you do know that in space, coffee is nothing like the real thing. It's better to get it out of your system now in preparation."

Llama snarls at Dr. Jog. He hands her a carton. She looks at it with a cross between adoration and a scowl, then pours it into a tin cup and places it on the camp burner. When it starts to steam, she snatches it from the burner and carefully handles the cup between her hands. She brings it to her full, pink lips and sips. I watch, entranced by those same lips that I kissed as the liquid takes effect. She straightens up, her eyes becoming brighter, her demeanor pleasant. It's like watching something that's solar powered get charged.

Dr. Jog catches me staring and laughs. Llama scowls. A fleeting fear that I've said too much to Llama pulses down my body as I remember the guilt from her words from yesterday. I shove it away. Llama likes me. I like her. Nation isn't going to stop this. Enforce won't. Llama's strong. And she hates Enforce.

A few more sips of the coffee and Llama has visibly relaxed. "Dr. Jog," Llama says. "When you went to space, did you do this too?" That's actually a really good question, and I find myself wanting to know more about Dr. Jog's space preparations and his mission.

"Yes," he says. "We did a cave training. There are records of astronauts doing cave training from before the Scientific Revolution. It's ingenious, really. Significantly less expensive than sending someone into space."

"We?" I ask, catching that detail.

"I had a partner for most of my preparation. Things didn't...- work out," he says. He slaps his palms on his knees and stands. "That's enough morning chitchat. We have work to do. It's important that we get our experiments underway. They didn't send us underground to sit around and talk all day. Let's go."

I stand, then extend my hand to Llama. She reaches out, and her hand is perfect in mine. I feel an electric current passing between our palms. I didn't know we could conduct like this. She stands and drops my hand. "Thanks, Reach." The smile she gives me makes me want to tell her everything about me. Why have secrets when you can have love?

Dr. Jog leads us out of the cavern, back to the cache of bags we left by the now-sealed-over entrance. On our way up, I discover a few tunnels off the main passageway that will work for our experiments. We've grabbed our bags and have each claimed a tunnel as our own makeshift lab space, when Dr. Jog comes to check on me.

"Reach, you're all good with your experiment?"

"Yes. I have two objectives: the experiment devised at Hub and providing a thorough map of this underground system. I was going to make the maps as I go, but the system isn't always reliable down here. I'm worried none of my data will save."

He nods, considering the seriousness of the situation. "You have the primitive tools, right?"

I hold up my compass, map paper, ruler, and planimeter.

"It's like Lewis and Clark," he whispers in awe.

"Who?"

"Olden days. The explorers, they mapped half a continent with nothing but those primitive tools."

I grin. Dr. Jog might be a lot of things, but he is always a scientist. The thought is comforting, because at least I can always predict his enthusiasm for learning. "I'll have to borrow your books about it when we're done here."

"Books? How did you know I have books on this topic?"

"Dr. Jog, I've seen your quarters. And Sublab has books that would never be available in libraries for the general public. Historical books are nearly impossible to find, but you have entire rare collections at your disposal. If there's a book to be had, you've got it. I'd really like to know how you got them, but for now I need to get going…"

He grins under my lamplight when Llama barrels in. "Go where?" she asks.

"Ah, Llama!" Dr. Jog still smiles warmly. "We were discussing our schedules and plans for the day, the experiments, that sort of thing. Do you need any assistance from me?"

Llama shakes her head. "Nope. I'm supposed to set up my station near Reach. We need to be able to freely share data. The protocol says that if one of us is indisposed, the other needs to know how to take over the experiment so the data and opportunity for progress isn't lost."

I'm a little embarrassed as I think about sharing only what Llama needs to know with her. We're supposed to be extensions of the other in space, able to jump in at a moment's notice and do the other's job.

Dr. Jog gives me a knowing look, then disappears back into the recesses of the cave system.

# 36

It's the last evening of the mission. Our time together was simple and predictable. We worked on our experiments during the day, and at night followed our prescribed schedules for sleeping and exercise. I kept some distance from Llama, unnerved by Dr. Jog's words of warning and her cryptic "wish" comment. I feel stretched taut between two poles. Eventually I'll snap.

Llama's science experiments have to do with chlorophyll in plants and the structures of the individual plant cells. Could plant and animal cells mutate? Could they combine to create a 'planimal'? Adverse conditions are perfect for cell mutations, so she's been trying to help the 'planimal' become a reality during this mission. Today we cleaned up her stations and packed everything in special packets and bags. The bags are waterproof, with pockets of air that will provide buoyancy for our samples and materials. Everything is protected from every possible disaster.

My experiments consisted of collecting rock samples for the geology department at Hub to analyze. Those samples have been packaged and placed near the cave entrance. The last thing I need to do before sleeping tonight is pack my equipment; it's still on the rock ledges I claimed as my experiment base.

Dr. Jog's experiments involved the water in the cave. But he also gathered data about Llama and me, and how effectively we worked together as a team. His reports will be the official record of what happened here. It feels crass to think of myself as a specimen, but in this instance, I truly am the human subject. It's frustrating to think that I'll be reduced to probabilities and statistics in his report. I know I'm more than a number, but the government doesn't care. They want a number to use in their calculations.

How do you do it? How do you reduce a person to a percentage? Some questions are best not asked.

We ate an evening meal together every day, and Dr. Jog started the tradition of telling us stories about his own space mission. Those stories weren't part of the movement. They were just practical and funny. He's in the middle of a tale now about the space toilet malfunctions he had to deal with when he suddenly stops. His eyes grow huge as he glances at the pool. He stands and shifts back on his feet. Llama and I are still laughing about the toilet water when he yells, "Run! RUN!" and takes off running toward higher ground.

I don't bother asking why. Dr. Jog is our mission leader for this endeavor, and if he says run, we run. Llama doesn't move. I glance at the pool and realize why she's staring. The pool that has been placid and calm for the past two weeks is choppy, the waves splashing onto the deck and growing in intensity and regularly hitting the five-foot marks. I watch a ten-foot mark get splashed.

Llama whispers, "How?" just before a tumultuous roar announces that the consistent gentle flow of a waterfall that has been ambient background noise is now a roaring, gushing torrent. The noise spurs her to action. She bolts headlong out of the cavern and up the passageway toward the entrance.

The cave makes a sucking sound and a whoosh of air blasts past us. The oxygen is being forced from the cave by whatever is happening. The sandstone is going to suffocate us. The walls begin to quake, stalactites crashing as debris drops from the ceiling. We have never run as fast as we are now. I know that Llama and I have surpassed Lift's expectations for our sprinting speed.

When we reach the area where our experiments were stationed, Dr. Jog slows. "Llama"—he pants—"do you need to gather equipment that can help us get out?"

She doesn't stop and continues to barrel along to the top of the cave. Dr. Jog looks back. I dart into my station and grab the three things closest to the passage. I don't even look at what's in my hand before I begin to run again, whooshing air continuing to belch past me as if the cave is gasping its own dying breaths before collapsing.

We crash into the barricaded entrance. Our bodies reverberate off the jumble of rock and stone that seals us in the cave. We don't stop. The three of us push, palms flat against the massive pile at the entrance. It's survival instincts taking over, not rational thinking.

Llama is the first to stop. She gasps. "We need a plan. And to"—another gasp—"assess the situation."

Dr. Jog breathes heavily, but he stands tall and drops his hands to his side. He glances back at the passageway we just ran along. "I think," he begins with a deep breath. "I think that there must have been a significant rain event above ground that inundated the water levels of the underground aquifer. If the cave system was a natural drainage collection point for mountain runoff, and there was a thousand-year flood in the vicinity...this would happen—"

I interrupt. "We have to get out."

A gust of wind cuts across us, this time from left to right, not from the back of the cave. The cave is collapsing, and we don't have time to think. We don't have time to hypothesize. We only have time to act.

I look at the tools I'm still holding in my hand: a rock hammer, a small ruler, and the marker I used to annotate the bags of samples. I run my fingers over the rock in front of me, and my fingers find a small crack in the boulders. Taking the rock hammer, I begin to hack along the small crack as Dr. Jog and Llama push and shove. There's a sudden burst of movement, and a sliver of light passes through. We throw ourselves at the wall with renewed vigor.

Rocks shift and crumble around us as the cave expels another blast of air. It throws us against the wall with such force that I feel my cheek slam into the stone and cut open. The seam we had been working on splits open as easily as a hot knife cutting through butter. There's enough leeway for us to squeeze through, but we don't know when or if the rest of the rocks will collapse and crush us inside the cave. We have to get out. Once we're out of this rock jam, we can breathe. Nothing about this situation is stable.

"Go!" Dr. Jog and I both scream at Llama. She crouches down and springs through the hole into the bright desert beyond.

"Run, Reach!" Dr. Jog hollers.

I follow Llama's approach, crouching down to spring off my feet and push through the narrow space. It is our one chance out of this imploding cave.

"I'm out!" I yell over my shoulder as soon as I'm through, blinded by the sudden appearance of the sun after days in darkness. I hear Dr. Jog coming through the seam when I feel another whoosh of air. This pocket of air is different. It's circular, like a tornado, not like the gusts that pushed us straight into the wall. I sense rather than see Dr. Jog's body flying through the air along with hunks of stone. I act on instinct, crouching and covering my neck with my hands.

My senses are inundated. The tremendous roar of crashing rocks assaults my ears while the dust and grit and sand and debris of the cave sting my body. The heat from the sun scorches and burns my hands. I can't see, so I can't move.

I close my eyes and curl myself into a ball while waiting for the noise to die out.

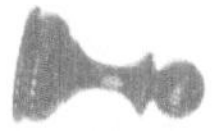

Silence after something traumatic is loud. I notice the loudness of it as I brush my hands away from my neck, shaking off a layer of gravel and sand as I go. I slowly blink open my eyes, giving them time to adjust to the brightness. A massive boulder, twice as tall as I am, is two feet from me. I was two feet away from being crushed by a rock. With that sobering fact, I survey the area for Dr. Jog and Llama.

My eyes track over the horizon as I search for my companions. A flash of orange catches my peripheral vision. It's Llama, scrambling over a jumble of rocks twenty feet away and trying to reach something. I squint and realize she's trying to get to Dr. Jog. He's lying on his back, face ashen, one hand pinned under a boulder and a leg bent at an impossible angle.

I run toward him, too, meeting Llama at his side as she drops to her knees and places light fingers on his heart. There is the tiniest flicker of movement as his chest rises.

"Llama, he's passed out. We have to get him out of here."

"His LEG, Reach! His leg!" She points wildly, turns green, and I can tell vomit isn't far behind.

I turn away from her, my attention back on Dr. Jog. "We have to get this off him," I say. I gesture to the rock pinning down his hand. "Can you find the communication device? Maybe we can get the aircraft here sooner for an emergency."

Llama extricates the communication device from his pocket and then moves to study the boulder crushing his hand into the sand. She still has her putrid coloring, but she speaks calmly. "I can't see the way his hand is set under the rock. We might hurt him more if we roll it, but I don't see another option."

I grunt my assent. Llama stays where she is and I walk around to take a position on the boulder by Dr. Jog's horribly bent leg. Together we push and heave until the rock subtly shifts in the sand, revealing a very crumpled, crushed left hand.

Dr. Jog is shiny from the sweat accumulating on his brow. He's unconscious from the pain, but I can tell from his labored, shallow breathing that he is in grave danger.

Llama pushes a red button on her alarm bracelet and calls "mayday." I didn't know the alarm could do that. Why was hers different from mine? She continues to push the button, each time saying "mayday."

A crackling response comes over the device after a few tries. "Loyal, responding mayday, coordinates for assistance."

Llama shoves her wrist in my face, knowing I know the coordinates from the GIS system. I speak coordinates into the device. "Captain Loyal, this is Reach from Global 1 Cave Training. This situation is a serious medical emergency for Dr. Jog. You were due to pick us up tomorrow. Hurry."

"Reach, copy." Captain Loyal's voice crackles with the static. "Changing course for rapid pick up. Emergency response protocol enacted. I do not have a medic on my craft, but I do have some supplies. Based on your coordinates, I'll be there in two hours. It's going to get dark and cold in the desert. Keep yourselves covered and as comfortable as you can."

The device blinks its red light, and Llama and I are left alone in the setting desert sun with nothing to do but will Dr. Jog to live.

# 37

THE SUN BEATING down on Dr. Jog is just as worrisome as the wait. I remove my jacket and try to fashion a tent of sorts over him. Llama does the same. The sun's rays burn her pale skin bright red, and I can feel blisters forming on my own body. It's almost a relief when the sun slips below the horizon and darkness envelopes the desert.

Llama and I sit next to Dr. Jog, staring at his chest, hoping for movement. There's nothing to do but wait. It's cold without the sun, but Dr. Jog occasionally shivers. He can't regulate his body temperature. When the lights of the aircraft descend on the plain, Llama and I are over-coiled springs, ready to snap.

Captain Loyal runs down the steps carrying a mesh hammock attached to a wire frame, an emergency stretcher. When he reaches Dr. Jog, his face blanches. "That's bad." He sets the stretcher on the ground.

"We know," Llama and I respond in unison.

Loyal looks at us with concern. "Are you all right? You're both cut and bleeding."

I'm not proud of it, but I snap. "Dr. Jog. We have to help him!"

I shout, the desperation filling my voice leaking into the cool air.

Captain Loyal narrows his eyes as they rove over Dr. Jog's still form in the sand. "We have to get him on this stretcher. I know some basic medical stuff, but this is way outside the scope of my abilities. We can shift the sand… No, we're going to just pick him up. It's going to hurt him no matter what we do. Llama, you need to lift his injured leg while Reach and I pick him up by the armpits. His good leg will just have to drag while we get him on the stretcher."

Llama says nothing, just closes her eyes and stands next to Dr. Jog's leg.

"On three," Captain Loyal commands. "One, two, three—lift."

We lift and heave. Dr. Jog's body is surprisingly heavy despite being distributed amongst the three of us, but we manage to lay him on the stretcher. Loyal and I pick up the ends of the stretcher as Llama runs ahead to the craft. Loyal's second-in-command officer is a short man who stands in the doorway of the craft. He waves Llama up the stairs and inside the *c*-shaped craft before he disappears. It doesn't seem like the appropriate reaction to seeing Loyal and me carrying an injured person, until a small hatch in the middle of the curve unfolds to create a tiny ramp.

Captain Loyal leads us up the ramp and into the bowels of the aircraft. Lights bloom on, revealing this area as a medical berth. Captain Loyal pulls a communication device from the wall and begins to bark orders to the man upstairs. "Take off immediately. We need to divert to Ward Two. Closest to route hospital. Leg and hand. Surgeon required. Imperative. Medics need to come aboard. We can't transfer the patient. Call the flight directors and inform them of the situation." He slams the device back into the cradle and gathers bandages and tape.

The craft heaves off the ground while Captain Loyal slams the drawers of metal carts open and shut. He retrieves a small device with a green screen. It looks like a gun, but when he points it at Dr. Jog, I see that it is mapping Dr. Jog's body. When the device arrives at his bent leg, there is not a singular bone there. Instead, there are hundreds of pebble shapes. The bone is crushed, pulverized. There's no setting a bone like that.

"Reach." Captain Loyal's meaty hand clasps onto my shoulder. "We're going to get him help. I can't do anything else for him, but I can treat your cut, your burns, and your dehydration." He hands me a bottle of water, pours antiseptic on a small gauze pad, and applies pressure to my cheek. It stings, but then numbs. He begins stitching, quiet as he works.

"It's not the prettiest, and I think you'll have a scar under your eye, but it's better than leaving it open for infection." He hands a small mirror to me, and I can see the ugly hashes crisscrossing my face from the outside corner of my eye along my right cheekbone. I shrug, not caring. I turn my attention back to Dr. Jog. Captain Loyal is setting out medical equipment on trays. There's an IV line, bags, pumps, and needles.

"You're not a doctor?" I ask just to break the suffocating silence. I know he's not. He's a pilot. Still, hearing his words is better than worrying over Dr. Jog.

"No. I'm not a doctor. But pilots have one course on basic medical treatments in school. And also we learn how to transport patients."

"And what does your one course tell you about him?" I gesture to Dr. Jog, who is lying pitifully on the stretcher. My eyes are steely. I can't show weakness, but the truth is that I am feeling tired and angry and afraid.

Loyal swallows and meets my gaze with a hard one of his own. "I know the bone in his leg is crushed. There's no setting that. His hand is probably salvageable. We're stopping at the hospital in Ward Two and will be taking their best Med team. The Ward doctors aren't as highly qualified as the doctors in the Citizen Cities or Hub, but every doctor has to complete assignments in a Ward before they can move into Citizen care. The ones we are taking are the head doctors at the hospital, the ones closest to being moved back to their Cities and Citizen care. Can I be honest with you, Reach?" I nod.

"He might not make it. But I'm trying."

I appreciate his sentiments, but the words that could acknowledge that won't come, so I stare at the floor instead.

The telltale drop of my stomach alerts me to our descent. One thunk later, and the same hatch Loyal and I used to bring Dr. Jog aboard opens. Twelve people run through it. They are dressed in dark navy blue scrubs with caps on their heads. On everyone's back is a large, white block number two.

"What are we dealing with here?" The first one in, a man with dark skin and a curl that's escaped his cap, directs at Captain Loyal. Others surround Dr. Jog, one placing the IV line, another studying his hand, and another his leg. Captain Loyal doesn't say anything, just hands the first doctor the scanner device and shows him the images. The doctor's lips tighten. He looks to Captain Loyal. "Permission to operate on craft, sir?"

Captain Loyal stands at attention. "Granted. Do it. All of it. We are going above deck now. The bay is yours to command. Channel 002 if you need to reach me."

The same meaty hand clamps down on my shoulder and propels me away from what has rapidly become an operating theater. He steers me through the belly of the ship as I numbly follow. We climb a flimsy staircase and arrive in the passenger area. I slump into a seat.

"Reach," he says kindly. "It's his best chance."

I look down just in time to see his brown leather shoes walk away. The worry has taken its toll—my eyes are too heavy to fight it—so I sink deeper into the chair and fall asleep.

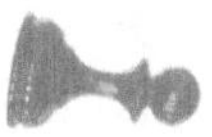

Some hours later I am awoken by Llama's head on my shoulder. The first streaks of light appear on the eastern horizon, and Llama's steady breathing is soothing. My body feels crumpled, and I need to move, though I hate to wake her.

"Hey," I whisper as I gingerly move my shoulder. She stirs. "Hey, Llama," I whisper more urgently and watch as her eyes flutter open. She looks befuddled, but adorable. I'd like to kiss her again.

"Sorry," she croaks. "We must both have needed a nap."

I shrug but notice that a white sheen covers her skin. It looks like an ointment rubbed on the burns.

"Any word on Dr. Jog?"

She shakes her head, but springs to her feet. "I can go ask."

"What? You're going to ask who? And where are you going to ask it?"

She sighs. "I can ask the cockpit. I helped Aero with the take-off procedures. You need two people to drive this thing."

"Can I come too?"

Now it's her turn for a noncommittal shrug. She walks around the seating clusters and finds a door marked *Private, no Entry*. She doesn't abide by the sign. She pushes it open and stalks up a flimsy staircase similar to the one from last night. She stops outside a set of sliding metal doors and presses a button. The doors slide open. She slips through. I follow suit before the doors can close.

Captain Loyal and his second in command, Aero, are seated in leather chairs as they fiddle with instrument panels.

"Could we get an update on Dr. Jog?" Llama asks as both Captain Loyal and Aero stand.

Captain Loyal glances at Aero for a moment before he responds. "Sure. Aero, you have control."

Aero salutes, then turns back to the instrument panels. Captain Loyal ushers us out of the cockpit. After the doors close behind him, he retrieves the communication device from the wall and pulls it from the cradle. "This is Captain, requesting a status update on the patient."

Crackle and static punctuate the silence for a beat.

"Patient is stable, but in surgery. Continue the course to Hub for treatment. Patient will require specialized care."

Captain Loyal shrugs, his large shoulders out of proportion with his narrow waist. The whole movement is bizarre. "I can't tell you any more than that," he says. Llama's face is a blank mask. I don't feel anything. Loyal reads our faces and takes pity on us. "He's stable. He wasn't when we brought him on board. That's good news. Give them time. These medics are due to return to Citizen population. They've experienced years of training. They might not be the best, but they aren't the worst. He has a chance, thanks to them."

Llama's nostrils flare, her eyes narrow, and her lip quivers. Captain Loyal misreads her facial expression and offers her a sympathetic smile. "I know it's hard for you, but this is the best we can do. He might be ok. He's closer to ok than he was yesterday."

I raise an eyebrow and wince as I feel the stitches I forgot about pull taut. Llama hears my sharp intake of breath and her ferocious gaze calms.

"I guess..." She grinds out her words in Captain Loyal's general direction. "That's good."

His response is to beam at her. "Keep your chin up, Llama. Aero told me you were a great help in the cockpit earlier. If you want to consider piloting, I'd be happy to recommend you."

A snort slips out. "You do know what we're training for, right?" I ask, making no effort to hide the snark behind my words.

"No. I don't know." Captain Loyal's voice turns frosty. "I know nothing. Because knowing nothing keeps us *secure*." He turns, punches the button on the wall, and strides back through the metal doors, leaving Llama and me alone in the corridor.

She blinks at me. "That was...I don't know. He doesn't know I'm from a Ward, but he thinks...it's a good system." She hangs her head. "I don't know how to act around people." She looks so dejected that I lean over and place an arm around her shoulder. I mean to comfort her, but she pulls into my chest, and suddenly it's a whole hug. "The way the system is set up. It's just so..."

"Wrong?" I supply, thinking about how hugging her is *wrong*, but also so *right*. Dr. Jog was definitely wrong. There is no reason for Llama and me to not be romantically involved.

"Exactly!" she says. "They make the medical teams practice in Ward hospitals until they're proven worthy of being the doctors of Citizens. It's like the Nons in Wards are just experiments."

I draw back at her words, dropping my hands from her body, startled. She gazes up at me, and as her eyes search mine, she realizes what she said. "I'm sorry, Reach. I didn't mean—"

"Forget it," I cut in, not meeting her eyes. She picks at her fingernail and then slowly trudges off toward the flimsy staircase.

I watch her go.

# 38

WHEN I FINALLY make my way back to the seating area, Llama is curled up like a cat, staring at the vast expanse of blackness that is Nation. She says nothing, so neither do I. We sit in uncomfortable silence until the craft docks at Hub.

The docking is preceded by the sudden stomach-dropping lurch and a thud as we hit the ground. A crew of medical personnel waits in the hangar. Llama exits ahead of me, but I can see the medics rushing in through the medical bay hatch. Dr. Jog is in the best of hands now.

Llama looks straight ahead, making eye contact with no one and marching with purpose through the throng.

"Reach!" I stop and search for the voice, certain I've heard it before. "Llama! Thank goodness you're all right!" I find the person moving toward us in the sea of people. My jaw drops open, pulling my stitches taut yet again, as I realize the woman walking toward us is Leader.

Llama tenses and stands taller. I step behind Llama because I have been trained to do so. Men's Manners, and all that. Second bustles along behind Leader. I don't spot Enforce, but I would prefer not to see her, ever, so I take this as a positive. Leader is only yards from us. She keeps going and doesn't stop. She reaches Llama and wraps her arms around her. Llama stands stiffly and doesn't quite accept the contact. This is by far the oddest government official interaction I've ever witnessed.

"Heroes! You are both heroes!" Leader gushes. Leader never gushes. Second is busy tapping away on her tablet and shaking her head. It's clear by the look on Second's face that this was not a scheduled part of Leader's Day. Leader is unperturbed by Second's scowl. She turns to me, and I freeze. I don't know if she's going to launch herself at me, but I hope she doesn't. Mercifully, she doesn't hug me, but she does place a cold palm on my cheek and softly says, "I'm sorry for this ordeal, Reach." It's a rare peek at what might be humanity. Whenever I've seen Leader, she's acted in an official position. This is not official.

She motions to Llama and me that we should both follow her. There is nothing else to do, so we step after her and away from the crush of maintenance workers in the hangar. She ushers us into a car, where we sit across from Second and Leader. When the door closes behind us, Leader's demeanor changes. Gone is the caring, almost motherly woman who met us on the tarmac. Second has put her tablet down, which is cause for alarm. Llama fidgets, pushing her jacket sleeve up and down along her arm while Second eyes her tattoo with interest.

Leader steeples her fingers together and focuses on me. "Reach. We need to know exactly what happened. We would typically have Dr. Jog debriefed with his supervising official, but since he is incapacitated, we need to hear from you both." She leans forward slightly.

Llama fixes me with a look that screams 'tell them' and then turns her head to gaze out the window. I launch into the story of the cave flood and implosion while Leader and Second listen in rapt attention. When I finish, Second reclaims her tablet and taps furiously while Leader grins broadly. "Heroic. Absolutely heroic. I think it's time to share some of the details with the Citizens. You are going on a space mission, and we need the support of our people. They will eat this up."

"What were the coordinates, Reach?" Second nods her head in agreement, but the abrupt change in topic stops me.

"Well, since we were underground, they aren't exact, but we were close to 34.9 North and 104.6 West."

Leader strokes a ring on her left hand with one of her other fingers, thinking. "And was there a significant rain event in the area at any point recently?" Leader inquiries Second.

"Not in those coordinates. But a weather station at 31.9 North and 99.9 West noted odd cloud formations on the second day they were on mission," Second answers.

"Hmm." Leader taps her fingers on her thigh.

I speak before I can stop myself. "Leader, ma'am. With all due respect, I don't think that makes sense." When neither Leader nor Second interrupts me, I keep going. "Weather tends to move geographically, from west to east. It rarely moves from east to west; it's possible, but an event like that would be an anomaly. Are there other observations from the surrounding areas?"

Second's eyes snap to mine, holding a warning, but Leader looks delighted. "Second." She waves a hand at her. "Get the media on this one. Call a Sty and set up film segments. Reach, that's great. We need to have you trained in media specialties. Llama, you'll have to be trained, too, since you'll be partners in space. I know it's not your area of expertise, but you'll have to manage. Reach can carry it."

I glance at Llama, who is sitting perfectly still with wide eyes.

"We'd like the public to be invested in you two. Second, can you get a Sty for Llama? I'd like the story of cave heroics and the weather event broken into two chunks. Weather one day, heroic saving of the esteemed space mission scientist Dr. Jog by future space missionaries the next. This will be fantastic."

"You do know they need to be indoctrinated in media protocols first?" Second asks dryly.

Leader shoots her a look, then waves her hand like Second's comment is an annoying fly she's shooing away. "We can do that as soon as Dr. Wave is ready. Call her, tell her I'm fast-tracking this."

Second pushes buttons on her tablet, pulls a microphone down from a headpiece dangling along her ear, and begins talking in low tones to someone.

The rest of the ride is silent. Leader stares at Llama and me. I get the sense she's sizing us up, but finding us agreeable. I don't know what she wants from us, but she's certain she'll get it.

I follow Llama's lead and look out the window, watching as the buildings I've seen from the confines of Science Hub grow closer.

"We aren't going back to Hub?" I ask, breaking the quiet.

"No, we're going to get you cleaned up at the Media Center," Second responds. "Leader, Dr. Wave is ready for them. It's a special session, so we can take them straight through."

"Good. What about Stys? I'd like this to hit today. The algorithm can help show the right audience the content, but it seems most effective when it's a large event."

"Stys are confirmed. I'll let Dr. Wave know that we want footage for a broadcast at..." She trails off and looks at Leader.

"The seven p.m. Citizen shows. We'll have to cut another broadcast for the Ward Media Center. The censors will need to work on it. I want this pushed through for the Ward top officials tonight as well. The more we have a common enemy, the better."

Second nods her head, tapping along as Leader speaks. The car stops. Second doesn't even look up. "Oh good, we're here. Dr. Wave will meet us in a moment."

Less than a minute later, a woman with short, spiky blue hair taps on the window of the car next to Second. Second flicks a button and the door retracts.

"Madam Leader, Madam Second," the blue-haired woman says with a small smile gracing her lips. I notice a dusting of freckles on the bridge of her nose. Apparently media specialists do get to see the sun sometimes.

"Dr. Wave," Second says coolly. "These are your charges. I've sent over the files. Reach is to be handled with care. Hub has all the samples they need, but we do require him back in one piece for this to work. The girl too."

Leader surveys Dr. Wave imperiously. "You know the precariousness of this situation. If you aren't sure, read the files again. I expect perfection, but that's never been a problem for you. Do your duty, and we'll be just fine."

Dr. Wave swallows. "Yes, ma'am."

"That's all. Take care with these two." Leader gestures for Llama and me to exit the vehicle. We stand on the curb in stunned silence as the car pulls away with Leader and Second inside.

Dr. Wave faces us and begins walking backward toward a tall white building with a menagerie of antennas adorning the top of it. "Hi. I'm Wave. I'm technically a doctor, but no one here calls me that. Wave is more my style." She says her words slow as molasses, but it's not unpleasant. "We've got a job to do, so I'll take you inside for your special media training session. Usually I don't lead these, but it's a special circumstance. After your training, you'll be sent to a Sty. After your Sty sessions, you'll be filmed. I have lines for you. But first, the training."

Wave uses her wrist to unlock the sliding glass doors and let us into the building. She calls over her shoulder, "Follow me."

Llama and I trail behind her, taking in the immense glass facade of the building. Every wall, door, and surface is glass. Some of it is colored so you can't see through it, but most of it is so clear it gives you the impression of floating. She leads us up glass staircases, down glass corridors, and through a labyrinth of invisible levels until we arrive at a set of frosted glass doors. She waves her wrist over the middle of the door and it slides open with a gentle hiss. The puff of air blows Llama's hair slightly, and I realize how bedraggled she looks. It makes me wonder how I look, but that thought disappears as quickly as it came when I step through the door.

There is a bold geometric pattern on the black carpet, curved metal beams artfully scattered through the space with brightly colored leather couches along the walls of a round room. There is a balcony around the edge of the room and a set of four steps that lead to a sunken circular area with tables and chairs. Along the balcony are different doors with words hanging on placards. I notice that one reads *information*, another *censorship*, and another *preparation room*. I don't have time to read every doors' placard because Wave steps down into the sunken area and summons us to a table.

Llama plops gracelessly into the chair. Her lip is split, she has cuts on her hands, and a burn on her cheek. She's less damaged than Dr. Jog, but she's been hurt too. A protective instinct flares in me. I want to curl my body around hers. I want to shield her from physical harm. But I can't. That type of thinking, that type of feeling, is forbidden.

I follow suit, dropping into the seat, too tired to care if I'm being lazy in my movements. Dr. Etiquette would care, but Wave is not Dr. Etiquette, and I want to sleep for the next three weeks.

Wave does not allow us to sleep. She strides to the edge of the sunken space and pulls a cord. It releases a white screen from a roll, like some of the old maps I've used with Dr. Geo. Wave reaches into a cart and tosses Llama and me each a tablet, identical to the one Second always uses.

"Welcome to your media indoctrination. I'm going to give you an expedited version, but I have the go-ahead from higher up to get you on the screen today, so we don't have much time. First, turn on your tablets. Please." Despite talking about speeding things up, Wave says this in an unhurried voice.

I power on my tablet and discover the seal of Nation lights up and remains on the screen.

"Click the app in the top left of your screen. It says MIP."

I click and am brought to a legal document. The font is tiny. I can hardly read the black-and-white text.

"Scroll to the bottom." There's a signature line. "Sign."

Llama and I glance at each other with looks of caution. Wave catches us and offers reassurance. "We will go over everything. This is an NDA that says you won't discuss the indoctrination protocols with anyone outside the Media Center, and that you agree to what we will be discussing. You have two minutes to read the document." I'm still trying to read the first of many paragraphs of fine print when Wave calls the time, but Llama huffs and signs her name on the screen with her finger. It's sloppy and unlike her usual handwriting. I grimace as I sign without reading the entire document. As soon as my name is down, the document disappears.

Wave nods once in satisfaction, then clicks a button on her tablet. A video begins playing on the screen. Short clips of children playing games are spliced with images of gentle breezes and quick nature features, and narrated by Wave. It's familiar…

"The media is an integral part of Nation's infrastructure. As part of the media team, you are responsible for upholding the standards and truths of our government. The media exists to serve. We serve our illustrious Leader, who boldly brings us each day into a future better than the past." The familiar cadence of the voice gives me pause. It was Wave who narrated the Men's Manners video. There is no way I can trust anything this woman says or does. My insides clench as if I drank a vial of poison. My signature is affixed to the document *she* presented us with.

"As a partner in the media, you must understand how important your role is. By participating in media appearances, you agree to uphold the view of Leader and the government of Nation both publicly and personally. Failure to provide proper support will result in penalties, including, but not limited to, removal of Citizenship status.

"Being a media spokesperson requires a level of engagement with people that most other Citizen professions do not experience. There is extensive training available for journalists in Nation.

"As a spokesperson, you will be the face of the government that enters into people's homes. You will be a touchpoint for the government and are responsible for bolstering the trust between the Citizenry and the government. Trust is imperative and is the function

you serve. Scripts and notes will be provided before each cast in order
to facilitate the continuity of this trust.

"As media, you are responsible for maintaining a level of attrac-
tiveness that suits your given purpose as instructed by your government supervisors. A government-approved style coordinator will be
assigned to you and report to you before each cast. Your style coordinator is responsible for augmenting viewership and creating appeal.

"We value stories of triumph and strength, excellence, and in-
tegrity. These are the stories we will broadcast in order to showcase
the government in the positive light it deserves. With Leader at the
helm and our fearless journalists following directions, the media has
been, and will continue to be, the star that guides Nation's Citizens
into the illustrious future Leader foresees for us."

The video stops. Wave steps forward. "Any questions?"

I can't help it. I wince as I think through the implications of
signing something before I knew the details. "What if I don't want
to say everything that's on the script?" I dare to question.

Wave smiles brightly at my question. "There's room for some
ad-lib content, but that's not until you've more fully developed your
media personality. For now, we can't leave something as powerful as
media to chance, so we use scripts to ensure the proper narrative is
told. We all exist to support the government."

I blink. Llama blinks. I choose my words carefully and slowly.
"The reason we all *exist* is to support the government? Did you mean
the reason our *jobs* exist?"

Wave flexes her wrists and stretches her hands. She exudes nonchalance. "Of course not." She smiles. "What purpose could you exist
for other than to serve the government and Leader? To serve *this*
government. It's on line eighty-five of the document you signed—
that you'll serve this government with all of your abilities and your
whole heart. It's actually the same clause that's in the Citizenry papers. I realize you haven't seen those papers yet since you're not quite
of age. But yes, Reach, the whole reason *we* exist is to support the
government, and the media must never forget it."

Wave isn't angry. She's not even alarmed. To her, this is the same bald truth as learning irrefutable math facts. Two plus two is four, and we exist to serve the government.

My brow creases.

Llama raises her hand in an uncharacteristically timid manner. "When can we see our scripts?" she asks as Wave acknowledges her with a head bob.

Wave's grin widens. "You'll see them and receive delivery coaching today. I'm finalizing a few details, but the best advice I can give you is to always give thanks to the government, especially if you forget a detail or start to misspeak."

I turn my face away, not comforted by the advice in the slightest.

"Oh, and Reach." Wave pulls my attention back to her. "You'll need to interact with the crowds, make them like you. If they like you, they'll like what you're saying. If they like what you're saying, they'll like Leader. It's really simple. I know you don't want to seek out attention, but your file does show that you have an aptitude for etiquette. That aptitude needs to be used to further Nation's progress." She continues beaming at me, then Llama raises her hand again and Wave's smile drops into a frown.

"Do they have to like me?" Llama asks quietly, her throat bobbing as she swallows.

Wave's eyes narrow and she considers her words carefully as she studies her fingernails. "It's not as imperative. You don't have the same aptitude that Reach has shown, so you'll need to follow the scripts and look appealing. You'll be making a lot of appearances with Reach, but sometimes Reach will make appearances on his own. I know it's more difficult for some people to put on a show, but you'll figure it out."

Llama's face is pallid, her eyes round as her mouth frowns. "What if they don't—" she begins to ask, but Wave interrupts.

"Your style coordinators are here. You can refer to each one as *Sty*, or by their number. You'll have Sty 8, Reach. Llama, you'll have Sty 78. That can't be right. The lower their number, the higher security clearance they have. You shouldn't have a Sty over twenty. If you have any concerns about your Stys, be sure to let someone on the media staff know."

Two women walk through the sliding doors before they stand in the shadows. I recognize one of them as my Sty from when I first arrived in Hub City. Both Stys have badges with large black numbers hanging around their necks. My Sty sees me and gives a small smile. The number eight is on her badge.

"Stys," Wave says dismissively. "Here are your charges. Can you explain this?" Wave points a long finger at the number 78 on the other woman's badge.

"Yes, ma'am," says my Sty, Sty 8. "She was the highest available with clearance for a cast in three hours. That was the indicated time frame; is that still the case?"

Wave frowns. "Yes. She has proper clearance?"

Sty 8 twists her mouth in a half-grimace, half-frown. "It's in process. It could be denied, but given the circumstances…" She trails off and looks at Wave with some trepidation.

"I'll have to supervise her. Seventy-eight, you're styling Llama under me. Eight, you have Reach since you've worked together. Let's get going, we only have three hours until they want the cast recorded."

"Yes, ma'am." Sty 8 says. "Would you please unlock the preparation spaces?"

Wave reaches into her pocket and pulls out a ring of old-fashioned metal keys. The ring is filled to bursting. She walks to a door and unlocks it, watching as Sty 8 walks inside. She gestures for me to follow, and I do. The door shuts, and as I hear the clink of metal as the lock turns, I realize that Wave has locked us in the room.

# 39

Sty 8 sighs as the door shuts.

"Hey, Reach," she says.

"Hi…Sty. I…I didn't know about the name and the numbers. I'm sorry," I mumble.

She's bent over at the waist, unlocking drawers in a rolling metal cart with her thumbprint. She pauses and looks at me with searching eyes. "I know you didn't," she says simply.

"What do you know about me?" I ask.

"I have access to classified information that's in your file. It's available to the cleared Stys. That's not to say I know much. I know that you're a half-pre-Citizen and need to be treated as a spokesperson for the media for now. You need to be attractive and relaxed for this cast, and you and Llama need to look like heroes."

"Do you know I'm half-Martian?" I don't know why I say it. I need to connect with Sty 8. I need her to know I don't have full humanity according to the powers that be either. I need camaraderie. I don't fully understand it, but I know it's important.

She turns and looks straight at me, not blinking. "Yes. I just thought you might not know that."

"There's a lot of miscommunication about who I am. Actually, there's a lot of noncommunication. Or communication that isn't accurate. I don't know what to expect from people here. I just…I understand that…" I don't have the words to formulate the thought in my brain, so I stop and just stare at her. Finally, I ask, "What's your real name?"

She looks me up and down. "According to the government, I don't have a name. I'm a Sty, *Sty 8*." I'm trying to think of a response to the sadness in her voice, but then she whispers, "My name is Shauna."

I nod as I remember all she had to do last time to prepare me. This time is significantly less intense. I wear my orange uniform, which is easy enough. I have to be fitted into a clean one, the sleeves of my jacket rolled to a specific mark on my arm. The jacket sleeves are held in place using double-sided tape that sticks to my arm hair.

Sty 8, *Shauna*, uses trimmers and clippers to trim my eyebrows and nails. Finally, she gets to my actual hair. Squeezing a lemon-scented gel onto her fingers, she massages it into my scalp, combing it into a swoop. I feel ridiculous, but then she pushes a cart of makeup over. I don't have a practiced eye for makeup, but even I can tell the colors she's selecting are ridiculously bright.

"Errr, are those really the right colors for me?"

*Shauna* smirks. "I am the professional here. It looks weird in person, but under the lights for a cast, you need more robust shades."

I have nothing to say to that. She busies herself with applying black eyeliner around my lower eyelids. I'm holding my eyes open as widely as I can, staring up at a fixed point on the ceiling and trying not to blink despite the intense discomfort of someone being so close to my eyeball, when the scripts are delivered. A page walks through the door and hands Shauna a manilla file folder.

"Script for Sty 8's charge." The page doesn't say anything else, just leaves back the way he came.

"How did he get in here?" I ask.

"Pages have keys for the prep rooms embedded in their DNA when they take the job at Media Center. Any door that's locked inside this center is available for them. But the coding has to be updated for each delivery. Only that page could have opened this door."

"Oh—" I begin to comment, but then catch sight of myself in a mirror. I know I'm tall, but I have to duck my head to see my face. Instead of my usual pale skin, there's a clown staring back. I look orange. My dark hazel eyes look massive, ringed by black paint, taking up too much of my face. My hair is gelled back and looks nearly blue in the harsh light instead of its regular brown color.

I bring my hand to my ear in relief as I feel the notch in my right earlobe is the same. Shauna catches my expression and laughs a real laugh, one that shakes her body. She begins picking up her makeup and tools.

"Read your script, Reach. You'll need to practice, and you might as well practice with me while I'm cleaning up."

I open the file containing my script and begin to read aloud. I don't bother scanning the words before I read them. My eyes are too tired. Instead, I hear the words as they dribble out of my mouth.

*In preparation for Nation's upcoming space mission to Station 51, my partners and I were training in a remote area of Nation. A significant weather event covered in a previous cast caused an emergency evacuation of our training site. Thankfully, the training provided by Leader for my teammates and me has been exceptional. This high-caliber training represents the best available training for any space-exploring astronaut. My actions saved the lives of myself, my mission partner, Llama, and the mission instructor, the esteemed scientist, Dr. Jog. Further detail and study of the weather event reveals that it was likely caused by Martian activity. These Martians used a type of gas to create a cloud over a body of water. From the seeded cloud, they then used electromagnetics to push it further, before it created a torrential flood. This was not miscalculated. They deliberately tested their technology over a sparsely populated area. They will use the weather to attack our Cities.*

I stop and stare at Shauna. "What?" I sputter.

"You say what's on the script. No questions, no chances, remember?"

"But that can't be true? Can it? Why would Martians cause a weather event? I don't understand."

"Your role in the game they play is to say what's on the script," Shauna supplies, but not in an unhelpful way. Her words make me think of Dr Jog and all the questions I'd like to ask, but I can't ask him anything. I'm not even sure if he's alive.

Shauna studies my face. "It makes no sense to *you*. Remember your duty and your *purpose*." She bites out the words in a growl that nearly stops me from the rest of what I have to say, but not quite.

"My duty and purpose to tell the truth? Or to tell *this* truth?"

She raises an eyebrow at the script in my hands, indicating which truth I'm supposed to tell.

"Is it still truth if there are two versions?" I whisper, remembering Dr. Jog's comments on relativism.

"There are two sides to every story," Shauna says, "but one side that gets told. Remember, it's not so much what you say as how you say it. And you're supposed to be charming. We made you look good, now you make us look good."

A different page bursts in. The official page uniform is the same one worn on Compound when delivering schedules: bright red pants with a white top and a red sash across one shoulder. Forming an *x* with the sash is a bright red canvas messenger bag. This page doesn't have a file folder or a pile of paper schedules in his bag, but a tablet. The people of Hub love electronics.

"Reach and Sty 8, Studio B is ready. This way." He doesn't wait for any acknowledgment; he just leaves.

Shauna scrubs her hand down her face and steps out after the page. I follow. We walk around the perimeter of the sunken room where Wave showed Llama and me the presentation and stop at a set of metal double doors. The doors slide open when the page waves his wrist over the center of the door. The page leads us into the studio and ushers us in. He points at me and then at a stiff leather couch. I sit. Wave appears. She was supervising Llama, so I look around, expecting to find her. She's not here.

"Great, you have your script. You ready? She'll be here soon, so let's go over it once together, hmm?" Wave hums as she looks me up and down. "Your posture should be more like this." She leans slightly forward, her forearms just above her knees, and relaxes. I mimic her. "Great. Let's get her here." I assume the word 'her' refers to Llama. This would be logical since we were both at cave training and the Media Center. Instead my ears are greeted with a clicking-clacking sound. High heels.

I look up and see Leader and Enforce walking across the studio. *Where did Llama go? Why isn't she here?*

Wave vacates her spot and Leader sits down, instantly adopting a relaxed but composed posture. "Ready, Reach?" she asks kindly.

I gulp in some air and say, "Yes, ma'am."

A camera crew enters, pulling cords and levers, flicking on switches and knobs and dials. Bright lights flash overhead. "Recording in ten…nine…" a voice counts down through the speakers.

"Relax, Reach. Just read the script. Editing will be done, you don't need to worry," Leader whispers. I lock my jaw because the voice is at number four. "Smile. Look happy, Reach. You're alive."

"Two," the voice calls out.

"Is Dr. Jog alive?" I whisper without moving my lips, keeping my face in a permanent smile.

"One," says the countdown voice.

Leader indulges me with a barely perceptible nod of her head.

"Live!" the countdown voice proclaims, and Leader begins.

I smile, nod, and look at the mark behind the camera where they want my eyes to focus. Leader asks me to make a statement. There's a teleprompter that projects my script. I read it verbatim. It's all going fine until Leader goes off script.

"Reach, you had a different type of upbringing. You're going to be sent into deep space to make Martian contact in a few months. What do you want the Citizens of Nation to know about you?"

I freeze for a moment, considering, and then I do something either insanely stupid or brilliant: I tell lies rooted in truth, but masked in flattery. I make a move on our metaphorical game board.

"My mother served a space mission and I have always admired that part of her life," I say. "I value scientific progress. I want you to know that I'm not a Citizen; I'm half-Citizen and half-Martian. I am prepared to make Martian contact and protect our people from a harmful way of life."

"Cut!" sounds across the speakers, and the bright light dims.

Leader's eyes narrow as she looks at me. "Divulging national security secrets on camera, are we?" she questions.

I shrug. "It wasn't on the script. I didn't know how to answer."

She taps one long finger on her cheekbone. "It is probably time to share that juicy tidbit with the people. Gives you more of a chance with the mission and puts our side ahead. Reach, we're about to be at war. I don't know how to play this. The Information Department will have to take a look as we figure out what's more helpful to our cause. Stick to the script next time."

I begin to interject—*But there was no script for that question!*—but Leader is already walking away, her high heels leaving little tapping sounds behind her as I try to understand the rules of the game and the implications of what I've just done.

# 40

A CAR DELIVERS me back to Hub after the media cast. I walk into my room in the RA quarters, fully prepared to flop onto the bed since it's after working hours but find Llama lounging on it. She moves to rub her eyes as if she was sleeping, but as she props herself up on one elbow, I can see the tear tracks still wet along her cheeks.

"What happened to you? I thought you'd be at the cast."

"They deemed that I wasn't ready to be in front of cameras." She shrugs in a valiant effort at nonchalance. She fails and laughs bitterly. "Too much gore doesn't make a woman look tough, it makes her look vulnerable, they say. They took pictures but sent me back here. They told me to wait for you but didn't say where, so I guessed this would be the best place to catch you."

I drop onto the bed next to her. "You didn't miss much. Except...I might have divulged classified secrets. I don't even know what's real and what's not real anymore. I kind of went off the deep end at the end of my interview."

Llama's mouth quirks downward in a frown. "What do you mean you went off the deep end?"

"I…I told everyone I'm half-Martian." The words rush out and Llama blinks in quick succession.

"You told them you're a Martian? That's like the most highly classified secret here at Hub."

It's my turn to shrug. "There was a script, but then she asked me about my unusual upbringing. I didn't know what to say, but I was trying to maybe make a move in the stupid game."

"Ugh. I hate the game," she whispers. "I know you're half-Martian, but not actually Martian, and I know your mother served a space mission, but I don't understand *why* the whole half-Martian thing."

Far away in the recesses of my mind, an alarm bell is clanging. The word *danger* tolls in my brain. I shove it aside. Llama is my friend—more than a friend, really—and she knows almost everything about me. Dr. Jog's voice tries to swim to the surface of my consciousness, but I push that back beneath the murky muddle of my thoughts. I need to spell out the truth. It's all too convoluted to process.

I go to my drawer and fish out the picture. I hand it to Llama. "This is my mother. And my father. And she was trying to save me, and also everyone, by telling all the lies. I had to say that Martians attacked us in the cave by making a weather event. The Three Powers want us to have a common enemy. I thought maybe telling them I'm half-Martian would…I don't know. Take away some of their power. Leader isn't happy, but they can edit anything they want out or into the footage."

Llama's eyes are round, taking up a significant part of her face. "Reach," she says slowly as she gazes at the picture in her lap. "You're the hope of the whole Resistance movement, aren't you?"

I gulp. "I think so."

"So space is…"

"Just another part of the game the Three Powers and the movement are playing."

"But why?" Llama asks sadly.

"My mother said she'd die anyway, but it would give me a chance. It would give everyone a chance to take it down."

Llama nods solemnly. "I can understand taking down the government. But why has no one told us everything in a way that we can follow?"

"I think it's like we're in a machine—and we only need to know our function and the function of the other cogs nearest us. That's how it was explained to me. I've been trying to understand this stupid metaphorical chess board since I found out about…everything."

Llama sits up fully and wraps her arms around my middle. She buries her head into my shoulder and whispers a quiet "thank you, Reach." She plants a kiss on my cheek, then slides to the floor and leaves the room.

I stare at the space where she disappeared from for a long while. Finally, I can't take the tension. I need to know what is happening between us. I step into the hall and am greeted by my arrow. I don't know why I have an arrow pointing me away from my room in the late evening, but I don't care. Thinking is too difficult right now, so I follow it to a research classroom.

Hero greets me with a small smile. "Reach," she says, "welcome back!"

"Hey, Hero," I say. I can hear the tiredness in my voice. "Why are you here off hours?"

"I have clearance to help with your data notes and observations. It's new, but I'm your official assistant. I think you've been working with maps?"

I nod. "Yeah, with Dr. Geo."

She smiles. "Dr. Geo will be joining us shortly. We need to analyze and write reports for your file. Since Dr. Jog is unable to act as your official head of project and I've been on the project the longest, they have me acting as an interim head. It's kind of weird. I hope you don't mind taking orders from me."

I grin. "Not at all. You're easier to understand than a lot of people around here."

"Ouch, Reach. Is that a thinly veiled insult directed at me and my maps?" Dr. Geo strides through the door with long legs and purposeful steps, kicking the heavy wooden planks shut behind him.

I grin some more, feeling relaxed to be around friends after the ordeals I've just been subjected to. "Not at all. But I have some questions maybe you could help with," I say.

"Sure. How can I help?" Dr. Geo asks.

"Did you see the data in the GIS system?" I ask.

Hero types something on a tablet and a three-dimensional projection of the cave system illuminates the center of the room.

"Woah," I say in awe.

"It's newer technology, but they decided it worked well for this type of information, so we got you access to it," Dr. Geo explains.

"Ok, well, we think it was a type of aquifer. But Leader and Second said something about significant rain events and gave coordinates to the east of this location. That doesn't make a lot of sense. Based on our geography, I didn't think that storm systems could go hundreds of miles from east to west."

Dr. Geo pushes some buttons on Hero's tablet, and suddenly I'm looking at a three-dimensional view of the ground. He zooms out and I can see a highly guarded secret: the shape of Nation. Why are they suddenly not concerned with me viewing it?

"It's very unlikely that a storm system would have the energy to push from east to west for that long. The nearest body of water is here, and your coordinates were here." He points to places on the model. "But if something of an anomaly happened, it could. Possible, not probable."

"Leader said Martians caused it," I blurt. Hero and Dr. Geo look at me, at each other, then back at me. "Would *that* be possible?"

"I doubt it." Dr. Geo chooses his words carefully. "Weather manipulation has never been a very cooperative science. Cloud seeding could have been done, but that would have required large amounts of chemicals. I don't think that's the case. I think they're trying to move your mission along and give the people some—"

"Something to fight against," I finish. "A common enemy that isn't them?"

Hero and Dr. Geo nod.

"Reach," Hero says softly. "I know you have a lot of questions and things to work through, but we need to get your data analyzed. Let's work on the task at hand for now."

Dr. Geo nods his support and I'm relieved to stop thinking of the labyrinth of truths and lies tangled in my mind. The kiss Llama pressed to my cheek burns in my memory. We work for the next several hours on my data, putting observations into the system and analyzing the aquifer and cave system's function, depth, and resource availability.

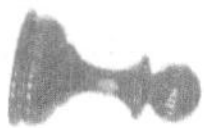

When we finally depart, I skip following my arrow to the cafeteria and march straight back to my quarters. I hesitate for a moment at my doorway, but doggedly continue on until I reach Llama's. She's sitting cross-legged on her bed reading a book.

"Hi," I whisper, watching as she jumps.

"Reach!" She startles. "You startled me."

"I know." I state it simply. "Llama, what I said earlier…"

"It's ok, Reach. We're both pawns. And I hate chess."

"No, I…Llama, the cave, and earlier. Kissing?" I feel the heat ignite in my cheeks as I try to get my mind to form words that make sense. I chance a glance away from my feet and at her pretty face. She looks amused.

"Kissing?" she repeats, grinning. "Sit here." She pats the spot beside her, and I obediently sit next to her on the bed. She takes my cheek in her palm, careful not to touch my stitches, and turns my head. Then she leans in and places her lips on mine for the barest of touches. "I think we can't do more than this for now, but I think we can be more than what they allow."

My brain isn't computing her words fast enough to understand what she's saying, but I nod along. I'll be anything for Llama. She sees me as a person—I'll be loyal to her forever.

"Reach, will you stay with me tonight?" she asks quietly. I nod, and as her eyes rove over my face, she must see my hunger for her because she shuts it down. "As my friend. We can't be romantic, but I don't want to be alone after everything."

I will settle for the crumbs she throws me. Time with Llama sounds better than a night of tossing and turning in my own room alone. There's a chair in the corner of her room. I drag it beside her bed and slump into it. The orange and pink sky outside of her window shows the evening.

"I'm exhausted," she says before she slips beneath her covers and stretches her hand out to mine. I am too.

I fall asleep with the comforting clasp of her palm entwined in mine.

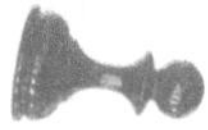

Weeks pass, Llama and I go about our business. We have training sessions with Lift, which now include self-defense and attack maneuvers, and breath control in oxygenless environments, which means sitting underwater in the deepest part of the pool for as long as we possibly can. We spend every night together. I curl up in the chair, she stretches out on her bed, and we hold hands. Sometimes I wake her from her nightmares, other times she wakes me from mine. Sometimes Llama presses a soft kiss to my head, and the gesture soothes me.

It's nice to have a friend who understands this kind of nightmare.

# 41

I RETURN FROM research time with Hero and Dr. Geo to find Llama as I usually do, crisscrossed legs at the end of her bed, a new book in hand.

"*The Adventures of Huckleberry Finn?*" I ask.

"Yeah," she says. "It's good. Dr. Jog recommended it. Very messed up society. I don't really understand all of it, but it's interesting."

Guilt grips my stomach. I haven't seen Dr. Jog since the craft dropped us off. I know we weren't allowed to see him at first, but Llama obviously has seen him.

"Did you see him?" I whisper.

"Yeah, today. Lift and I went after a special training session. Sometimes I have two sessions with Lift while you are doing your research stuff with Hero and your map doctor."

I force myself to swallow. "How is he?"

"He sent me to his apartment to get this…" She looks up at me with tears pooling in the corner of her eyes. They well over and spill down. I watch the tracks, mesmerized as the tears flow over her freckles. "They…they ruined him."

"Ruined him?" I ask, confused by the abrupt topic change.

"They amputated his leg," she murmurs. "They had to amputate his leg. He'll never run again."

"Amputate?" I question, knowing the word's meaning but in denial that they'd do that to him.

"The bone was so shattered that they cut—CUT—it off, Reach!" she screams, hysterical. She grips her bedspread so tightly her knuckles turn white. She fights for composure and gains some. "He has a prosthetic, but it's not enough. He can't have full Citizen duties anymore."

My face blanches. "What?"

"He's not complete. He's not whole. He can't be a full Citizen. He's not useful enough." She spits her words.

"But he's an esteemed hero. He served a space mission!"

"There's only those who can further Nation's progress and those who can't. He's not dead because of his status. But I don't think he would have lived through the surgery if it wasn't for his role here."

My eyes narrow as I consider her words. I've never met anyone with a disability. That seems genetically impossible. "Is that…normal?"

Llama shakes her head sadly. "Yeah. The Wards are full of people with odd bodies. If your body isn't optimal, you aren't furthering Nation's goals."

"That makes no sense," I state angrily. "So what happens to people who are *different?*"

"You should probably go ask him. He can give you more information about it than I can. He asked about you."

My head spins. I slink into my chair and grip Llama's hand. "I'll see him tomorrow," I whisper to her before closing my eyes.

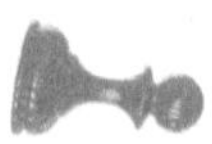

*The darkness presses in on all sides. There's a glimmer of light, and I stretch out for it. I can just squeeze through the crack in the cave before it collapses, but I'll have to stop bracing myself against the back wall of the cave, and*

I startle awake, my legs flailing under the blanket I draped over
my lap, my hand wildly grasping for anything to clutch onto. My
nightmares haven't gotten to that part in a long time. Llama usually
wakes me well before the mortal panic sets in.

I scan the room. Llama isn't in her bed. Sometimes she slips out
to use the bathroom. I sit and work on breathing techniques. When
fifteen minutes have passed and she's not here, I know something is
wrong.

I brashly drop the blanket to the floor and stalk to the hallway.
It's dark except for the floor lights that cast a dim glow at night so
people can find the bathroom. I growl a curse as I turn toward the
women's bathroom.

"Llama?" I call softly as I pass the space. She doesn't answer, and
I don't hear anything inside, so I keep going.

The air feels sinister. There's a heaviness as a sense of unease settles into the depths of my core. Half-asleep but tense with worry, I
meander the hallway, looking for Llama. She's the only one who will
understand what I'm afraid of. I have to find her. I have to know that
the dream isn't real.

The research assistant floor is a circle. I follow the loop, ending
up outside of my own quarters, where I stop and melt into the shadows. I hear a low murmur of voices inside—voices I'd recognize anywhere: Llama and Enforce.

"He doesn't come here at night," Llama says in a low voice filled
with hatred.

"And what is your report?" Enforce asks coolly.

"Defector. His father is actually a defector and his mother made
it all up. She did it so the Resistance would have a figurehead."

My mouth goes dry. Llama is betraying me? She can't be. I stand
still, frozen, listening.

"Interesting," Enforce supplies. "I suppose that's a psychological
tactic I hadn't considered."

"The things you don't consider could fill books," Llama mutters.

"Manners! Llama!" Enforce snaps.

"Sorry, ma'am," Llama deadpans.

"Back to the matter at hand, Llama dearest," Enforce pushes back with sarcasm. "You were saying…"

"That his mother is…it's all planned. I don't understand how, but if you want to hurt him, you'll want to go after his mother."

My stomach cramps as the weight of Llama's words settles.

"Not you?" Enforce prods, her voice dripping with amusement.

"I've done enough for you!" Llama growls. "If you hurt me, you'll make him hate you more. His mother would be…more confusing for him."

"Confusion isn't what I'm going for here, Llama," Enforce retorts. "Do you have proof of these things?"

There's a rustling in the drawer. I'm still in the shadows, but she holds the deodorant tube at Enforce, and I nearly step out.

"Why would I want male deodorant?" Enforce scorns.

Llama shakes her head and puts it back in the drawer. "I thought there was something in the drawer…but there isn't anything."

"Is he suspicious?" Enforce asks.

"Not of me, but of you." I clench my fists and hold my breath to keep from screaming.

Enforce arches a thin eyebrow.

Llama grows more volatile. "Fine! You. He will fight you. He will fight your ambitions. He doesn't like you. He suspects…things. He doesn't know what your endgame is, but I do—and he will get in the way if you harm me."

"Interesting game theory, but that never was your strong suit, then, was it?" Enforce intones, the menace dripping from her voice.

"I've done what you asked," Llama spits.

"You've done it well," Enforce states, calm in the face of Llama's rage. "I think you've expertly led him to have feelings for you. Divulging information is difficult for some, but you got him to spill his secrets. I suppose that is what we agreed to."

I bite the inside of my cheek so hard that I taste blood.

"So?" Llama asks, desperation lacing her words. "So she gets out?"

"That *was* the deal," Enforce replies. "You should go back to your little love nest. He might realize you're missing."

I slink back further into the shadows as I hear movement. Llama's head swivels when she crosses the threshold. I close my eyes and hold my breath. She doesn't see me, just turns to her quarters. Moments later, Enforce strides out of the doorway. She taps vigorously on a tablet. Her heels tap against the tile. She passes me without a second of hesitation.

I slip into my room and sit on my rumpled bed. Llama had been sitting there—I can tell because she has a habit of rubbing the edges of fabric between her fingers when she's nervous. I hang my head and sort through what I just heard.

Llama, the girl who I have been in love with, the girl who I am going to space with, the girl who has seen me as a friend, the girl who has been with me for years as we undertake this ordeal, has betrayed me and recommended they go after my mother because *that* will hurt me the most. The girl who held my hand, who hugged me, who kissed me in the cave, who had the same nightmare as me…the signs were all wrong. I've been playing chess with three opponents and didn't know it.

Llama hurt me.

Llama used me.

Llama is a traitor.

My mind latches onto the word traitor. I stand and grab the bowl from the washstand. I hurl it against the cinderblock wall. I don't care that it's the middle of the night, or that I'm going to wake people.

I shout the word "TRAITOR!" as the bowl shatters into hundreds of pieces.

# 42

THE SUN HAS the indecency to shine brightly the next morning and wake me from where I curled up, crumpled among the shards of pottery. A fuzziness spreads through my veins as the events of the previous night flash back. Fury rises in my chest. The need for revenge grips my soul.

I'm hungry, so I march to the cafeteria. It's not my appointed breakfast time, but I don't care. I stride to my purple kiosk, scan my wrist, and take the food without looking at anyone. Not making eye contact is one of my specialties.

I plop onto a stool and begin shoveling food into my mouth. I'm so focused on eating that I don't register the sudden silence that replaces the buzz of conversations.

"Reach." A hand comes down on my shoulder. My eyes track from the hand up the navy blue sleeve and land on Second's face. "Come with me, please." She takes a step back as I stand. "Leave it." She points at the trash. "They'll get it." She looks oddly lost without Leader in front of her, but she manages to command the room regardless.

I follow her, the fury thrumming in my veins from earlier replaced with ice. She leads me to an office in the Administrative Wing of Hub. It's appointed with comfortable chairs, carpets, and soft yellow light.

"Sit." She snaps her fingers at me, and I sit in a puffy, overstuffed chair with purple flowers all over it. "You are in a unique position. I say this because you are only being informed, as a courtesy of the services you are about to render to the government of Nation on a space mission. Otherwise, this information would be given to you through different channels." I stare at her blankly. "Your mother has been arrested and will be executed in due course."

I continue to stare. My jaw works as I realize that Enforce wasted no time. I lick my lips, stalling, thinking, trying to grasp at anything to keep me grounded. "My...mother? When?"

"Yes. And when exactly is classified. You'll be made aware, of course. You'll need to be there."

"The Citizen who served a space mission?"

"Yes."

"Why?"

"Treason. I'm sorry, Reach. There's nothing more to do." Second sounds genuinely apologetic. Her apology doesn't keep her from the status quo, though. Treason equals death.

"Treason for what?"

Second has the decency to look abashed before she responds in an official voice. "That's classified."

I sigh. There's nothing more to do. The exact words Second said moments ago float through my mind. *I'll need to be there.* "Will I...- can I see her?" I ask.

Second's mouth twists. "Yes. As her direct family, you are required to sign."

I feel my mouth fall open. *Sign.* "I have to sign for my mother's execution."

Second shakes her head in assent. She's looking at me like I'm fragile, like she's sorry she's breaking me, like she has compassion. I can't merge this version of Second with the official one I've always seen.

"What if I don't?"

"Sign?" Second asks. "You won't refuse." She stares sadly off over my shoulder before standing abruptly. "That's life, Reach." Second's demeanor is uncharacteristically subdued. "She knew what she was doing when she did it. When she did *all* of it." Her eyes meet mine in a piercing gaze. "I really am sorry."

My lungs aren't functioning. It takes sheer will to push the air into the chambers, to convert the oxygen and carbon dioxide, to keep my heart beating. Second's words hang in the air, echoing off the furniture and walls, reverberating in my core. She is right. My mother knew. She knew everything. She told me as much. I have never been more than a pawn in a game. I have been used by everyone and *she* knew. She knew it all along.

Second places her hand on my shoulder and gently squeezes. "Remember your loyalty, Reach," she speaks softly into my ear and then slips from the room. The door clicks closed behind her, leaving me seething.

Llama's betrayal is a fresh wound, Second has poured saltwater over it, and the feeling of helplessness and exploitation leaks out in tears of anger and frustration. I begin making a list of everyone who's used me, everyone I want to hurt in my desire to get my revenge.

*Mom*
*Leader*
*Enforce*
*Second*
*Llama*
*Dr. Jog*

When I get to Dr. Jog, I pause. I told Llama I'd visit him today. Some of us can actually keep our promises to people. Some of us don't have relationships with people just to use the person. I like Dr. Jog. He became more than an ally, he became a mentor, a friend. But the game theory, the Resistance, the constant pushing and pulling from the government—it's all too much. He deserves to know. I'm done. I'm not a figurehead. I'm not going to do it. I'm quitting the game. I'll go off grid. I'll…find Freedom. I'll escape. They'll kill Mom whether I sign or not. There's nothing to fight for anymore. I can't protect anyone.

Resolve powers my body through the doors and around Hub as I make my way to the hospital wing. There's a man sitting at a desk beside sliding doors. "Name and reason for visit." His monotone voice lacks any inflection, and he stares at me with a look of complete boredom. For the first time since I left the administration wing, my anger begins to ebb. Perhaps this wasn't such a good idea.

"Err. Dr. Jog. I mean, I'm Reach. To see Dr. Jog."

The man presses a button and a buzzer sounds as the doors slide open. I walk through the sliding doors and discover the antiseptic smell that permeates the hospital wing extends to the features. It's all bright light, white, and, despite the brightness and the whiteness, dingy. How air can be gray is beyond me.

"Can I help you?" A small woman whose head comes only up to my shoulder intercepts me at a hallway junction. She's wearing a nurse's uniform, the medical symbol of the staff and two snakes embroidered on the breast pocket of her coat.

"Hi. I'm looking for Dr. Jog. He's been my project…mentor." I stumble over the words, from both pent-up anger and realizing how foolish this plan is.

"Of course," she says. "This way." She turns right and walks down the hall until she arrives at a heavy door. "I'll see if he's available." She twists the handle on the door and it opens slightly.

"No need," I growl and push past her. When I'm in, I kick the door shut.

The figure in the bed startles at the loud noise. "You know what *she* did?" I whisper the words, but even in a whisper betrayal is loud.

Dr. Jog struggles to sit up against his pillows. His face is ashen. He looks smaller than I've ever seen him, fragile, weak. The expression "on death's door" is cliche, but it fits.

"Who?" he rasps. The room has the same gray pallor as the hall.

"Everyone. Everything. You've known all along?" I accuse.

"I don't follow, Reach. I've been...here." He gestures around helplessly. I don't feel pity. I feel rage.

"Llama," I spit. "My mother will be executed because of her. And her cozy chat with Enforce."

"Oh." Dr. Jog's face falls as his eyes widen. "Enforce is very persuasive. What happened?"

"Llama has been passing inside information about *me* and *my mother* to Enforce. I heard them last night. She used me. You've all used me. Even Mom, who's going to die. I'm so tired of being used. You should all feel the shame that comes from this."

Dr. Jog grasps for a glass of water with shaking hands and sips. His one hand is wrapped in bandages, the one crushed in the cave implosion. He's shaking, and half the glass spills onto his face, his neck, his blanket. I stare and refuse to offer my help. "Reach. I know that you haven't had a say in anything, and I respect that this feels...heavy." I snort in derision. "But maybe there's more at stake here than your feelings."

My voice has the venom of a thousand cobras. "Like Llama's feelings? Or yours? Or my mother's? She'll feel so much when she's dead."

Dr. Jog seems to shrink even more, his shoulders hunching under the thin blue-striped blanket, then shakes his head. "No. Llama's actions weren't part of any official plan. She cracked under Enforce's pressure, that I'm sure of. But the plan, the real plan, the one your mother put into place—she knew she'd eventually be discovered. You have a purpose, Reach. One that I think you're trying to get out of."

"I don't like being manipulated. I am not a pawn. I am not a piece in some game."

Dr. Jog shifts. There is a determined set to his shoulders. His voice is firm. "We are all pieces in the game. That's why it matters. That's why *you* matter so much."

"I could go off grid," I respond carelessly.

"You cannot," Dr. Jog replies. "You cannot *yet*."

"I don't want to do this anymore. And I don't want to sign any papers."

"Then don't sign them—it doesn't make a difference," he whispers weakly. "Reach. I was hoping to accompany you into space. My leg is…gone. I can't go with you." He shudders, and I notice the vials of pills lined up on a tray next to him. My eye snags on the prosthetic leg propped next to his bed. I have a morbid fascination with it. I can't stop staring at it, imagining someone using such a device.

Dr. Jog draws my attention away, gesturing to the pills with his wrapped hand. "These make me sleep. But the pain…I have to learn to live with the pain." He points at the pills as his hands shake. "I can still help. But don't give up on the game. Llama was wrong, and a woman will die, but that woman isn't really innocent under the law. She knew it, and she prepared for it."

Remorse courses through me as I study my mentor. He's been an ally, just like my mom said. He's tried to protect Llama and me. He warned me about Enforce's special interest in Llama, and he treated me as a piece in the game of power being played against the government. I don't understand the melancholy that cools my ire, but sadness bubbles down my limbs.

"I'm so sorry, Dr. Jog." Our entire conversation has been a whisper, and these words are no different.

"Me too, Reach," he says before slumping back against the pillows. His eyes flutter closed. The woman I rudely pushed aside bustles through the door with another burly man in a medical uniform.

"Is everything all right in here?" she calls out. The echo of her voice is startling after our harsh whispers.

"Yes," Dr. Jog says. "Reach is like a son to me. And this is distressing."

The burly man sizes me up as he walks closer.

"Well, visiting hours are over," the woman says in a clipped way, decidedly at odds with her earlier demeanor in the hallway.

I turn to leave.

"Reach," Dr. Jog's calls to me, his voice small. "Don't hate her."

I give a tight-lipped smile and nod my head before leaving the room, his words rattling down my eustachian tubes. The problem is, I don't know who I'm not supposed to hate.

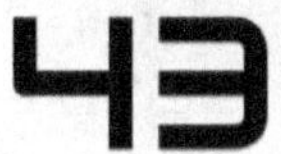

# 43

Avoiding Llama is my new pastime. I manage to make it an entire week before we're forced together. I'm fairly confident that Dr. Jog meant I shouldn't hate Llama, but I have confusing feelings about my mother too. I opt not to hate my mom, even though she set me up for a life like this, knowing *she* might be killed and putting pressure on me to keep her alive, and focus my hatred on Llama instead.

It must have become obvious to Llama when she returned to her room after chatting with Enforce that her cover was blown. She hasn't tried to see me. If anything, we've both been avoiding each other. Obviously, I'm better at it than she is. I don't sell out my friends.

I've been eating at strange hours. At eleven a.m., instead of heading to a fitness session with Lift, which I have been skipping, I stalk back to my quarters. I'm not paying attention as I walk through the archway and slam against a solid barrier. An *oof!* escapes, and a small laugh meets my ears. I look around and discover a man in the hallway, gathering tools into a bag.

"Congratulations," he says. "You've earned a door. Your space mission is scheduled. You'll be given official quarters in the scientist wing when you return, but for now, Second asked that you and your partner be given this distinction."

"I've earned a…" I feel my eyebrows rise as I stare back at the barrier. "…a door." I run a finger down the heavy wood grain, a sense of awe at this basic privacy being granted after years. *Privacy.* I don't remember the last time I felt that I had something that was truly my own.

Tears form in the creases of my eyes. I blink them away. How odd that a door makes me emotional.

"Yep." The man grins, revealing a missing front tooth. "And they wanted me to give you this note." He passes me a small square piece of paper.

I unfold it and read the neatly written words.

*Media appearance required today. Your schedule exists for a reason. Follow the arrow, Reach. -2*

I stare at the number. "From Second?" I ask the man. He nods. I glance at my arrow, and since it is pointing away from my lovely new door, I suppose I have to follow it. I begin to walk down the hallway but stop and call back over my shoulder, "Hey, thanks," to the man.

His grin gets even bigger in response. He bobs his head and whistles while he gathers his tools.

My arrow leads me to the entrance of Hub. There's a white car waiting in the loop. The doors to the outside don't typically open, but since my arrow is directing me outside the building, they whir open. I climb into the vehicle, still euphoric about the door, and am confronted with my nightmare. There is no one else in the vehicle. No one else except Llama.

I snarl in her direction, but she's stoically staring out the window opposite my door. I know from experience that it takes several minutes to drive to the Media Center. I stare at Llama, my gaze harsh and unyielding. She senses it. She doesn't look at me, but when she shifts subtly, I know my intimidation tactics are working.

"Why did you do it?" The words gush from my mouth without any consideration for what the answer might actually be.

Her head turns slowly, her eyes boring into mine. "I was never good at games."

I snort. "You were plenty good at one of them."

Her face falls as her eyes rip away from mine. "I didn't do anything right." She leans her forehead against the glass.

"Enforce would disagree," I retort.

"I'm sorry, Reach, ok? I'm sorry!" she shouts at the window. "I didn't do it right! Everyone's so obsessed with the stupid game metaphors! Fine! I played the cards wrong! I messed up the game theory! I'm stupid! I'm wrong! I'm a traitor to everyone! Everyone can go on hating me now! I'll just be here, the girl who can't do anything right!"

Her bluster is a facade for what she actually feels. I've always known this about Llama— that instead of feeling emotions, she acts. She's not good at a lot of things. She *deserves* hate.

Dr. Jog's words about hate flicker in the distance of my memory, along with the picture that she kept hidden. She could have handed Enforce the last remnant of my time with Mom—she was going to, but she stopped and pulled back. I still have it, in the deodorant tube. The shred of humanity in her betrayal… I ache with too much emotion.

Tamping down the conflicting feelings of betrayal and hatred and gratitude that she didn't lose all her humanity, I clench my teeth before I grind out what I need to understand. "I really don't understand why."

Llama scrubs a hand down her face, pulling some of her hair out of the tie with her fingers. "I was trying to save my mother," she mumbles.

"What?" I snap.

"Enforce said that if I had information about…things, I could get my mother out. Maybe. If I could help her with her political ambitions, I could be rewarded. I asked for that."

"You asked to give up my mother in exchange for yours?" I attempt to clarify, because this doesn't sound right.

"No. Enforce wants to have more power. I don't know exactly what that means, or how, but she has political aspirations. Her words, not mine. Anyway. She told me that she had suspicions about Global 1 and the Resistance movement. She wanted to know if I had any information that would help her, and promised to reward me. I asked if she'd let my mom go. At this point, my mom has been in prison for so long she's no threat to anyone. She's not…right…psychologically. After Dr. Jog got hurt, I wanted to protect us. And your mom knew what she did and was prepared, and I thought it was the best option for all of us to get what we needed."

"That makes no sense, Llama."

"I know."

"My mom is going to be executed. I have to sign the papers. But Dr. Jog says it doesn't really make a difference if I do or not. They'll still kill her anyway."

"I'm an idiot. I'm a fool. I'm a…" She gulps. "It didn't even matter. My mom's dead now too. And everyone is right to hate me."

I reel back in shock. "What?"

"I told you I'm not good at games," she says bitterly as she hangs her head.

The car rolls to a stop outside the Media Center and Wave steps to the doors. "You made it—great! We have a cast in a few hours. We're going to kick off your space mission! How exciting!" Wave finally notices the solemn mood Llama and I are both in. "Woah, who died?"

It's insensitive at best, cruel at worst. Wave is one of those people who has no filter. It's to be expected with the government puppets.

I shrug. "Her mom, my mom. Dead. Or about to be."

Wave's eyes widen. "I…I'm sorry?"

"I doubt it," Llama retorts, shocking me and Wave into stunned silence as she stares up at the Media Center tower.

Wave scowls and doesn't respond. She steps in front of us and walks briskly into the building. We follow her through the labyrinth of glass halls and arrive at prep rooms.

"Stys!" Wave yells. Sty 8 and Sty 78 appear from the shadows. "Here. Good luck." She pushes me at Sty 8. *Shauna*, I remind myself. She shoves Llama toward Sty 78 and states clearly, "Don't try too hard with her."

Wave storms off in the opposite direction as the Stys lead us to the preparation rooms.

An hour later, I'm seated on the tufted couch. I remember Wave's advice about posture and try to reenact it. Llama is ushered in looking utterly ridiculous in a too-small shirt and too-tight pants. She sits next to me, looking as uncomfortable as I have ever seen anyone. I don't want to be near her, but there's nowhere else to go.

Taps clack on the wood and I look across the set floor, expecting to see Leader. Instead, I see Enforce. Enforce grins, her face lighting up with joy as her eyes rake over Llama and me. She approaches slowly, stopping just close enough so that we can hear her words. "Ready for your mission? We have some *loose* ends to take care of first though. Reach, you'll be coming with me after this."

A small buzz reverberates through the air. She steps back, still grinning as Leader comes into focus. Enforce moves to the side of the set, staring at me with the same 'preparing to strike prey' look I've seen her give Llama. She doesn't so much as look at Llama.

"Enforce, off set." Leader snaps her fingers at Enforce as she settles beside me on the couch.

Enforce slinks away, her lips contorting into a grimace of disgust as the lights flash on and the countdown begins. I realize no one has given us a script.

"Relax, Reach," Leader says. "The people need to see you as calm and confident. You're our secret weapon."

"ACTION!" Leader launches into the cast.

"Good evening, people of Nation. I'm here to share the exciting news that our newest heroes, Reach and Llama, will be launching on their space mission within the next week."

My eyebrows shoot up. I didn't realize that *soon* meant within a week.

"I wanted to take this time to introduce you to our youngest space missionaries. As you know, Reach has been part of a secret project. Since Martian activity is a real risk to Nation, our esteemed scientists have constructed, with great foresight, a genetic anomaly. Reach is a specimen of half-Martian, half-human descent. He will be invaluable in making contact with the hostile Martians and bringing them under control. Llama is a language scholar. These creatures don't speak our language and will require training if they are to reach their full potential. Llama will help us understand how we can communicate with them. Folks, we are at war. Reach and Llama will be our front-line soldiers. They deserve your full support and best wishes as they embark on this journey. Llama, Reach, I speak for all of the Citizens of Nation when I wish you the best of luck."

I've been staring ahead at the mark on the wall, just like last time.

"CUT!" sounds out over the speakers.

"Great job, Reach." Leader gives me a friendly gesture as she stands up. "Llama." She nods sternly at her.

"But we didn't do anything," I say, confused.

"But you will. The public has a strong perception of you. You embody *loyalty*. You embody all the things that make the *game* worth playing. Don't you think?"

My breath catches when she emphasizes the word *game*. I will myself to not look suspicious. I will myself to not react. That code word triggers alarm bells.

Leader places her hands on my forearms and leans down, her mouth dangerously close to my face. "Loyalty. Games. Games. Games. I hear you're quite good at chess. We should play sometime." I shrink back involuntarily as Leader laughs. "Then again, I prefer to play with greater pieces than pawns."

Enforce approaches as Leader gives her a sharp nod. "Let's go, Reach." One talon-like hand is on my forearm, and a fingernail snags on my orange jacket. She pulls me up before I can attempt to stand

and shoves me in front of her. I manage to walk, but only barely. She pushes me down hallways, around offices, and finally into a tunnel. The tunnel is not part of the Media Center. I can tell because the Media Center is all pristine glass and white shininess; the tunnel is dark and dingy and moldy. It goes on for miles, or maybe yards. The twists and turns make it impossible to tell.

We enter a gray building. It smells like cabbage and dirt.

"Great. You're here," Enforce says to a woman with lifeless eyes who stands in a corner, watching the tunnel entrance.

"Yes. Reach, I am Dr. Trauma." The woman's voice has no inflection. "I'll be working with you today. Follow me."

The woman turns and I wonder if she's blind, because she doesn't seem to blink.

"Follow her!" Enforce hisses as Dr. Trauma begins to walk away. I do as I'm told. Dr. Trauma leads me to a small room with a mirror on one wall. There's no window, but there is a table in the middle of the room and a chair next to it. Overhead is one small light bulb that casts the room in grimy shadows.

"Sit," Dr. Trauma says, pointing to the chair. I sit. "My name is Dr. Trauma. I will be working with you today. You may share any of your feelings and emotions with me. There is no penalty for feelings and emotions at this time."

"At this time," I repeat the phrase back to Dr. Trauma slowly. She ignores me and produces a single piece of paper from the front pocket of her coat. It doesn't have the medical symbol and hangs on her frame in a way that's both too loose and too tight.

"Sign here." She points to a line at the bottom of the paper.

"Why?" I ask.

"You must sign," she insists. Her voice is still flat, one-dimensional, and odd.

I read the paper.

*I, as a Citizen of Nation, hereby renounce the accused and sever all ties with them. The accused is to be disposed of according to the best interest of Nation and its future progress.*

*Signed,* ______________________

*Relation to Accused* ______________________

"I'm not signing this." I stand as the reality of the situation wallops me like one of Lift's medicine balls.

"You are upset." Dr. Trauma pulls a notepad out of her other pocket and begins making a note.

"What's wrong with you? With all of you?" I yell.

"We're here to talk about your trauma."

"I'm NOT signing this." My voice approaches hysterical levels.

"We're here to talk about your trauma," she repeats again, not reacting to my heightened emotions.

"You ARE my trauma. This IS my trauma! Do you even know what trauma is?" My shouting doesn't faze her in the slightest.

"Trauma. Noun. A disturbing experience that results in significant fear, helplessness, confusion or disruptive feelings intense enough to negatively affect a person's attitudes, behavior, or other aspects of functioning."

I stop. The inflections, the lack of response to my emotions, the lifeless eyes, the dictionary definition. "You aren't human, are you?" I state.

Dr. Trauma stares back at me, unblinking. "One moment, please." She moves to the door, pulls it open, and leaves the room. The door remains ajar. There's nothing keeping me here, so I follow.

She opens a door halfway down the hall and slips inside. I wrench the door further open. It's a utility closet, full of cables, wires, and switches.

"Prototype not ready for subject's questioning." The whir of machinery hums momentarily, and after a female voice coolly announces "power off," whatever Dr. Trauma is collapses on the floor.

"Well, Reach, that was enlightening, wasn't it?" Enforce's voice startles me as I stare in horror at the non-human Dr. Trauma.

"What *is that?*"

"A prototype. Feelings are so cumbersome. Shame it wasn't ready." Enforce clicks her tongue.

"How many are there?" I feel the vomit rising from my stomach.

"Enough," Enforce scolds. "Now, since you won't sign, I suppose you won't have the benefit of full Citizenship ever, but it's not like it really matters. Would you like to see her?"

I nod as I clutch my stomach.

"Say please," she singsongs.

"P-please," I stutter, bending over and trying not to expel the contents of my stomach. The sound of footsteps gives me something other than the nearly human-robot making me feel ill.

"Step out of the closet, Reach," Enforce commands.

I listen, turning toward the sound. My eyes meet the form of my mother and my heart wrenches into pieces.

"Mom!" I shout and begin to run toward her. "Mom!" I slow. I haven't seen her in years. She wears a sad smile, is bone thin, and dons a dirty scientist uniform.

"Reach," she says, voice husky. "I am so glad I get to see you one more time."

"I didn't do it, Mom. I didn't. I wouldn't. I didn't sign. I don't know what to say." Everything I want to say feels inconsequential. What do you say when someone you love is facing imminent death?

Mom's eyes rove my face like she's memorizing a map. When she speaks, her words are whispers. "Reach, I love you. I would do it all again. I knew this would be the outcome eventually. Don't feel guilty. We all die in the end. Don't give up. Don't let it be in vain. Carry the torch, the flame, the spirit of Greg. Please, Reach. Please."

Enforce's beady eyes soak in this emotional moment, observing weakness, but I do not care. I need to say it.

"Mom. I know that you used me. I know that you *know* you used me. And I need you to know that I forgive you."

Mom extends her hands toward me and pulls me into a hug. "Reach, I love you. I'm so sorry it was this way. If I could have found a better way, I'd have done that."

"Touching." Enforce's sarcasm punctures our hug. "Wrap it up."

"Never forget, Reach, that I love you." Mom swallows and inhales. "I'm ready." She speaks the phrase with dignity and directs her statement at Enforce. I know the words are meant for me. She's saying she can go in peace, and that I can too.

Enforce snaps her fingers, and the bouncers that brutalized the scientist at the banquet materialize from the recesses of the dark hallway. They grip Mom by the elbows, but she doesn't fight. I stand in the dim light and watch as she marches away.

"Mom!" I shout, feeling desperate. My feet begin to run. I'm following her, and there is no plan, but it doesn't matter. I have to get to her. "Mom—I love you! I love—"

Something heavy and hard hits my head and there is no more sight, no more sound, no more anything.

# 44

THE RHYTHMIC CADENCE of beeps is the first thing I register. The second thing is my name, in the form of a hiss. I wrench open my eyes. Llama sits by my head. A feeling of profound disgust washes over me, but I can't remember why.

"Reach," she whispers urgently. "Reach. Come on, Reach, wake up."

I fix a scowl to my face and move my head so I can tell her to go away. "Go." I have to draw another breath before I can force out the next word. "Away."

Her eyes are bright. She looks healthy. I remember with sudden clarity that she betrayed my mother, and my mother was executed.

"Reach." She grasps my hand. "She's not dead."

I snarl, but she interrupts me before I can dispute her.

"She got out. She escaped. They're madder than anything I've ever seen, and I've seen a lot."

Dr. Jog's face swims into view. "I think, Llama, that Reach might need to hear this news when he's woken up fully. And probably not from you…"

I purse my lips. "I'm awake now."

Dr. Jog pushes a cup into my hands. His previously bandaged hand is reconstructed.

I sip the water, buying time before I cave and ask, "What happened?"

Dr. Jog sits in a wheelchair. He looks thin, but brighter. Llama stands next to him. "You had a concussion, but they kept you unconscious for a few days as they sorted out what they knew about your mother. They knew she was important to the Resistance, but they didn't understand how important."

"Good thing too," I retort, slinging the barb at Llama. She flinches away from me as Dr. Jog begins speaking over our odd chemistry.

"Anyway. Your mother had a plan, and she managed to escape the holding area. Because Enforce incapacitated you before she escaped, you aren't in trouble. Enforce didn't take into account the security system in the Pen tunnel. It's new, and she overlooked it. But Enforce is in a lot of trouble for excessive use of force. On you. The consensus is that had Enforce not hit you on the head, which caused confusion with the security teams, your mother wouldn't have evaded them. The security team witnessed Enforce hit you with her shoe and came rushing to get you medical help. Higher government officials informed them that no harm was to come to you."

Dr. Jog's logical voice is calm and even, but I still don't understand. I consider this information for a few beats. At first I feel relief, but too soon it morphs into disbelief. "Where is she?"

"They don't know. She's off grid, Reach," Llama whispers reverently. Like it somehow absolves her betrayal.

"Why?" I lick my lips. "Why wouldn't they hurt me?"

"Leader's publicity stunt has aired. They can't have you injured if you're about to be a national hero," Dr, Jog explains with kindness in his tired voice. "And you're going to be launching in forty-eight hours."

My brow furrows. "I am?"

"*We* are," Llama replies, a small smile playing on her lips.

"But I don't like you," I say.

"Well, isn't it all water under the bridge anyway?" Dr. Jog offers.

"Not to me."

*Where is Mom? How? What happened? Enforce hit me with her pointy shoe? They got it on camera? What does it mean? Leader called me a pawn, told me about chess…* The thoughts spin cartwheels in my mind. I turn my aching head away from Llama and Dr. Jog. I don't understand anything about what they are saying. I hear Llama's soft shuffle as she retreats and the whir of Dr. Jog's wheels as he pushes away from the bed.

A nurse arrives and hands me a stack of papers. "Discharge instructions. Drink water. You'll be fine." She pulls a tube out of my arm, then flips some switches on the machines, and the beeping stops.

When I step into the hallway, there is no arrow. I have no schedule. This is odd, but somehow also freeing. I pass by groups of research assistants. I haven't seen Cyto and Mitch since they disappeared to separate Wards. El sometimes sees me in the hallway, but he hasn't attempted to play chess with me since Cyto and Mitch were removed from Hub. My friends have a way of disappearing. Even my *mom* disappeared.

The word *friend* makes me think of the people I'll miss when I head to space. Space missions have a notoriously low return rate. My mother might have escaped her death, but the opportunity for my own life to end looms large. A piece of my heart wants to leave everyone and everything behind. Another piece of my heart says I need to say goodbye. This place, Hub, has been home for years.

Without considering it, I find myself headed to the gym. When I push open the door, it's empty. Lift is usually in his office if he's not training anyone, so I tread lightly to the back wall. The door is shut, but I can see the form of two people through the glass window. And I can hear their words.

"Just think about it. Please," a woman's voice pleads.

"I can't commit to that."

"It would make it all worth it if you were with me."

"I wish I could. But you know the punishments."

I don't know if I should knock and interrupt or run away with my hands over my ears because this is definitely a private conversation. I'm frozen in indecision, but it doesn't matter because the door swings open and Lift steps out. He's followed by Britta, the woman who helped me to the hospital when I got my first concussion.

Britta has a stony look on her face. Lift looks abashed. He sees me and straightens. "Reach. How long…have you been here long?"

I shake my head. "No, I only just got here." Both Britta and Lift exhale. "But I heard," I whisper.

Britta snaps around to stare at me and Lift whispers, "What did you hear?"

"Nothing, really. Just punishments? I was about to knock, but then you opened the door before I could and…I'm sorry."

Britta's eyes bore into mine, causing me to shrink back in terror. This woman is a force, and I don't know what I heard. She cracks a grin when she sees my retreat. "Reach. It's good to see you again. Congratulations on space. Good luck. Lift, think about it." She gives a small wave and leaves.

"She's scary. In a friendly way," I say.

Lift runs a hand through his hair. "That's accurate. What brings you here today, Reach? We're done training now that you have less than two days to launch."

"I came to say…goodbye. And thanks." The awkwardness of my words, coupled with my worry about death, does not help lessen the tension in the room.

"Reach. It was an honor to train you. And Britta was asking me to go with her to a competition. It's something I'm not permitted to do while employed at Hub."

"I think you should do it." Lift's eyebrows raise and he squints one eye down at me. "She's really good. You're really good. Can you get a pass or something? You did just successfully train two space missionaries. You should get a reward for that."

Lift's smile is wry. "I'll think about it, Reach. There's always more happening here than meets the eye." He clamps a hand down on my shoulder and I stare at him. He clearly reads my thoughts about death. "You can't think about it, Reach. You have to stay positive. Mindset matters. You've trained. You're prepared. You will survive. Just follow the protocol. It's there to keep you safe."

"Ok," I mutter.

Lift pulls me into a brotherly hug and thumps my back once.

"Don't dwell on it!" he calls out as I leave the gym.

I spend the rest of the day dwelling on it. I want to say goodbye to Dr. Geo and Hero, but I can't bring myself to. I'll miss them the most.

I plant myself on my bed. With the door shut, it's quieter than ever before. *Is this what death sounds like?* I wonder. No one comes to me, no one bothers me. I exist. Alone.

I have to eat. Nutrition is imperative before a space flight, so when the morning breaks over the horizon, I wander to the cafeteria. I'm melancholy. Thoughts about death won't leave me alone. This is why I am completely taken by surprise when I step into the cafeteria and find Leader standing in the center of the room. She's standing with Second, Dr. Geo, Hero, Lift, Llama, and Dr. Jog, who sits in his wheelchair. Flanking the group are a few people with large cameras hoisted on their shoulders. Llama motions to me and I start to walk forward. She gives a bright, exaggerated smile while she cuts her eyes to the cameras.

I plaster on a fake smile and approach Leader, stopping at a respectful distance.

Leader gives a curt nod and begins a speech. "Our brave space missionaries will be departing us shortly. We have been honored to form such wonderful young minds. The future of Nation's progress rests on the youth who are passionately pursuing science. Reach,

Llama, you are the future of Nation. I speak for all of us when I say to you, good luck."

The camera people unload the equipment from their shoulders and Dr. Geo steps forward. "Reach." He says my name warmly, quietly, soothingly. "When you return, you can apprentice with me."

I beam at him, but there's something else in his eyes. I sense he can't say what he wants, given the audience. I nod. "I'd like to be your apprentice, Dr. Geo."

He nods back, taps Lift on the shoulder, and the two of them walk off while talking. Lift gives me a small salute before sauntering away, our goodbyes already completed. Leader chats with Second, observing the group as she taps and types on her tablet. It's oddly comforting to see the two of them interact.

Hero steps up to me and throws her arms around me in an embrace. "Reach. I'll miss you," she whispers as she squeezes me fiercely. The air whooshes out of my lungs.

"I'll miss you too, Hero," I wheeze.

"Oops, sorry." She grins as she drops her arms. "I'm happy for you. They've offered me a position as Dr. Jog's official head assistant. I'm accepting." She looks sad, and I sense Leader's interest in our interactions. I remember that Hero and I are officially an approved match. Which would be great if we were interested in each other in that way.

"Don't you…" I choose my words carefully. "Wouldn't you rather be somewhere else?"

She smirks at my very unconvincing word choice. Clearly I'm alluding to Freedom in the most obvious way possible. "No. No place I'd rather be than here. Right here. Helping. Dr. Jog,"she says pointedly.

"Oh. I'm glad you're helping him," I say.

Hero wraps me in another unexpected hug, although this one is gentler. "You've got this, Reach. It's been a long journey, but there's so much more to do." Hero presses two fingers to her lips, then pushes her fingers to my cheek. She leaves and I stare after her, wondering what her future will be.

All that's left are Dr. Jog, Llama, Leader, Second, and myself. Leader pushes fully upright and dusts her hands on her pants. "That's that. Reach, Llama, time to go. Also, Reach, it would be very helpful if you would smile and wave when we arrive at the launch pad. Llama, you too. Just try not to make it look like you're a giddy little girl." Leader's condescending tone chills me. I don't like Llama at all, but Leader is speaking to her as if she's scum. Something uncomfortable unfurls in my belly. Anxiety, again.

Second bustles over. "Time to go. For real."

Leader and Second lead the way through the cafeteria, then out of Hub's sliding glass doors to an official vehicle. Llama pushes Dr. Jog's wheelchair. When we get to the vehicle, the group climbs in. When I look out the window, I see Llama standing on the pavement, looking from Dr. Jog to the car.

"Get in the car, Llama," he urges.

Llama responds with concern. "How will you get in?"

"I don't think I will." He flushes at the words.

Second climbs back out of the car to stare at us. "What's the hold-up?" She points to her watch. "We have a schedule to keep."

Llama points at the car, then at Dr. Jog's wheelchair.

"Oh." Second's eyes widen as she understands. "We've never..." she trails off and bites her lip.

I climb out. "Llama and I can lift him in." My words are rash. Dr. Jog looks at me indignantly. "Please. I want you to come to the launch," I whisper before he can protest. His hands tighten on his armrests and he nods once.

Together, Llama and I lift him easily and place him on the bench seat in the vehicle. The wheelchair folds with the pull of a strap, and we cram it into the vehicle as we climb in. We're smushed in the vehicle, every available space taken up by a body or Dr. Jog's wheelchair.

We ride in silence to the launch bunker. It's almost as if we are afraid the vehicle won't hold words in addition to our group. After only an hour outside of Hub City, the scenery changes dramatically. The green and clean city fades away, and dirt, mud, and scraggly plant life take over the view.

When we arrive at the launch pad, it looks like we've arrived on the moon. A circle of charred grass for a half-mile radius around the bottom of a tall white rocket sits next to a towering structure with two smaller towers attached on the north and south sides of the tallest part of the building.

The car pulls to a stop, and we extricate ourselves with difficulty. Llama and I place Dr. Jog into his wheelchair. He doesn't mean to, but he sighs in relief as he hits the seat. "I'll never get used to that," he whispers, knuckles white.

Second steps forward. "Dr. Jog, Reach, your materials are on the north side tower. Llama, your Sty is on the south side tower. We will meet in the central tower in one hour."

The ground is pitted and bumpy, but I pick a path and roll Dr. Jog toward the north tower. He's jolted and jerked but doesn't complain.

We enter the tower, and I step into my uncertain future.

# 45

Fluorescent white light blinds me. There are scuffs on the floor, grime in the tile grout. The floor is uneven and bumpy, the disrepair made more noticeable because I'm pushing Dr. Jog's wheelchair.

"You'd think," I mumble, "they'd want to make the launch pad a little nicer for all their proclamations of progress."

"Reach. You need to know things." Dr. Jog shifts in his seat and grasps my wrist. I look down at him in wonder.

"Now. You want to tell me things *now*?"

"Yes. But keep walking. We have to multitask," he says. I walk forward, approaching the door at the end of the hall. "Put your wrist over the door," he says. I follow the instructions and it opens just as it did for the pages at the Media Center. I stare at my wrist in wonder. The arrows, the door—what else have they coded to recognize my DNA?

"Ahem." Dr. Jog clears his throat and I shove him through the doorway, following behind. We've entered a white room. Hooks from the ceiling with hangers support my spacesuit. It's bulky and cumbersome to carry, but once we're through the initial phase, I can take it off and wear my regular orange uniform in the tiny confines of the space capsule.

"My job is to help you with this, but I don't think I'll be much help," Dr. Jog self-deprecates.

"I'm sure I can manage…"

"Reach," he interrupts, his voice laced with urgency. "You have been playing blind for too long. We made you think you were a pawn. They think you are a pawn. But you're about to be promoted. Pawns can become queens."

I nod. Pawn promotion is one of the more fascinating aspects of the game.

"This situation is…challenging. And you're the only one who can make the move. I know you know about the Resistance movement, about your mother, Freedom, Llama's parents, Dr. Geo, me… There's so much more that has happened. What's important right now is that you know what moves are available to you. The government knows you're the son of a defector and a powerful scientist mother who escaped execution for treason. They also know Llama is the child of Resistance leaders. They want to give the people something to focus on, something to cheer and hope for by sending you on this mission. They want to use you, but also be rid of you."

I nearly drop the heavy space bodysuit. "They want to be *rid* of us, or just want us to disappear?"

"I grew up a Ward of the State because my father was a dissenter. I thought if I proved myself, I would clear my name. It was my life's ambition. It was everything when I was selected for a space mission. I did it all—the training, the learning, everything. I was sent to 51, the furthest station. It didn't take me long to understand, once I was in space, that there was no Station 51. My mission was a way of executing me without getting their hands dirty."

"But you came back."

"I came back." He frowns. "And in exchange for not telling anyone what I knew about the deep recesses of space, I was allowed to live and help train new recruits. Since they wanted me out of the

public eye, they sent me to Compound. I already knew all the classified things about space I wasn't supposed to, so there was no harm in
putting me on your project. I played my game, and honestly, I won.
You can win too. You can force a checkmate, Reach."

"How?"

"Go rogue. Don't accept the mission they wrote. But, Reach, if
you do that—if you choose to actively override the mission—they
will know. If you do this—if you actually do it—you have to get to
your father's colony. We don't have the resources to overthrow the
government on our own. We need the colonists. They aren't at 51.
They're underground on Mars."

"What happens to the Resistance if I redirect the mission? Right
now it's coded for 51?"

"Right now, your mission is a silent execution meant to rally the
people of Nation into a war against a fictional threat, which will ensure that the government maintains power. If you force their hand,
the Resistance will continue training, infiltrating, and learning. The
colony can make contact with the Resistance if it wants to."

"But they never have?"

"They did once."

"When?"

"When your mother tried after you were born. There was static,
a blip, and nothing. But she could see there was a connection."

"You've known all along? You've known this entire time that
this mission would be an execution? And that the colony *is* on Mars?"

"Yes." Dr. Jog shifts uncomfortably, his hand reaching down to
his absent leg. He scratches at the air. "I sometimes forget that it's
gone," he says softly. "I knew the most. No one but me ever had all
this information at one time. Look." He straightens, suddenly busi-
nesslike. "The colony has no interest in the Resistance unless it concerns you or your mother. The government is overplaying its hand.
They took the farce too far and created what they feared. You are the
only hope for us, but there are consequences to those actions."

"Why were you in charge of our project if you knew so much?"

"Because I'm not a threat. Silence was the price of my life. I've been a good servant for all these years, but actually, I'm just a good liar. It was good for their image to have me training you."

The bulky fabric of the heavy spacesuit is stiff and overly insulated. I'm uncomfortable. "Recode the mission? Reprogram? Go to Mars? Hope my father's colony has an interest in me and will return to Earth to overthrow the government? Is that what I'm supposed to do?"

Dr. Jog shrugs. "Or you could go to the nonexistent Station 51 and things can continue as planned by the Three Powers. Of course, if you do that, you're choosing death for yourself and making the decision for Llama. If you did that, you'd be an executioner."

I swallow hard. I'm many things, but I'm not a killer. I might despise Llama, but I don't want her dead. And I'd really like to live.

"Reach, you're a fighter. It's what your entire life has been about. The repercussions for the greater good are significant." A buzzer sounds over the intercom and Dr. Jog wheels himself to the elevator in the corner of the room. "Time to go, Reach," he says with a small smile. I shuffle to the elevator, which dings open with the tinkle of a bell. "Reach. It's not hard. There are hundreds of thousands of people who are oppressed here. You can change that. That's your purpose. But it's your decision now. No one can make it for you. And Llama doesn't know all of this. She can't influence you."

I start to nod, but stop short. "What if I do it? Won't they know about you?"

"Yes," Dr. Jog says simply. "I have outlived my usefulness. I'd rather know it wasn't in vain. And Llama—she's more than she seems. You'll know more when she tells you."

The realization that if I do what he wishes, if I recode the mission and go rogue, I'll be sentencing him to death steals my breath.

"Could you get out?" I whisper.

Dr. Jog knows what I mean. He looks pointedly at his leg and smiles. "Others will have the chance."

"I don't know what to do. This feels impossible. I can't. I can't do that to you."

"Reach, I'm not afraid. I know enough about death to know it's not worth fearing. There's more. All that philosophy wasn't just for you. I'll do everything I can, but if I must lay down my life for someone else, I'll willingly do it. The hope of a better future means that much to me."

I swallow. "Thank you," I breathe, tears pooling in the corners of my eyes. "I never knew quite what you were, but you really were a mentor. An ally, actually..." My mom's words float through my memory as the elevator rises. "You've been a friend."

Dr. Jog laughs. It's a full-bodied laugh, and I marvel that even with a limb missing, his laugh is the same. "All that game theory, Reach. Don't waste it." He pats me on the spacesuit, which is awkward because I can't feel it, but then he rolls back a little. "Go, make your move."

The elevator doors slide open. On the other side, Llama and some technicians stand idly, waiting for us. Dr. Jog can't accompany us in his wheelchair. He gives a wave to me, our goodbyes having concluded. Llama rushes to him, attempting to bend her body in a hug. He smiles and pats her gently. "...be with you. *Be you.*"

The technicians grab her from the elevator chamber and usher us inside the rocket capsule as they call out instructions to one another. Llama and I say nothing as we are strapped into the seats. When they have completed their checklists, they each offer us a wave and a 'good luck' before they disappear from the hatch.

The countdown begins, the engines ignite. I close my eyes and prepare for liftoff. When it comes, it's smooth—much smoother than the videos we watched of liftoffs before the Scientific Revolution. Progress really has been made in some regard to space science.

The roar of the engines as we throttle into space prevents any conversation. When the thrusters detach and fall back to Earth, the silence pierces my soul. I know enough philosophy from Dr. Jog to understand the idea of a soul, even if parts of it are hazy. In this moment where I can see Earth in all its blue and green and white glory from the porthole window, I think I understand what a soul is, what *life* is.

I shrug out of my gloves, unbuckle, and begin the arduous process of removing the spacesuit. Finally I'm out. When I look over at Llama, I discover she has done the same thing.

*Chess,* I think. It's all just a game of chess. The government thought Dr. Jog was on their side. They thought they owned him. They thought he wouldn't tell me. He's been playing three-sided chess for decades.

I open the coding sequence. It's the same system the GIS uses, and fairly simple. It doesn't take me long to delete the Station 51 directive.

Llama coughs. I look at her, observing her confusion. It dawns on me in that moment that, for better or worse, in sickness and health, it's now just the two of us in space, openly rebelling against the government that put us here, and she doesn't know I changed our mission from a silent execution to a coup.

"I just made my move."

## THE END

*Keep reading for a sneak peak of Book 2!*

# RISING

It's a strange thing about space, that when you're looking out into the vast expanse of blackness, speckled with light from distant suns, you need sunglasses. Ours also provide biofeedback data in the lower left corner. I've tuned out the blinking beeps and blips telling my heart rate and pulse ox levels. Llama and I both wear the special glasses as we go about our duties on the spacecraft. These duties aren't the ones we were sent here for though. No, these duties are the ones that make us rebels, openly defying the corrupt government that was probably attempting to kill us in a dramatic way. For the sympathy, and the ability to unite a people on the brink of rebellion against a different, less nefarious cause- martians.

Dr. Jog's final words before I left Earth were about Llama. *"She's more than what you know,"* play on loop in my mind. I asked her moments ago- "Llama, what exactly are you?" Her response: a Cheshire cat grin and the words, "I guess it *is* time to tell you." Now, I sit here with baited breath, wondering what other secrets my space mission partner could possibly be keeping from me.

"You know the story of my parents," she says as she manipulates

** This is an unproofed copy of Chapter 1 and is subject to slight change.*

a knob. The inky cosmos is visible over her shoulder. I can't stand to look at her after what she did, after what she showed herself to *be*. But, I want to know. I probably *need* to know everything about her. This is the time in the game where secrets between the two of us are more likely to kill us than bring any advantage. She looks directly at me, I feel the heat of her gaze tingling over my spine. I hate that she betrayed me and I still find her attractive. I'll need to work on that.

"My father was killed resisting arrest. My mother was already pregnant with me, so she ended up in Pen 1, where she lived the rest of her life as a high security prisoner, with inadequate care." I nod, knowing all this. I also know Llama's mother was killed despite the bargain Llama struck with Enforce. It was all useless. "My father resisted arrest because he wasn't an Earthling."

My eyes snap to her face, my eyebrows arch so sharply, I wonder if they've simply left my face. She has the nerve to look bemused.

"Your father was... wasn't? Isn't? I'm *not* half, but *you are?*" She still looks bemused. Anger at her courses through my body, hot and fluid.

"Of course not. I'm all human too. But it's likely that there are some genetic differences between us and the general population. Given that our fathers came from difficult conditions — we saw what happened with my planimal experiment."

I continue gaping. I actually didn't see what happened with her planimal experiment. Trying to force plant and animal cells to mutate into a combination of both was her experiment in cave training. I thought it was a blow off, something to do that didn't really matter. Maybe it actually did.

"Llama. Please tell me our fathers are not..." I trail off unsure how to phrase this. "Please tell me that we have different fathers."

Her posture stiffens and she bites her lip. "As far as I know, they were different. I just know that my father was sent to scout on Earth."

"Wait, you're older than me, right?" I prompt.

"Yeah, according to the official records. I'm a year older," she replies and I watch her lips curve into a half smile. I breathe a huge sigh of relief. I have trust issues with Llama, I've kissed Llama, I do not want to think about kissing Llama, except now I *am* thinking about it, and I am really glad she's not my half-sister. Except I still can't stand her, the lying, conniving, sneak. "So we can't be brother and sister based on when your dad met your mom."

I had already arrived at this conclusion. The story of my life began when my mother, a renowned scientist for the esteemed scientific community of Nation served a space mission. While in space, she was contacted by a scout from a colony on Mars. The colony was full of the descendants of people who fled Earth just before the Scientific Revolution. My father, a man named Greg, asked my mother questions about Nation and life on Earth. She asked him questions about life on Mars. His colony wasn't full of the power hungry, corrupt leaders who ruled Nation.

The way of life in the colony was so appealing to my mother that she turned from a life of loyalty and service to the government to an active rebel. They fell in love, but he left to return to his colony before my mother knew she was pregnant with me. My mother had no way to contact him while still in space, so she did the only thing she could think of. She returned to Earth with the claim that I was half Martian and lived on Compound, the top secret government classified experiment scientist base. She fudged data in the experiments that were waged on me, along with Dr. Jog, who has been mine and Llama's mentor for the training and this mission.

The government let me stay with her until I was fourteen. Then, they brought me to Nation Hub, where I began to train for this mission to space. Of course, my mother was an active member of the resistance movement, which meant that I was inadvertently part of it too. In fact, without knowing it, I became the face of the resistance movement. She had insisted I learn the game of chess when we lived on Compound. Every move I made at Hub was part of a game for power, played against the Three Powers, (Leader, Legislate, and Litigate), and their scary Punishment and Retribution Head, Enforce.

Enforce has a habit of hurting people for fun. It's not an ideal character trait. She likes to inflict pain, especially emotional. She convinced Llama to get close to me romantically and to tell her any secrets I revealed.

Now, Llama and I are in space. Together. Despite the betrayal and romantic tension and downright loathing I feel for her. I'm supposed to gather data at Station 51, and along the way to it. Whatever data I send back is data they can use.

But Dr. Jog made it clear that Nation does not want Llama and I back. Nation sends people to Station 51 to get rid of them. No one has ever come back from it alive, except Dr. Jog. And he knows the terrible secret: There is no Station 51. Station 51 is a silent execution. A way to get rid of trouble but give the people heroes who died: martyrs, to unite them.

This is why for all our training, we used game theory against the government, waiting on the powermoves of the government before we showed our hand. And this is why, I'm in space, and not heading to Station 51 with Llama to die.

I'm headed to Mars. *We're* headed to Mars to find my father, and maybe Llama's father too. The mental gymnastics I'm doing to keep everything straight are high-intensity. Thankfully, I'm very proficient at shoving my own thoughts and feelings aside and getting work done.

I've reworked the code. There isn't anything more we can do except wait. Getting to Mars takes a long time, but we've trained specifically for a long-term space mission. And there are *people*, who live on Mars who will meet us at the end of it. There's not much for Llama and I to do as we float through space.

I watch the stars and planets from my new perspective, just a tiny speck of insignificance in this vast, unfolding cosmos.

# AUTHOR'S NOTE

Writing a book is a lengthy process. It's even lengthier when you've been writing in fits and starts for a decade. There would be no *Reach* without many very important people, who I must thank. But first, I want to thank you, my reader, for taking a chance on a debut author who still has very little idea what she's doing. I'm grateful for you. Thank you for choosing to read *Reach*.

To Caitlin, editor extraordinaire. You are amazing. Thank you for taking an ok story and helping make it better than I ever could have dreamed. You are a blessing, indeed.

To Benita, what a beautiful cover you made! I can't believe that this gorgeous art sits ontop of my story. Working with you was incredible. I have loved connecting further over faith, regency attire, and of course, book design stuff.

To Madelyn, author bestie. Thank you for being the best cheerleader, ever.

To Mary, I am so fortunate to get to write with you in person! Thank you for sharing your dream with me, and supporting mine.

To all the bookstagram authors and readers who have answered my many questions. Leah, Claire, Drew, Mary, Paige, and Rachel. You have my undying support and gratitude.

**Olivia McCarthy** lives with her husband and five children in Michigan. When not chauffeuring children to/from activities, Olivia can be found running long distances or making sourdough bread. This is the first of many books.

*You can connect with Olivia on Instagram:*
@oliviamccarthyauthor